ELEVEN PERCENT

ELEVEN PERCENT

A Novel

MAREN UTHAUG

Translated by
Caroline Waight

ST. MARTIN'S PRESS
NEW YORK

This is a work of fiction. All of the characters, organizations, and events portrayed in this novel are either products of the author's imagination or are used fictitiously.

First published in the United States by St. Martin's Press, an imprint of St. Martin's Publishing Group

For information, address St. Martin's Publishing Group, 120 Broadway, New York, NY 10271.

www.stmartins.com

Designed by Meryl Sussman Levavi

The Library of Congress Cataloging-in-Publication Data is available upon request.

ISBN 978-1-250-32964-6 (hardcover)
ISBN 978-1-250-32965-3 (ebook)

Originally published in Denmark by Lindhardt og Ringhof

First U.S. Edition: 2025

1 3 5 7 9 10 8 6 4 2

In one account of creation, Lilith was Adam's first wife. They were created on the same day, by the same God, of the same earth, and lived side by side in the Garden of Eden.

One day Adam said, "Bring me some food."

"Go get your own figs," said Lilith.

"I must always be on top when we have sex," Adam continued.

"No, for we are equal," Lilith answered, twisting free from underneath him.

Since they could not agree that Adam was in charge, Lilith left the Garden of Eden. Frustrated, Adam went to God, who sent three angels after Lilith to persuade her to return and submit herself to Adam.

"Never," Lilith said, and the angels had to go back empty-handed.

This made God angry.

"Your punishment for demanding equality with man is that you shall be persecuted, loathed, and mocked."

God then created Eve instead.

"I have made her from your rib, from a part of you that neither walks nor thinks nor speaks, so she shall be ready to obey your will," said God to Adam.

And she was.

Especially after she saw what happened to Lilith.

Thereafter, man ruled over woman for thousands of years.

But all things come to an end, even injustices. One day the universe decided to redress the balance, tipping the scales in the other direction. And so it was that all the Liliths of the world had their turn to decide who would be on top.

MEDEA

SHE'D GOTTEN THE BLOODY MIXTURE IN HER HAIR AS WELL. Sticky-handed, she wound the stray locks into the knot on her head.

Go away, Medea communicated telepathically to the male dog. It stared dumbly back at her.

"Go on, get away," she shouted when it nudged again at the bowl on the table, slopping yet more over the rim and down her dress. A pool of red spread across the uneven surface and dribbled down onto the floor, where the dog tried to lap it up.

Irritated, she tugged it away from the table and into the corner of the kitchen, where the young female was asleep. Quiet as ever. The male settled down discontentedly beside it.

For one thing, the chocolate mixed in with the blood would give it a stomachache; for another, those drops were precious. Now that Silence was the only one bleeding in the convent, there was twice as much chocolate in the lovecakes as Medea's carefully refined recipe stipulated. But since she couldn't get any more menstrual blood, there was nothing to be done but to use more roots and more chocolate.

The male leaned over, stretching its tongue toward the puddle of blood. It could almost reach. It was the largest of all the wolfdogs they'd had in the convent over the years, with a head that came up to Medea's shoulders—which was partly because it was gigantic, but also because she was only four foot seven.

The wolfdogs grew bigger and bigger every time they had pups. So big that sometimes they got stuck in the birth canal, killing themselves, their mother, and the others in her belly, and

Medea, crying, had to feed the stillborn whelps to the snakes while they were still warm.

Luckily, since she had determined the right dose of snake venom to help with the most difficult births, this was rare. Experimenting with the venom had cost a few pregnant females their lives, but it had been more than ten years since she'd killed a dog instead of saving it. She had a whole row of little bottles marked on top with a red dot, ready for the next litter to be born. They were clearly differentiated from the yellow-dotted ones, which she used to ease an old dog's passing when its suffering grew more than she could stand.

Dogs weren't really her area of expertise. They had belonged to a sister at the convent, now deceased, who had been able to make hers do everything from tidying to foraging for mushrooms and herbs in the old parks, where the flora wasn't as weighed down by ancient ruins, shattered asphalt, and other fallen detritus from the patriarchal times.

Unfortunately, the sister hadn't lived long enough to train the male and the little female, so they obeyed no one. Medea tried every day, but even coaxing them with food she couldn't make them listen. It was different with the snakes. They moved in concert with her thoughts.

She needed to go and see Pythia. Yesterday she hadn't wanted anything to eat, even though this was the week she was usually fed. Instead, when Medea entered the basement, she had shrunk away. She'd never done that before. Ever since Medea carried her over the threshold of the convent as a baby python, Pythia had sought her out. At first, she lived beside Medea's bed, in a little crate she replaced whenever Pythia grew out of it. After a few years this became unsustainable, and Pythia—at thirty-six feet and just shy of two hundred and twenty pounds—moved down to the basement, where the heating pipes in the floor kept the temperature appropriately warm. That first year Medea had spent every single night with Pythia. It was only because the sisters thought that soon she'd be more snake than human if she didn't have a few nights to herself that she began to sleep in her own room again, on the first floor of the convent, where in those days the twelve other sisters' rooms were too. But once a week at least, she slept curled up with Pythia in the basement. Or with the other snakes beside her, when one of the new hatchlings was sickly or a snakelet had trouble shedding its first skin.

Medea quickly wiped the blood off the floor and set the bowl containing the mixture higher up, out of the dog's reach. The chocolate, blood, and roots would benefit from being left to stand and draw strength from each other before she shaped the mass into little cakes and baked them.

The winter sun still gave a wan light as she ran down the stairs to the basement, to her snakes. With every step she took her breathing calmed, and her shoulders dropped into place.

I'm coming, she thought, sensing eighty-seven snakes coil to the rhythm of her breath.

She took her time in the anteroom. If she was stressed when she went in to see the snakes, they would be too. The two-headed ones were most easily rattled, the surest way to make the two heads attack each other, even though they were attached to the same body.

Pythia knew she was coming. Medea could feel it in her soul. She would let herself begin with Pythia tonight. Particularly given that she was out of sorts.

Medea took off all her clothes and dressed in the long golden cloak, splashing a few drops of ylang-ylang on one wrist and sandalwood on the other. She parted her hair into three sections and braided each one into a long plait. The snakes loved to crawl on them: the little ones, especially, were often playful. Finally, she put her hand out the window and—a stroke of luck—drew two birds out of the baited trap. Checking their sex, she was irritated to find that both were females. Now she'd have to sacrifice one of her two male white cobras. Pythia had always preferred males to females when Medea brought her food. All snakes and small animals sated her, of course, even the females, but there was a special glow and greater energy to Pythia when the creatures she ate were male. Since her illness, male white cobras were the only meal that perked her up.

On catching sight of her, the two white males darted to the front of the vivarium. She reached her hand inside. Last year she had twenty white cobras; now only the two males were left. Partly because she'd been unlucky with the youngstock, and partly because she'd fed the ones she did have to Pythia. The males slipped silken-gentle through her hands. She picked each up in turn and examined them closely. At any other time she would have fed Pythia the one that was more robust. Today, instead, she chose the weaker one and put it in her pocket. The healthy one she'd use to make more young. Although she didn't have a white female for the male, she had a plan.

It had been a mistake to sell her young white cobra female. She hadn't thought it would be a problem, because she still had the old white one, which was with eggs, so a new clutch of white cobras would soon come trickling out. She had regretted the sale many times since. For the old female died, and in the new eggs there were only males. She'd never seen it happen before, but then again, there was a time for everything. In any case, it meant she could rear no more white cobras.

Had things been the way they were in the convent's heyday, she wouldn't have sold the young female, but money had been so tight that month she'd had no choice. Either she sold it when a buyer came along or more of the animals would starve to death, and maybe she would too, and the boy and Eldest. Silence rarely ate at home.

Not long after that, Pythia began to sicken so badly that the hatched male cobras went more quickly than expected. Now, besides the one in her pocket, she had one lone male left in the vivarium.

Her plan was to persuade the buyer to let her borrow the white female and birth a new clutch. When the eggs had hatched, the buyer could have it back. Maybe even with an extra white cobra thrown into the bargain, as thanks for her trouble. It was a piece of luck that Medea had such a close relationship with the woman who had bought the snake. It was bad luck, however, that the woman was a Christian priest, and as such it was against the rules for her not to keep her snake with her at all times.

Medea had been waiting for the young cobras to become sexually mature. It was almost time. Tomorrow she would ride the train to Himlingeøje, where Wicca lived, and convince her to let her borrow the snake. An alternative might be to bring the male cobra with her to Himlingeøje and let the female be fertilized there, but Wicca didn't take good care of her snake, so it was doubtful they would be able to get them to breed willingly under those conditions.

She checked that the cobra's heater was working properly. Compared to areas like the one where Wicca lived, they didn't have much energy supplied to the slum, and hardly any to the convent. Heating the snakes took up more of their total consumption than Medea had ever admitted to Eldest.

The door leading into the room at the end of the basement creaked. In wartime it had been a bunker. A green, thirty-six-foot body came gliding toward her.

"Here," she said, holding the white cobra out to Pythia. "It's a male," she coaxed, setting it on the ground. "You need to eat something, love," she said anxiously, stroking Pythia's beautiful skin, which was usually glossy but now had dulled.

Pythia flicked out her tongue and tasted the cobra's scent. Then she opened her mouth and swallowed it whole. Afterward she slithered into the corner and looped herself into a heap. Medea watched her with concern. Then she went in to see the other snakes, sharing the birds between them.

She yawned loudly. The exhaustion of the last laborious months made her legs heavy and the basement steps almost unclimbable. The thought of giving up and settling down beside Pythia for the night nearly won out. But she couldn't. Even if there hadn't been lovecakes to finish, there were still plenty more mouths to feed.

The dogs gazed pleadingly at her as she passed them in the kitchen.

"You've eaten today," she told them, stroking their oily coats. They followed her with their eyes as she opened the cupboard with herbs and dried food and took out the rosemary. Once again, the dogs hadn't had enough to eat, given how big they were. But she had to ration the food equally between dogs, birds, snakes, and people. They were running out of supplies. Hopefully she'd get something decent in exchange for the lovecakes on the Street so they could all go to bed on full stomachs. The birds in the front room were mercifully quiet, content with the smattering of seeds she'd given them yesterday, but as soon as one of them noticed the hunger in its belly and began to prattle, the others would follow suit. Best to enjoy the calm while it lasted.

She glanced up at the ceiling. It was around this time that Eldest generally grew impatient and banged on the floorboards if she didn't get her dinner. It was easier with the boy, who just ate when there was something to eat. He was sweet and placid. So far.

The sun would soon be hidden behind the few rooftops still standing in the Frederiksberg slum; she'd have to get a move on if she wanted to take advantage of the daylight. They needed to save the power for Eldest's radiator. Now that her aging body spent all day lying down, she felt the cold more.

The convent was always cold in winter. The last few had been piercing. Maybe because there were only three people left to keep the walls warm. Four, counting the boy, if he could be counted. Or maybe it was because she was lonely, now that Eldest wasn't popping in and out day after day. She used to rise with the sun and her birds, gather herbs and seeds and groom the creatures' wings, train them to fetch the things she couldn't reach on the uppermost shelves or in the treetops. But in the last year or two she'd gone downhill. With every day that passed, it seemed like there was less Eldest could do, until at last all she did was lie in bed upstairs, in the room with the boy. The worst thing wasn't the physical decline. Worse was that her memory was crumbling, and conversations that had once been full of life were now truncated, riddled with misunderstandings that made Medea feel even more alone.

Medea shivered and undid her braids. Her matted hair fell down her back, reaching the hollows of her knees. Though some of it was damp with the blood, the heavy locks were warm. She always wore her hair in braids or piled up; anything else was impractical. But when it was as cold in the convent as it was that winter, she left it loose, glad of the faint heat. The price she paid was that blood, bird shit, things from the vivariums, and whatever else she picked up along the way got caught in it, making it impossible to keep neat. Not to mention the dirt when she was out foraging and her hair dragged across the ground.

She tried to comb it out with a fork. It got stuck halfway. Giving up, she left it where it was. She would cut off the bottom four inches next full moon. When she was small, her mothers had always told her there was no point growing your hair longer than your knees. All five of them had kept their hair so short they looked bald. It felt best, they said. Medea was sure they were right. She just wasn't willing to give up the magical power contained in long, strong hair.

Turning to the bowl with the blood mixture, she made seven straight rows of cakes and left them to warm. The sun was low, and the light scarce. Swiftly she poured hot water over the sprigs of rosemary, wiped her hands on the tattered dishcloth, and hugged herself for warmth, rubbing her arms. In half an hour the water would have taken what it needed from the rosemary, drawing out whatever it was that prompted Eldest's memory. Not that it worked miracles, but Medea did whatever she could to get even a single moment of clarity with her sister.

The wind stole in through the cracks around the window, drawing eddies in the dust on the sill. The convent couldn't afford to maintain the house, and of course nobody was interested in keeping up the buildings in the slum. They were waiting for the whole lot to be swallowed up in earth, so they could build something new and round.

At least there was hot water in the taps, which was more than they had in the few remaining buildings in Nørrebro or Vesterbro. It was probably only a matter of time before nature reclaimed the last two bridge districts, as it had Østerbro the year before. In Frederiksberg, meanwhile, several residential areas were still standing, mostly big houses like the one the convent had used for over a hundred years. Sadly, some were uninhabitable, ruins almost, because they'd stood empty so long. Medea thought it was a shame. There was no denying that the angular houses and straight roads were a reminder of patriarchal times, which no one wanted to think about, but these were old, historic buildings. She hoped a miracle would happen, that the people in charge of deciding these things would find a vein of nostalgia and take pity on the aging homes. But not many these days were inclined to indulge the past, and the notion that the slums might be integrated into some sort of urban plan along with the round areas was too naive. She should just be happy that as long as the walls stayed upright, houses like the convent would be left untouched. Nobody these days approved of the old-fashioned masculine enthusiasm for razing walls and leveling buildings with machines. Nature must be allowed to take its course, to devour and obliterate humanity's earlier self-destructive attempts at a society. Men had spent centuries wrecking everything in their path, so it was no wonder it would take nature centuries to redress the balance.

Although the convent leaked and needed a caring hand more or less everywhere, Medea loved the dark old house in spite of its straight walls, ceilings, corners, and rectangular windows. It wasn't houses, after all, that had made society bad, but the people who had lived in them. Medea thought about it a lot but had never said so out loud to anyone but Eldest, who sometimes agreed with her.

The sun was gone. In fifteen minutes the rosemary would be finished steeping. She got the rest of the meal ready on a tray for Eldest and the boy. It was lucky she was so familiar with the kitchen, because she couldn't see much. She jogged on the spot to get the blood circulating, then crept stiffly into the warmth between the dogs in the corner, who made room for her. She lifted the male's large paw and placed it over her, drew the young female close to her body and gave herself permission to doze off. Just until the rosemary was ready.

She woke with a start. The birds were screeching in the front room. The moon shone through the dull panes. How long had she been asleep? The rat snake slithered noiselessly past her, already on the hunt for rats, of which there were unfortunately plenty. It was because of the rats that this was the only one of her snakes allowed to move freely through all the rooms. It was the last of its species. A year ago she'd had three, but she found two of them dead in Eldest's room within the span of a few months.

Medea had asked if she knew how they had died. Eldest had begun to cry, so Medea had to console her instead of getting an answer.

Where she was supposed to find a spare rat snake she didn't know, but if the last one died and the rats got the upper hand they were done for. Huge numbers of rats were currently being released in the area. Only females. They were too clever to fall for the traps Medea had set in the garden. But luckily not too clever to be nabbed by a rat snake.

Three angry stomps on the floor above. Medea looked up. Eldest, once the convent's most even-tempered sister, now had daily outbursts of rage.

The dogs protested sleepily as she pushed them aside and stood up. Wrapping an extra shawl around her shoulders, she briefly looked in on the birds, which were fussing about the lack of food.

Later, she thought to them. They shrieked querulously.

The rosemary water was cold. Medea took a few sips before she hurried upstairs with the tray—there was no harm in clearing her own mind a little. Eldest was eating less and less these days, and when she did clean her plate it was usually because the boy had finished it for her. He was in the middle of a growth spurt. The cut-off tunic that used to belong to one of the sisters who had died was beginning to look too short.

"What do you want?" snarled Eldest when Medea unlocked the door and set the tray in front of them. The boy grinned cheerfully at her and took a carrot. He had thrown off the tunic and was naked despite the cold. All he wore was the cloth bag. Eldest had sewn it for him four years ago when he turned three, from the same blue fabric her skirts were made of. On it, in the middle, she had embroidered a red raspberry, because raspberries were what he most liked eating. The boy loved that bag. He always carried it, even when he was naked.

Medea could never get used to seeing the fleshy appendage between his legs and preferred him to wear clothes.

"Dinner," said Medea to Eldest. "It's broccoli today." Picking up the tunic, she tossed it in the boy's direction. He put it on obediently.

"Ugh," snorted Eldest, spitting out the food and glaring at Medea with childish defiance. Her thin white hair was pasted to her scalp on top and bristled awkwardly at the back.

Medea felt impelled to smooth the hair—she couldn't bear to see Eldest this way. For eight years they had been the only sisters in the convent. And Silence, of course. But Silence disappeared into the slum every day, often all night too. In any case, she never said a word.

"Drink this," said Medea, holding out the rosemary water to Eldest. Eldest sniffed it and stuck out her tongue.

"Ugh, I don't want that."

"Take a sip, you'll feel better."

"I'm fine. Fine fine fine." Eldest rocked back and forth, repeating the word to a tune Medea had heard her sing to the boy when he was little and going to sleep.

The boy sang along, although his mouth was full of food. Picking up the glass of rosemary water, he lifted it to his mouth. Hastily Medea grabbed it back. She had no idea what rosemary did to testosterone and had neither the time nor the energy to experiment.

"Drink this instead." She gave him a glass of water.

The boy didn't seem to have noticed that Eldest wasn't the person she had been before. So long as he had a warm human body to nestle up to, someone to sing with, and enough to eat, he seemed content.

Nor did it seem as though he needed more space than the two cramped rooms where he had always lived, at the back of the first floor. They had built an extra wall so outsiders couldn't tell there were two rooms. Not that guests ever saw the upper story, but it was best to be on the safe side. The handful of people who visited the stall never went inside, merely hurried on. Only those who bought snakes from Medea came indoors, but briefly and only as far as the basement. Nobody wanted to linger among witches longer than strictly necessary.

Eldest fell asleep, mouth open and head propped against the wall. The boy crept up beside her and drew the blanket over them both. He pointed at the fork in Medea's hair and laughed, his green eyes narrowing to slits. Medea smiled, tugged it out of her hair, and gave it to him. He tried at first to wedge the fork into his own white mop, but Medea had cut off too many tufts for her experiments for it to stay put. Instead he rested the fork against his cheek, like a teddy bear, and shut his eyes.

Medea shut the door carefully and went down the corridor. Outside Silence's door was a cup of menstrual blood. So she was home, then. The smell of sweet clover was as intense as ever outside her door. Silence hated the rat snakes—her door was always closed and every gap stopped. Instead she held the rats at bay with the stench. Or perhaps Silence thought it smelled nice; she was obsessed with the plant and believed it could be used for everything. As far as Medea knew, it was good for nothing but keeping out the mice and rats.

She picked up the cup. At least Silence could still be helpful with a drop of blood, though it was becoming increasingly meager. Medea wasn't sure exactly how old Silence was, but she'd have guessed late forties. Where she was going to find blood for the lovecakes once Silence was also keeping her wisdom's blood to herself, Medea didn't know. Maybe she could try the dogs'. But they rarely bled, and it was difficult to collect. She'd tried once with chicken blood, but that was lying to her clients. She had too much respect for her profession to hoodwink people like that.

Medea went downstairs, giving her usual deferential greeting to the goddesses and Pan, each of whom had their own bust on a shelf along the stairs.

The birds screeched when they heard her approaching the kitchen and the front room, which were adjoining. Madam, a glossy black myna with an orange beak, was hopping hysterically from twig to twig, blue bow tie bobbing furiously. Eldest was very attached to her birds, but especially to Madam, who was nearly fifteen years old. Her absence upset the bird, which showed its distress by being more angry than usual. Medea would have to take it out flying in the morning. Madam needed to stretch her wings. The crows weren't demanding; they could happily sit and doze for a few days, so long as there was enough food.

You'll be let out tomorrow, she tried telling Madam with her mind. It cocked its head and stared at her blankly.

"Tomorrow," she said loudly. Madam gave another squawk and a shake of the head, took flight, and landed on another branch in the cage. In fact, it was capable of opening the cage itself and flying out whenever it pleased, but it would be in a huff for days if you didn't heed it by opening the door. She gave the birds a few handfuls of seeds each. Madam scowled and turned its back. It was used to better. Medea shook her head resignedly and put a blanket over the cage.

Silence came into the kitchen while Medea was cleaning up after baking the cakes.

"Are you going out?"

Silence looked straight past her. Mute as always.

"In this cold?" Medea went on. "Don't get your hair wet again. I can't make any more cream for your scalp fungus until the spring."

Silence didn't look back as she went out the door, but she waited a moment for the little female dog, which often trailed her when she left the house. The door slammed behind them. Through the poorly insulated windows, Medea could hear the ground frost crunch under Silence's boots. She sighed. She ought to go out too. Dig for loveroots for the next batch of cakes and find male animals for Pythia. But the chill would have made the soil as hard as stone, and it was too dark for catching animals. She would have to wait until tomorrow.

She listened. The whole house was asleep. Making hardly a sound, she went downstairs and took her clothes off in the anteroom, not bothering to fasten the golden snake cloak. Moments later she was shutting the door behind her, and Pythia was curling happily around her body. With Pythia, she didn't need to speak out loud to be understood.

The lovecakes were ready by the time she got up. The sun wasn't yet in the sky, and she still had a few hours until Eldest and the boy woke. While she ate some of what little food there was, she wrapped up the cakes one by one. A couple of them were going to the stall outside the convent. The rest she had promised to Lars from the Street. Lars was always up early, caring for the little ones he nursed. He slept a few hours during the day and worked with clients in the evening, as well as through most of the night. He had ordered an extra batch of lovecakes this time. Medea hoped he'd trade her some more energy for the radiators in exchange.

"My clients are still obsessed with those cakes," he'd said with a laugh. "I haven't lost a single customer in all the years I've been serving them those things. I do it before they put their clothes back on. One of these days you've got to tell me what's in them—I'm certainly not eating one. I'd probably end up falling permanently in love with you."

Medea had laughed. "If I hand over the recipe, I'll have nothing left to trade with."

"Just promise me you won't give the cakes to the other man-ladies on the Street. I want to be the popular one. You can have whatever I can get my hands on in return. Once my clients get their first taste of a lovecake, they'll pay anything."

The cakes only just fit into the backpack, which she put onto the large male dog. She slipped a pick into the side pocket, then went into the front room and snatched the blanket off Madam's cage. She opened the door.

"Coming?"

Madam, not usually shy when it came to making noise, glared at her irritably. It took flight, swooped once or twice around the room, and then landed between the male dog's ears. The dog shook its head, making its ears flap back and forth, but it knew if it protested too much then Madam would dig its claws into the dog's scalp and force it to carry the myna anyway.

The male dog trotted along good-naturedly beside Medea. It always came along when she went gathering. It helped her carry home crops, herbs, and roots, or anything usable she found among the ruins. Madam cocked its head, darting glances to either side as it looked for a more exciting perch.

Medea tugged the hat farther down onto her head, trying to keep out the frost. She drew the dogskin more tightly around her waist and hiked up the woolen socks inside her boots.

A ratgirl stood near one of the sagging houses by the Street, holding a basket crammed with rats. Although the general agreement was to wait as nature took its course, clearing away the negative energies of the past, people turned a blind eye to the ratgirls, who had taken it upon themselves to give nature a little nudge, to speed up the process of swallowing old walls and roofing tiles. As for why they weren't so strict about preaching slowness to them, it was presumably because the ratgirls' weapon was nature itself.

They went around with their baskets in the early hours of the day, setting down rats that chewed through foundations, ancient wires, and other patriarchal debris, and left the houses riddled and crumbling. In the summer months the ratgirls planted Japanese bamboo, which grew at an explosive speed and bored through everything, all sharp roots and pointed spears.

Disputes would arise at regular intervals as to whether nature was really natural if it was being helped along. Philosophers argued, debaters met, and days passed as the subject was discussed around the country. Then the conversation ground to a halt. At no point did the ratgirls stop setting out rats in the areas they believed were due for clearing so that new, round things could be built instead.

The ratgirls had been targeting the area around the convent relentlessly for the past few years. It was because of the Street, of course, which many people wanted swallowed up by nature more quickly than the clayish soil could manage on its own, but unfortunately, they seemed to think that the surrounding buildings, like the convent, should go down with it. Probably they were hoping Lars and the other manladies would scatter to the winds, that they might be forced to give up their trade instead of simply moving a few houses down.

Medea had never understood why so many people frowned on the Street when they accepted Centers like the one at Lolland without batting an eye. Men at the Center didn't even choose when they wanted to wake up or use their voices. Meanwhile, the manladies on the Street were free; but then again they weren't real men but women with silicone fakes.

The ratgirl followed Medea with her eyes. The woman was over a hundred years old, and the basket's weight made her shoulders sag. She walked stoop-backed among the ruins. When the ratgirls had first started to take a real interest in helping nature in this part of Frederiksberg, Medea had tried to scare them off with formulas and curses. To no avail. Then she'd tried to make friends with them, so that they would spare the convent the rats and bamboo.

"We're not hurting anybody. This is our home," Medea had said, offering several of the ratgirls cakes made with pacifying herbs. Only one had accepted. The rest had tried to recruit Medea instead.

"You can make a difference too," they'd said. "We can always do with an extra pair of hands. It's been hundreds of years since the Evolution first picked up momentum, of course, but it's still a huge task repairing all the nature the men destroyed. Don't you want to help our planet breathe freely again?"

Medea had kept out of their sight ever since. Her defense was to let the rat snakes loose around the house.

The big window that overlooked the Street was dark. It was the only one in the former supermarket where Lars lived. In the seven years they'd known each other, Medea had never been inside. She'd never had a reason to be invited in, so she'd been no farther than the covered terrace outside the window, where Lars had set out lanterns, armchairs, and warm blankets. The terrace was where his clients waited if he wasn't finished with the job currently underway, and his was the nicest on the whole Street. She suspected it wasn't just the lovecakes that made him popular.

Medea stood for a moment outside Lars's window. The Street was unusually peaceful. A couple of the other manladies poked drowsy heads out of their little homes but disappeared when they saw it was only Medea.

She didn't want to wake Lars, or disturb him if he'd finally gotten one of the little ones to sleep. Instead she went around to the back, where she always dug up loveroots for the cakes. A heating pipe ran along the edge of the wall, which was good for the plants. The trouble was, the ground was frozen.

"Come," she called to Madam, pointing. Eldest had used her birds to peck the soil soft. Madam lifted obligingly into the air, then passed elegantly over Medea's head and on above the houses.

Stupid bird, she thought, taking the backpack off the male dog's back and fishing the pick out of the side pocket. From a corner of the garden she fetched the green blanket that she used to protect her knees when she dug. She shook the cold out of it and folded it a couple of times before laying it on the ground.

A jolt rattled up Medea's arm as she swung the pick into the frozen dirt. Madam came sweeping overhead and landed back on the dog.

"Come on," she repeated imploringly. She tried to mimic the gestures and sounds Eldest had used to make the birds obey. But Madam only preened its feathers and pretended not to hear. Frustrated, she scraped at the ground with the pick but couldn't get down far enough to reach the roots. She looked at the dog, which stared back as it tried to make the bird let go, wriggling clumsily and scrabbling with one front paw. Madam only clung on tighter, even as the dog yowled, bolted out of the garden, and hared off down the Street, vanishing out of sight. Madam's delighted chortles grew fainter, until at last they were inaudible. Medea sighed and hacked with all her strength. Sweat ran down her back beneath the shaggy dogskin. After a while she could see the top of a root and started pulling. She landed on her back, winded, with the root in her hand. Tiredness stung behind her eyes. It wasn't enough, but it would have to do. She got up and called the dog. It didn't come. Medea took the cakes out of the bag to make room for the root, then walked back toward the Street. If Lars was asleep, she'd leave them on the terrace.

He wasn't there. Just as she was about to put down the cakes, she heard footsteps farther up the street. A group of women was marching purposefully toward Medea. They were all dressed in velour and too clean to belong in the slum. Usually people like that came alone, or with a friend or two at most, if they were going to the Street or the convent, and they didn't stride down the pitted roads that way—they were tentative, either ashamed or exploring. These velour-clad women had to be here for something else. Medea froze. It was happening: they were coming to take her. Someone had found out about the boy upstairs. Eldest would be dragged away, despite her age, and Medea and Silence would be taken and put in with the *pensives*. The snakes would starve and devour each other until not one was left, Pythia would never be well, she would waste away and turn to dust, and the birds, unused to finding their own seeds, would die. It was happening, now, the thing she'd feared for seven years, ever since they hid the boy. Tears collected in her throat, and her hands shook as she bent to put the cakes on Lars's terrace. At least he would have those. The last cakes he'd ever get.

A woman in velour grabbed her arm. She wanted to run, but her legs refused. She couldn't even scream. The cakes never made it to the terrace; she clutched them to her body instead, feeling them deform under the pressure. She was so certain it was her they were coming for that she didn't even hurry away when she was pushed aside and the women in velour barged into Lars's home without knocking.

"These, they're the ones he used to poison me," one shouted.

"Careful, don't touch that," another one howled.

"What are you doing here?" Lars cried. Something toppled. A child screamed.

"Take that cake, we need to have it analyzed," the first voice said.

Lars was bundled out onto the terrace, gazing startled at Medea, who still hadn't moved a muscle. His silicone penis flopped lazily between his legs as he tried to pull his coat over his swelling bosom. Noticing the cakes in Medea's arms, he shook his head unobtrusively.

"Grab her too, she's stealing," he said, pointing at Medea. "Look, she's stolen a whole armful of my cakes."

One of the women in velour tore the cakes out of Medea's grip. "Don't eat those, they'll poison you and make you do strange things," the woman said as she began to troop off up the street with the rest of the group. They had a firm hold on Lars, who was complaining loudly.

"Those cakes are harmless—don't tell me you believe in magic? They're just a bit of fun. There's nothing in there but chocolate and a few spices. You'll only end up embarrassing yourselves!"

"Be quiet. You might as well get used to it—you're going to be pensive for a long time."

They disappeared around the corner.

More than a minute passed before Medea got over the shock. Clutching the amulet around her neck, she ran. Across the Street and down the road toward the convent. She crashed head-on into the ratgirl from before, knocking them both off their feet and tossing the basket into the air. Rats scurried away in every direction. Medea managed to get up—the lack of food and sleep made everything spin. She forced herself to carry on, first with a few unsteady steps, then at a jog, until she reached the convent.

The male dog sat outside. Madam was perched in the big chestnut tree, which filled the whole sky above the building. It was whistling a march. Both of them followed her inside. She threw off the dogskin and sat down in the kitchen, breathing heavily, then burst into tears.

Madam, circling the ceiling, mimicked her sobs.

"Stop it," she wailed at the bird.

"Stop it," Madam repeated.

Medea crawled tearfully to the fridge and took out a bottle of nettle juice to fortify herself. It was moldy around the edge. She drank it anyway.

The dog licked her forehead. Medea leaned against it, into its soothing warmth. Relief, because it wasn't her the women in velour had taken, soon calmed her breathing. She dozed off for a moment, tears still dripping onto the dog's damp fur, but woke with a start at the thought of what would happen if they found out who had made the cakes. She was about to cry again when Silence came in from outside. There were icicles in her wet hair, and she gazed in astonishment at Medea's tearstained face. The female and the male dog, reunited, launched into a vigorous dance that knocked Medea sideways. At the same moment, Eldest thumped angrily on the floorboards above.

It had been six months since Wicca's first and only visit to the convent. Whenever they were together it was at her place, in Himlingeøje. Medea told herself it was better that way, because she could take the opportunity to check on the little white cobra Wicca had bought, but the real reason she went to Himlingeøje was that she was ashamed of the convent, especially compared to the roundhouse where Wicca lived. She didn't even consider inviting her over. Which suited Wicca just fine.

"That convent is just too disgusting," she'd said.

It wasn't as though Medea went around all day thinking how dirty it was, but the slum was the slum, and she couldn't help it that the convent smelled, given how many dogs, birds, and snakes they kept.

Wicca, like the other priests who'd knocked at the convent door over the years, had been looking for a snake. A cobra. Not many of them came. The Christians preferred to breed their own and were loath to have anything to do with witches' snakes. That some had come at all was because Medea was known for rearing exceptionally healthy snakes. Every once in a while, enthusiasts even traveled from abroad to buy a rare specimen from her brood. Her white cobras and two-headed orange milk snakes were particularly sought after, since they were near impossible to find in acceptable condition elsewhere. The single-sex black worm snakes were also popular, of course. They could reproduce without mating with a male, and all the eggs they hatched were females. But their popularity tended to come in waves. She bred them because she had a standing agreement with a group of researchers who hadn't given up hope of being able to continue the human species without the need for males. If the worm snake could clone itself without its genes becoming too homogenous, then humans should be able to as well, they reasoned. "There are plants that can do it too," they said. "One day, it will be our turn."

Medea thought this was unlikely. Snakes and people just weren't all that comparable. But the researchers were paying her enough that she chose not to share this opinion with them.

Sales of the items produced at the convent had been declining year after year. In its heyday they'd sold scented oils and magic creams, read fortunes in tarot cards, stars, and greenflies. People had bought amulets made of snail's shells, petrified sea urchins, adders' fangs, and teeth, nails, eyelashes, and locks of hair from the strongest of the sisters. Things weren't like that anymore. Medea had to sell whatever could be sold.

Wicca hadn't come to the convent on the strength of Medea's reputation. She came because she was desperate. Her last cobra had died, another in a long line of snakes Wicca had been unable to keep alive.

She'd come trudging through the door one day in summer, sweaty and sullen from the long walk through the slum. Didn't bother knocking. It was the hottest day of the year, when the sun was high and there was no shade to be found on the dusty streets. The little female dog snarled, but Wicca swept it aside with a wave of her hand. The dog slunk discontentedly into the corner and lay down. It was rare for the female to be anything but friendly.

"No—don't tell me humans *live* in here." Wicca put her hands on her hips and wrinkled her nose. "There was a bird outside with a bow around its neck, chasing me. I think it was shouting curses at me. And it shit on me right on the doorstep."

"Welcome," Medea said, but only half turned. She was making lovecakes. She knew immediately that Wicca was a Christian priest because around her neck was the snake-green stole they always wore. They only took it off when they slept, or when they wrapped the real thing, the cobra, around their necks at services. Medea also knew they didn't like to be kept waiting, but she had to make sure the chocolate and blood were at exactly the same temperature when they were stirred in. Otherwise there'd be no magic in them.

"Just a minute, I'll be right with you," she said, sticking an investigative finger into the dough.

Silence entered the room, wet-haired and carrying a bowl of sprouting aquatic plants. Like much of her other vegetation, they probably needed the extra warmth on the windowsill. Silence glowered at Wicca, who stared back at her indifferently. She seemed more interested in the plants.

"You should have some orgasms next to your plants. It'll give them a boost of energy," she said. "Looks like they need it."

Silence kept going as though she hadn't heard.

Madam fluttered through the window and into her cage. Underneath it, Eldest was asleep in her rocking chair. Last summer she'd still been coming down to the front room during the day. The chair creaked. Madam mimicked the sound with every rock.

"There it is again, the silly bird. Does it live here?" Wicca asked irritably.

"How can I help you?" Medea wiped her hands on her apron, which was already stained with dried blood.

Wicca was barely five foot five, but that was tall enough to look down on Medea, especially if you took her attitude into account.

"I thought you were a child." Wicca didn't even try to hide a smirk. "Your dogs are as big as you are."

"I'm not tall," Medea said patiently. "Is it a cobra you want?"

"Yes, mine is sick. Well, actually it's dead. I'm a priest, I *must* have my own snake."

"Of course. This way." Medea took off the apron.

"I thought they'd mostly gotten rid of patriarchal buildings like this," Wicca said, eyeing the dim windows and blotched walls with distaste as she followed Medea down to the basement.

"We're hoping our area will be spared. These are old buildings, historic. The house is many hundreds of years old. Built at the end of the twentieth century."

"I guess there's a chance they'll let the house remain, as a kind of Auschwitz—a perpetual reminder and a warning to posterity."

Medea nodded. She had no idea what Auschwitz was. Apprenticing in magic had its advantages over ordinary schooling—general historical knowledge was not one of them.

In spite of Wicca's disgust with the convent, Medea felt drawn to her. Her body fat danced erotically under her thin red dress. The fabric made a contrast to her skin, which glistened with each ray of sunlight that fell through the gray glass. Probably the walk in the heat. The snake stole undulated behind her as she walked. Painfully aware of how grubby and unkempt she must look, Medea tried hastily to neaten her hair as she walked down the stairs, with Wicca following.

"You can wait here," she said and went into the anteroom to don her golden cloak and fragrances. Through the crack she could see Wicca leaning impatiently against the wall, staring at her nails. Biting a cuticle and glancing incuriously around the dark basement. But the expression in her eyes shifted abruptly when Medea emerged in the cloak, long hair braided.

"You look different," Wicca exclaimed, eyes sweeping her up and down.

"Come in," said Medea, smiling.

The snakes were reticent and wouldn't come out like they did when Medea was alone. While she was changing, she'd told them this was a day when she'd brought a guest. And that one of them, the right one, would be going to a new home.

"I heard rumors you had two-headed snakes, but I didn't

know whether to believe it." Wicca bent over the vivarium where the larger of the two double-heads lived. Both heads hissed suspiciously up at the stranger.

"Are you selling them?"

"I thought you only used cobras?"

"Yes, but it might be interesting to have one with two heads. I've got a daughter who's nearly seven. She'd think it was fun."

"They're not easy to look after," Medea said, trying not to sound too dismissive. "The heads tend to quarrel and attack each other. If one of them has just been fed and it smells of food, the other one occasionally decides to eat it, even though they're attached to the same body. Sometimes I have to keep the heads separated with a board when I feed them. More than once after selling one it's died soon afterward."

"What are your female cobras like? The last one I had got parasites. Just disgusting. It wasn't symmetrical at all, it had bulges everywhere. In the end it died."

Medea looked at her dubiously. "Cobras aren't that hard to keep."

Wicca shrugged. "Maybe there's something wrong with my vivarium."

"My old white cobra is with eggs, and I only have one female left from the previous clutch. It's still young. It'll be a few months before you can use it in church. Not until winter, probably." Medea picked up the little white female. It wove happily in and out between her fingers. "It's a female you wanted, isn't it?"

Wicca nodded.

"It's not big yet, but with the right diet and care it'll grow nicely, and you'll be able to wear it around your neck."

Wicca gazed in fascination at the small white snake. "No one else at church has a white cobra. They'd be very impressed if I showed up with one."

"You'll have to be careful. My white cobras' venom is strong."

"Oh, I've been trained up since childhood. I'm from Walborg's bloodline—does that mean anything to you?"

Medea shook her head. "The white cobras are a little more difficult to care for than ordinary cobras, so perhaps you should try and find out why your last cobra didn't thrive?"

Several of the snakes had ventured out and were hanging off Medea's arms, slithering up and down her legs and around her waist.

Wicca was looking at her hungrily. "Maybe you could come to my place and take a look at my vivarium?"

The first time Medea visited Wicca in the round district at Himlingeøje was a week after she bought the little white cobra. Medea went to check on the snake, and to be sure the vivarium wasn't broken, but also because she couldn't stop thinking about Wicca's dark beauty. Usually, only snakes intrigued her like that.

From the moment she woke up on the summer morning they'd arranged her visit, Medea was nervous. Even the night before, she'd struggled with insomnia and had to go downstairs and lie with Pythia to catch a few hours' sleep.

She'd never been inside a house in one of the round districts before. She'd only seen them from the outside, racing past on the train. She brushed the dust from her snake cloak, spit-dabbed a few stains off the front, and put it on. It felt silly, getting all dressed up when it wasn't for the snakes. Silence watched in surprise as she passed her in the kitchen, wearing the golden cloak. For once, Medea was glad she didn't speak.

She chose the least dirty and overgrown paths through the Frederiksberg slum, hoping she wouldn't be too repellent when she arrived, and walked as slowly as possible so she wouldn't get there sweaty.

As she crossed the Street, Lars swapped a nursing infant from one breast to the other and waved to her from his terrace. She waved back, fighting the urge to run up and tell him what she was doing. Instead she went on, past what remained of the town hall tower, along the old park and toward the outskirts, where the train stopped to drop off and pick up curious ramblers or shame-faced visitors to the Street. The slum's inhabitants themselves rarely had any cause or desire to leave. Medea was so excited she couldn't help smiling. Not even the two gray-haired ratgirls, waiting with their empty baskets, brought her down.

The stops near the slums were nothing but wooden footboards, provisional structures designed to be easily removed the minute nature had finished swallowing the past. To build anything larger would be counterproductive, making it even harder for nature to clean up.

Getting off at the Himlingeøje stop was a very different experience. Medea had only used the stop at the Center in Lolland, but she'd seen the others from the train on her way there. Unlike the wooden boards in the slum, the other stops were a sensory experience, ornamented with beautiful paintings, plants, and poetry at once entertaining, moving, and expertly crafted, which changed according to the seasons and the passengers' moods.

You never had to wait long for the train. The cars ran all the time and in every direction. It took no more than twelve minutes to reach Himlingeøje from the Frederiksberg slum, but getting from the train to the convent was another matter. In the slum, the only mode of transport was your feet. Medea, however, had found a rusty old scooter that she rode if she needed to go farther than the Street and the back garden where the loveroots were—although only if there was no ice on the roads. She had found the scooter under a pile of rubble in a ruined garage. Speeding across the bumpy roads felt like taking her life in her hands, but she loved how quickly she could get around, gathering plants from the various sectors of the slum.

When Medea got off at Himlingeøje, the ratgirls stayed on

board. There was nothing for them to do in the round districts. The whole area had been cleared of the past and was now soft and accommodating.

Wicca had given her detailed directions to the roundhouse where she lived with eight other women and their children. The curving paths and gorgeous flowers that hung above them were the loveliest things Medea had ever seen. Their scent was so beautiful that she felt ecstatic walking there. At several points along the path, smaller branches curved away toward other roundhouses. They were like oases among the hills, dotted with old trees, new trees, plants, and animals grazing where the land was flattest.

Following Wicca's instructions, Medea turned right, down a path where the plants, flowers, and musical notes exploded in cascades of purple. The arch above the entryway glowed faintly as she stepped in front of it, and minutes later Wicca opened the door.

"You found it." She smiled, grasped Medea's arm, and drew her inside. She was wearing a dress in a deeper red than the one she'd had on when she bought the snake. The fabric seemed light around her large, voluptuous body. Medea had never seen someone so beguiling: the mere sight of her somehow eased her longing for all the things she hadn't known she craved.

Wicca let go of her arm for a moment, but only to take her hand.

"Come on," she said, leading Medea through the house, a rippling succession of soft materials and muted tones, one after another without edge. It was like moving through well-being. Clean and fragrant. Medea felt even grimier and more matted than usual.

"Here's my room," said Wicca, closing the door behind them. The space was oval, taken up mainly by two beds, one large and one small.

"My daughter Wendy sleeps here with me, but she won't be

back until tomorrow." Wicca went across to the vivarium. "Here's the snake—as you can see, she's fine."

Medea reached her hand down to the small white cobra, which gladly wound itself up her fingers and around her wrist. Medea shut her eyes, enjoying the feel of its warm, silk-soft body against her skin.

"She likes you more than she likes me," Wicca said, sounding aggrieved. "She slithers off if I go to pick her up. The minute I get anywhere near the vivarium she starts hissing."

"Nonsense," Medea said, without opening her eyes.

"I hope she'll warm up to me. Because she seems stronger than the other snakes I've had. The last ones were all a bit floppy. Easier to handle at services, of course, but they died at the drop of a hat." Wicca reached out for the small cobra, which immediately darted into the opening of Medea's sleeve.

"There, see," said Wicca, disappointed. "I was really looking forward to showing her off. I haven't even told my mother about her, because I want to surprise her at the first service I take her to. I can't wait to see her face when she realizes I've got a more interesting snake than she does."

"Give her time," Medea whispered, kissing the cobra. "She's young. You can't use her for a few months anyway, so you've got plenty of time to get acquainted."

"I hope you're right. I'm tired of having to borrow a snake from my mother, plus I can't keep doing that if I want to move up the ranks." Wicca sighed. "Now why don't you put the cobra down and come over here?"

Medea gave the snake another kiss, throwing a disapproving glance at a turd in the vivarium, which Wicca had not removed. She decided not to comment. Instead she put the cobra back and climbed into bed beside Wicca, who was about to put her arm around her when she stopped and eyed Medea critically. "Maybe you should take a bath?"

"Okay," Medea said, chastened.

"Just down the hall. There are warm towels in the closet."

The curved bathroom door was locked when Medea turned the handle. Puzzled, she tried again. She hadn't thought locks were used in round areas.

She leaned patiently against the wall and waited. Everything about this place made her feel inadequate. The walls were hung with old maps, tracing roads and buildings that must have long since fallen into ruin. *Aarhus, Risskov*, she spelled out in her mind. She could write and spell, of course, despite her piecemeal schooling, but mostly just ingredients, when she had to jot down a recipe.

She slid her hand into her pocket, holding her snow quartz for calm. Sorting through the stones in her other pocket, she found the yellow citrine and felt faith in her own worth flow up her arm and into her heart.

The door opened with a jerk, and an angular face surrounded by wispy hair poked out.

"Sorry, I have a tendency to shut the door in a way that makes it stick. Come on in," the woman said. "My name's Eva. Are you Wicca's snake-tamer?"

Medea nodded, crossing the threshold hesitantly. She knew it was rude, wanting to be alone in the toilet or the shower, but she preferred it that way purely out of habit. There'd been so few of them in the convent for so long that she mostly bathed alone. Moreover, the house was so old that it was blessed with numerous small toilets and bathrooms, unlike newer buildings, which only had one large bathroom, often the biggest room in the house. This one had space for at least ten people, with multiple toilets and menstrual tubs and various different ways to wash.

Eva was in her forties and seemed twice Medea's height, although the difference was probably no more than eighteen inches.

She wore a tight blue dress that made her look even taller and more raw-boned. Out of her pocket peeped a rat.

"She sent you to take a shower?" Eva shook her head and laughed kindly at Medea. "Typical Wicca. Don't take it personally. She says and does whatever she feels like. The only person she respects is her mother." Eva dabbed her lipstick with an embroidered handkerchief, which she then crumpled and threw away.

"Well, I did come in from the slum," Medea said apologetically.

"No need to be ashamed of that. I lived there when I was a child."

"You lived in the slum?"

"Yeah. It can be pretty homey, actually. At least you're left in peace." Eva smiled. "But I think I've seen you before. Down at the Center in Lolland, maybe?"

"Maybe." Medea hesitated.

"I'm a doctor there. I used to be in the breeding department, and now I work with the juvenile males, so I don't know much about what goes on at the spa. Do you visit us often? Maybe you've got a favorite type? Most people do."

Medea didn't have time to answer before Eva remembered where she'd seen her. "Wait, you're the one demonstrating outside the Center every Friday!" The affable tone was gone. Eva took the rat in her hand and then put it on her shoulder. "What exactly are you hoping to achieve by protesting against the Center?"

"I just think . . ." Medea began.

Eva raised her voice. "You want men loose on the streets, do you? You don't think history has proven how much of a threat they are to us humans?"

Medea bit her lower lip. She regretted having ventured into territory as unfamiliar as the round district. She was sure of herself in the slum, but here she wasn't on home turf. Men were often a touchy subject, although mostly among older women. They'd had foremothers on the front lines, women who had lived long enough to tell tales of bygone traumas from the age of their great-grandparents. The younger generations were slower to anger. They preferred to enjoy the society their foremothers had fought for rather than spend time being outraged by the injustices of those early days. The past to them was a topic to be discussed in class, a subject for history lessons. At break time they spoke with a shudder about what it must have been like to live under male rule day after day, night after night, every minute of every hour. But once you left school, life got too busy. It was rare to see someone of Eva's age getting so riled up.

"You do realize that ninety-six percent of all murders were committed by men, back when they were walking among us? You've got to remember that it's not the human species that's murderous, it's men. You know, the ones you feel so sorry for. If your project ever does succeed, I sincerely hope I'm not still here to witness it." Eva turned on her heel, then changed her mind and took a step back toward Medea.

"I don't know if you witches are even able to read or write, but you might want to consider why there are so many words that don't exist in feminine forms. Like gunman or henchman. Or warlord."

Eva strode off down the corridor, the rat's tail dangling down her shoulder blade. She disappeared into another room and slammed the door behind her.

Medea had tears in her eyes. All she wanted was to close the door—lock it, even. But she left it open, afraid of breaking more rules, as she took off her clothes and got into the shower. Thankfully, no one came. Nor, to her great relief, did she see anybody else as she hurried back down the corridors and into Wicca's bedroom.

She should have been used to people disliking her when they

found out what she was. She wished she didn't care, like Eldest and the other sisters, but she had to admit it stung when people wouldn't meet her gaze, when they rolled their eyes or insulted her like Eva had.

As a Christian, Wicca should have been more firmly opposed than anyone to what Medea was, but either she was as benevolent as her religion directed or, perhaps, she was seeing Medea through a fog of infatuation. Of lust, really. Probably.

When Medea came back into the room, her long hair so wet that she dripped puddles of water wherever she stood still, Wicca received her with arms outstretched. She wrapped them lovingly around her, and Medea felt enveloped in a greater warmth and desire than she'd known in all her life. The last traces of unpleasantness faded as she allowed herself to be lifted onto the bed and Wicca's ample belly enclosed itself around her slim, slight frame.

After Medea's first visit to Wicca's, they began to see each other regularly. Mostly on Fridays, when it was convenient for Medea to stop by on her way from Lolland after the protest. Missing Wicca wasn't the only reason she visited Himlingeøje. Once the weather turned cold, it was more comfortable, because she could get warm before she continued on home. And she could make sure the snake was doing well. Over the fall she cured it of colds, constipation, and mouth infections, and helped it shed its first skin. Wicca showed no particular interest in the creature. Really, she had no business owning a snake at all.

"It could stay with me," Medea had suggested one day, when the snake was dull-eyed and lacked its usual appetite. "You could come and pick it up on the days you need it." This was before Medea knew how badly she needed the female cobra.

Wicca snorted. "I am a descendent of Walborg, who led Christianity back to its matriarchal origins and to the Mother.

I have to keep my snake with me to protect it from external influence."

"I'm just worried about it," Medea said quietly, tickling the cobra under its chin.

"Well, now I've got you to help me look after it, haven't I?" Wicca said affectionately, drawing Medea away from the vivarium. Medea enjoyed the sensation of disappearing into Wicca's embrace. Wicca's daughter, Wendy, came into the room singing, and Wicca contented herself with discreetly stroking Medea's breasts. It felt like a delicious warning of what to expect once Wendy went into Eva's room to embroider, which they did together every afternoon.

One Friday, Medea and Wicca fell asleep after making love. Medea awoke to Wendy shaking her mother, trying to rouse her. "Look, Mama, I lost it!"

Wicca grunted drowsily and turned over. Medea stretched indolently in the bed—she was warm all over.

"Mama, look."

Wicca still didn't respond. Medea leaned forward.

"What have you lost?"

"My first tooth." The girl held out a flat palm to Medea, and on it rested a small, square tooth. Medea picked it up and studied it from all sides.

"That's lovely. What are you going to do with it?"

"Mama just said to be careful I didn't swallow it."

"You could make an amulet." Medea was looking forward to the boy starting to lose his teeth too, back at the convent. Then she could experiment with them. Maybe she could crush them up and sprinkle them onto the animals she fed to the snakes. His testosterone might have a positive effect on Pythia's ailing health. She'd tried his hair, nail clippings, and urine, but no luck there. The next step could be a drop of blood or other bodily fluids.

"What's an amulet?" Wendy clambered up onto the bed, shoved vainly at her mother, and ended up wedging herself between them after Medea moved instead.

"An amulet is something that protects you."

"How can my tooth protect me?"

"It isn't necessarily you it protects. It could be your mother. Here, look, I've got teeth from my first snake in a little pouch around my neck." Medea drew out the chain that lay between her breasts and showed the amulet to Wendy. "Don't touch, but you can look."

"And if you put it around your neck, nothing can happen to you?"

"It helps me make decisions that keep me out of danger," said Medea. Wicca's eyelids fluttered, and she hurriedly stuffed the amulet back between her breasts.

"Wendy's lost her tooth," she said loudly, getting out of bed. She had no time for idling anyway. She got dressed, kissed Wicca goodbye, and climbed out of the window, followed by Wicca's laughter. After Eva's outburst on that first visit, she had no desire to bump into either her or any of the other women in Wicca's household, and used the window when she came and went.

FINDING A WIZENED OLD LOVECAKE UNDERNEATH A PACKET of elixirs for bad breath at the stall outside the convent, Medea's heart began to race. If the women in velour saw the cakes here, they might connect Medea with Lars, and she'd be found out. They'd throw her in with the pensives too. She fed it to the male dog, which had trailed outside after her. It gulped the cake down hungrily, and moments later it was rubbing up against her leg in devotion, howling with longing. What a waste. She could have traded several days of heat and light for that cake. But not now, of course. Not now that Lars had been taken.

Hands moving quickly, she rearranged the few items on display. It had been a long time since anyone had stopped to buy anything, but even so, they had to be ready. The convent couldn't afford to lose any income, no matter how small. Now that Eldest had stopped leaving her room, Medea had managed to convince Silence to mind the stall a couple of times a week, but more than once she'd gone abruptly missing, so Medea had to keep half an eye on it anyway.

Once she'd fed the animals and prepared dinner for Eldest and the boy, so that all Silence had to do was take it up to them, she hitched the dogskin tightly around her waist, grabbed the scooter, and sped off toward the train. She didn't want to get back too late, because tomorrow was a Thursday, but to be on the safe side she took the long way around, giving the Street a wide berth. Just in case anybody in velour was still sniffing around.

Outside Frederiksberg Gardens the scooter skidded on some ice, but at the last second she managed to regain her balance.

Half the entrance to the park was still aboveground. The rest had sunk so far into the earth that it would never be visible again.

"All right, what's so important you had to ask me face-to-face?" Wicca demanded, pulling her into an embrace as soon as she'd climbed through the window at Himlingeøje. She kissed Medea passionately, although Medea wasn't really in the mood. That wasn't why she'd come. Still, she let her do it. Let herself be lifted up and carried to the bed, where Wicca attacked her greedily.

"Why don't you start showering at home before you come over?" Wicca said between kisses, removing one of Medea's long hairs from the corner of her mouth.

"Okay," Medea said, concentrating all her energies on satisfying Wicca. It was crucial to get her in a good mood.

Afterward they lay side by side, breathless.

"It's just," Medea began, "in my last clutch of white cobras I had nothing but males."

"When the other priests see my white cobra for the first time on Saturday, I guarantee they'll all want one just like it," Wicca said. "You'd better make some more. My mother's bound to want one too, even though she's got seventeen cobras at home already. But she doesn't have any like my white one."

"That's the problem," said Medea. "I can't make any more white cobras because I don't have any females. So would you mind if I borrowed yours? Just until she has hatchlings, then you'll get her back. I'll throw in an extra snake as well. For free. And one for your mother!"

"No, that's not possible," Wicca said with a yawn. "I'm going to start using her soon—once I get my period. You'll have to find another snake to make babies with."

"Could my male come here, maybe?" Medea asked desperately.

"I can't cope with more than one snake, I've got more than enough to look after as it is."

Medea was inclined to agree. In any case, it was too risky to leave her only remaining white cobra in Wicca's vivarium.

"Are you sure I can't borrow her? You can have an ordinary cobra in the meantime . . ."

"Yes, I'm sure, and I'm also sure you're not leaving without one more go." Wicca laughed and threw herself for a second time on Medea, who pulled out all the tricks she knew Wicca liked best. Afterward, she gazed at her expectantly.

Wicca leaned contentedly back into the pillows.

"You know what," she said, "after the service on Saturday I'll bring the cobra to you. You get her fertilized and afterward I'll take her straight back. Can't you stay, sleep over tonight?"

"Sorry," Medea said, giving her a delighted kiss on the lips, "it's Thursday tomorrow."

"Ah, yes, big day for witches." Wicca grinned. "You'd better hurry up and be on your way."

She waved to Medea as she ran back down the path, the dog-skin flapping in her wake.

THURSDAY WAS THE LUCKIEST DAY FOR MAGIC, FOR HARvesting plants, studying crystals, stars, scents, and whatever else could be read. It had always been the busiest day at the convent.

For Medea it was the day she milked the snakes of venom.

She was in a cheerful mood. On Saturday the white female would be back, and then there'd be a trickle of small white males, and Pythia would get better. She hummed all the way through the slum.

The moment she opened the basement door, the snakes sensed her exuberance. The ones free to move in and out of their vivariums darted toward her, coiling up and around until she was covered in snakes.

Laughing, she walked with legs apart toward one of the two-headers and gingerly gave each head a piece of squirrel from the trap. The vine snake took umbrage at not being fed anything, changing color from green to black, but it calmed down when Medea gave it a hind leg.

"Crazy kids," she scolded affectionately.

She waited until she couldn't ignore Pythia any longer before shooing off all the other snakes. She could sense her inside the bunker, shifting restively back and forth along the wall.

Medea allowed her to coil up one leg and around her waist, where she squeezed just enough for Medea to relax. She sat on the floor and rocked back and forth. The snake wound itself up her neck and around her head. She felt groggy, but there was no time for a nap. Instead she gave Pythia half a rat, left uneaten by the rat snake. Pythia explored it with her tongue, but slithered into the corner without swallowing.

"Just hang on a little longer and I'll get you all the white cobra males you can eat," she said.

The snakes were happy to provide their venom.

She got more in the vials than last time, when she'd been tired and distracted and the snakes had punished her by not wanting to be milked. She put the vials in a row in her laboratory, which adjoined the changing room. Maybe it was a stretch to call it a *laboratory*, makeshift as it was, but since nobody else went in there but her, she could call it what she liked. And to Medea, it was a laboratory. It was where she extracted the snake venom, diluted it, mingled it with herbs or the venom of other snakes. She used drops in creams and salves, and even in her shampoo—it was why her hair was strong enough to grow so long. Although the lab might seem chaotic to outsiders, Medea knew exactly what went where. She knew that much of it could kill a grown human, and was meticulous about labeling everything correctly.

Reemerging from the basement, she was swathed in the sense of calm she always felt working with the snakes. She drank a cup of tea in the kitchen, closed her eyes for a moment, and smiled blissfully. When Eldest banged on the floorboards, it made her jump.

"Breakfast, I want breakfast," Eldest said reproachfully as Medea came into the room.

"You've had breakfast," said Medea, stroking her thin hair. For a moment, Eldest stared at her in confusion, then she gave a terrified scream and pulled her legs up beneath her. The rat snake slithered under them and disappeared into a hole in the wall. Eldest had never been afraid of snakes before. But then again, many things were different now.

The boy rushed over to Eldest and threw his arms protectively around her hunched body.

"It's not dangerous," Medea said, sitting down by the radiator. "Only to rats." At least she could soak up a little warmth while she was here.

In the old days, she and Eldest had had many conversations about what to do with the boy. Many, of course, had revolved around what they should do when he grew up. Should they hand him over to one of the Centers? Could they live with themselves if they did? Was there any other choice?

Most of their talks, however, had turned on questions of professional interest. What they could use the testosterone for if they milked him, once he was old enough for it. What effect his sperm would have in the lovecakes as compared to the menstrual blood, once he started secreting it. What might occur if they mingled blood and semen.

There was power in some creatures from the moment they were born. Baby cobras could do damage from the second they came out of the egg, while other snakes took time to develop their potential. The samples Medea had taken from the boy so far showed nothing useful. She and Eldest had agreed they'd most likely have to wait until he got bigger—which, of course, was a risk they weren't sure they were willing to take.

It had been a long time since she'd been able to talk to Eldest about the boy's developing potency.

"Bring me Eldest, I have to tell her that the birds need more space," Eldest said. More and more these days she spoke of the previous Eldest as though she were still alive.

"Your eldest is dead," Medea said cautiously.

"Nonsense!" shouted Eldest, lashing out at her with a clumsy swipe. "She's right outside the door, let her in, she's got her hands full."

"Eldest is dead," Medea tried again. The grief began in Eldest's bottom lip and rose up into her eyes, which filled with tears.

"Actually, I just had a word with her, she said she'll drop by later," Medea said. She didn't have the heart to do otherwise. Eldest grew calm again, and Medea felt lonelier than ever.

"The birds are calling, I must go down to them." Eldest had gotten out of bed and was making for the door. The boy gazed at her quizzically with his narrow green eyes, then followed.

"You stay here." Instantly Medea was on her feet. He didn't usually try to go with them when they left. It must be a new stage in his development. It might mean the testosterone in him was now more powerful. Luckily, he was still small enough that she could hold him back while she shut the door. She locked it and hurried after Eldest, who was already halfway down the stairs, blue skirt dragging behind her. She could hear the boy banging on the door and crying. Two long howls and a brief gasp, the way it sounded when he was most upset. She hesitated for a moment, but the boy would have to wait. All of a sudden Eldest was surprisingly agile: she'd already made it to the kitchen. There she'd stopped, and was peering about her with a look that told Medea she didn't know where she was. Catching up to her, Medea took her hand and led her into the front room, to the birds. They gabbled excitedly. Madam immediately opened its cage with its beak, flew out, and perched on Eldest's shoulder. It cocked its head in delight, blue bow dancing at its throat. Eldest gave Madam a frightened look, which didn't seem to bother it in the slightest. Cooing happily, it plucked affectionately at her hair with its beak.

"Shall I let the others out for you?" Medea asked. Eldest shook her head in fear.

"Let's try one." Medea opened one of the crows' cages. The crow landed on Eldest's disheveled gray head. She might not remember the bird, but it had no doubt who she was. Cautiously, Eldest reached her hand up to touch it. A smile broadened across her face. Medea opened the cages of the other birds, which flew out and surrounded Eldest in a whirl of chirrups and flapping wings. She lay down on the floor, the blue skirt like a swelling sea beneath her, and spread her arms so that all the birds could find a place to sit.

At the sight of Eldest with the birds, tears came to Medea's eyes, and she went into the kitchen to compose herself. It was like seeing Eldest when she was still herself. Seven years had passed since the first sign that something in her aging mind had begun to fail.

It was the summer night the boy was born.

IT HAD BEEN AN ORDINARY DAY IN AN ORDINARY WEEK, THE evening too like all the rest. Medea had spent the afternoon in the basement with the researchers, who had struggled as always to choose which worm snakes to buy, agonizing over which would give them the best chance of success with their research. They'd wanted to take more but weren't sure if they had room.

"If we do, we'll send someone to pick up two more tonight," they'd said. Medea was cheerful: they'd made enough from the sale to live on for months.

Eldest was tending to the animals, settling them down for the night, when there was a knock at the door. Few people liked to approach a witch's house after dark, so Medea had assumed it was the researchers' courier, come to get more snakes, and asked Eldest to let them in while she went down to the basement to put the single-sexers in a box for them.

Eldest, who had been feeding the dogs with offal from a hen, went to answer the door.

"Medea," she called. "Come quick."

When Medea reached the top of the stairs, carrying the snakes, she found Eldest in the hallway, propping up a heavily pregnant woman who was moaning in agony. Short white hair hung in knots around her face, which was twisted with pain. Her green eyes stared fearfully at them, until she was overwhelmed by another contraction. Medea rushed to support her from the other side. The top of her head barely reached the woman's shoulder, and she leaned against her big belly to help her balance. The woman's tight leather dress rubbed against Medea's cheek, and it crossed her mind how uncomfortable it must be to wear tight clothes in the summer heat. Then the woman let out a shriek and clutched her lower back. Above her swollen belly was only one swollen breast. The other was tightly bound. An amazon. It had never occurred to Medea that they gave birth too. "We'd better get her into the kitchen," Eldest said, and together they maneuvered the laboring woman up the steps and into the kitchen, where the dogs picked up their heads and stared. Silence burst in from the street, wild-eyed. She rushed past and up toward her room.

"Where have you come from?" Medea asked the woman, sitting her on the stool in the kitchen. "Are you alone?"

The woman nodded, accepting the glass of water Eldest gave her. She drank in greedy slurps. Another contraction, now the kind that made her push.

"I think it's coming . . ." she said hoarsely, but only once the urge to push had faded. Her blonde hair was pale, so pale it was almost as white as Eldest's. Sweat had pasted it to her forehead.

"We need to get you into bed." Eldest helped the woman to her feet, ordering Medea to fetch extra blankets, pillows, and towels. The pregnant woman managed to climb the stairs and reach the back room at the end of the narrow corridor, a bedroom that had once belonged to one of the now-dead sisters. Then a contraction brought her to her knees.

"Have you given birth before?" Eldest asked the woman as she lay down on the bed. It creaked under her weight.

She shook her head.

"Have you ever delivered a baby?" Medea asked Eldest.

"I don't have any children," Eldest replied, confused.

Silence was in the doorway, drawn by the screams. This time of day the house was usually so peaceful you could hear the rat snakes rustling.

"Silence, do you know how to deliver a baby?"

Silence held up her hands in a gesture of denial.

Medea stood there for a moment, arms limp and despairing at her sides. Then the woman arched her back with a loud scream and pushed as hard as she could.

"All right, well, it can't be all that different from hatchlings and pups," Medea said resolutely. She rolled up her sleeves and sat down between the woman's legs. The amazon was sobbing with pain, and she grabbed hold of Silence, who had edged closer out of curiosity and now tried to squirm out of her grasp.

Medea attempted to tug the snug leather dress up over the woman's hips, but had to give up. The sweat wasn't making the leather any more cooperative.

"Do you need anything, are you hungry?"

The woman shook her head and stared desperately at Medea until another contraction surged through her. The dogs didn't eat anything either in the days before a birth, so that made sense to her.

"Maybe someone from the Street could help?" said Eldest.

The woman nodded and made to sit up, but was knocked back by the next contraction.

Eldest and Medea didn't have time to say another word before the woman screamed again.

"Surely it's not supposed to hurt this much," Medea said. The dogs barely squealed when they had pups, unless the pups were too big; then they groaned and panted until Medea helped them. The snakes' eggs just slipped out. Even when it was a species that had live young, the little ones would pour out effortlessly.

"Perhaps the baby's too big. Like the pups," Medea said. Suddenly Eldest was looking old, and tired. She sat down on a chair in the corner and dropped her head into her hands, as though she'd forgotten what they were doing there. At the same moment, Silence twisted out of the woman's grasp and ran out of the room. Medea was alone, left to hand-hold and peer up the woman's dress to see if anything was coming out. The zip was at the back. Grabbing the scissors she always kept in her belt, Medea cut the dress open, freeing the belly and the single bulging breast. The other lay beside it, flatter but still taut. She gave a sigh of relief: the woman could breathe properly now, unconstrained by the thick leather.

She ducked her head between the woman's legs. The area was red and swollen, but she couldn't see a baby.

"Why isn't she coming out?" Medea said, scrabbling in her pocket for the snow quartz to calm her nerves, but she couldn't find it before the woman gave an even louder roar.

"Get the tonic I use for the dogs when they can't push out the pups," she cried to Eldest. "Anteroom, shelves, second from the top, one of the little bottles with red dots. *Not* the top, *not* the yellow. Quick."

Eldest stumbled off, disoriented, and Medea thought she should have fetched the drug herself.

Eldest returned just as the woman gave a primal bellow, flinging herself back against the bed so hard that the old wood gave way. Half of it collapsed beneath her. Eldest unscrewed the top and gave the bottle to Medea, who swiftly put it to the woman's mouth. She swallowed its contents between two screams. When she looked at Medea, there was a wildness in her eyes. The bellow came from deep within her core, and as the child slid out it grew increasingly guttural. When the noise stopped, so did her breathing. Eldest, who seemed lucid again, quickly swaddled the baby, while Medea tried to help the woman lie more comfortably on the broken bed. Her eyes stared vacantly to the right, and her chest was still.

"You can wake up now, it's over." Medea gently patted her cheek. There was no life. Blood oozed from between her legs, and the placenta slid lazily out, landing with a flop on the boards, not far from the bottle top that had been on the snake medicine. On it was a yellow mark. Medea stared in bewilderment at Eldest, who was looking stunned as she cradled the child in her arms.

"It's a male," she said. "She's given birth to a boy!"

The hours afterward were hazy for them both. Medea tried to squeeze milk out of the dead woman's breasts, but in vain. Neither breast, large or small, would give so much as a drop. The boy sobbed miserably, hungry and afraid of the world he'd tumbled into.

Medea and Eldest, frightened of what had happened and of dealing with a male, tried to let go of the fear.

"Let's try giving him some sugar water. That's what I give the pups that can't suckle. He can probably survive on it until we know what we're going to do with him." Running down to the kitchen, Medea quickly returned with a small serving in a whelp bottle, and the boy gulped it down. Soon he was asleep in Eldest's arms.

The woman lay in a pool of blood on the mangled bed. Eldest, who had found new energy, wrapped the boy firmly to the front of her body and dragged Silence out of her hiding place to form a circle around the woman. The three of them sang her soul away to other spheres, asking the gods in the same breath what to do with the dead woman's body.

"If we report this, people will think we killed her," Eldest said. "Every time we've been in contact with the outside world it's brought us trouble, and interfered with our right to be left in peace. This might mean they shut the convent down, make us pensive."

"Maybe we did kill her," Medea said. She'd smashed the bottle and the lid with the yellow dot, scattering the shards at the bottom of the garden where the thistles grew. But if it was snake venom that had killed the woman, it wouldn't be hard for a doctor to discover.

"What do you mean?" Eldest said.

"The venom! You gave me the bottle with the yellow dot. If it can kill a large dog, maybe it can kill a human too."

"Why did you ask me for the yellow one, then?"

"I asked you for a bottle with a red dot, not a yellow one."

Eldest's gaze wavered for a moment, then something changed, and she glared at Medea with a contempt she'd never seen in her before. "You're not blaming me," she hissed.

Silence began to cry. If the convent was shut, she'd have nowhere to go.

"I'll come up with a solution," Medea said wearily. Leaving the boy in Eldest's care, she went to sit among the snakes. It was how she thought best.

The next morning she removed the large emerald ring the woman wore on her right hand. She wrapped up the leather dress and boots and hid them at the back of her closet. She called Eldest and Silence, who helped her drag the corpse down to the basement, to Pythia.

As they danced around the body, holding hands, the snake approached. It circled the body once or twice, then struck out at the legs. It ate the woman whole. Afterward, her shape was visible inside the thirty-six-foot python. It slithered a little laboriously into the corner and settled down.

It didn't eat again for three months.

The boy was screeching with hunger. They tried everything they could think of, and there were moments when each of them in turn gave up and felt like handing him over to the Center in Lolland. But always, one of them held the others back. There was a reason, after all, that they'd been demonstrating against the treatment of the men there ever since the convent's foundation.

In desperation, Medea hit upon the idea of satisfying his hunger with watered-down loveroots. They had a sweet taste and a good effect on the nervous systems of adult humans, so maybe they would also soothe a baby male. While Eldest and the boy slept, she went down to the garden in the dim light of early morning to grub up roots. On the way she passed the Street, where one of the manladies was sitting naked in a rocking chair, nursing a red-headed infant. His silicone penis lolled to the right, and his breasts were impressively large. The child was clutching one with both hands, drinking greedily with its eyes open and gaze fixed on Medea.

Medea had seen most of the manladies on the Street before, of course, but back then she'd never spoken to any of them. It was only fatigue and the sense that she had nothing to lose that made her overcome her usual reticence and walk up to the terrace.

"Can I buy some milk from you?"

The manlady eyed her skeptically, then broke into a loud laugh. "I see, so that's what you're into, is it? I thought you witches just sat around casting spells with your herbs and roots and filthy animals. Are you the one that's the snake oracle?"

Medea was too exhausted by the past few days to take offense. "What do you want for the milk?" she asked.

"What have you got?"

Medea emptied her pockets of crystals and a sprig of herbs and gave them to him. He laughed again. "That's not going to buy you anything naughty, little girl."

"You can have lovecakes?" Medea said hopefully. "You can make anybody fall in love with you if they eat them."

"Really?"

Medea nodded.

He put the red-headed baby in a basket, went inside, and got a cup. He pumped it rapidly half full of breast milk and handed it to Medea.

"Take this home. You'll get the other half of the cup when you come back with those magical cakes of yours."

That was the first time she'd met Lars.

That afternoon, Medea went back with a few cakes. Lars kept his word and returned the favor with another cup of breast milk.

They had one peaceful night where the boy slept in the crook of Eldest's arm, his tummy full, but the next morning he was screaming for more milk. Medea went back to the Street with a basket of lovecakes to beg for more. The terrace where Lars had been breastfeeding was empty.

"He's with a client," said the manlady sitting on the rickety windowsill of the house next door, his breasts dangling.

"Can you tell him I was here?"

Medea set the basket on the terrace and went around to the back garden instead, to dig up more roots. She was suddenly going through more of them than usual.

That night there was a knock, and Lars's neighbor stood on the doorstep with a container full of milk.

"Lars said to give this to the little girl who lives in the black house. Guess that's you?" he said, looking Medea up and down.

"That's right," she said, so relieved to finally have something to feed the boy that she wasn't even annoyed at being called "little girl," despite being past fifty.

"Lars says you can have more if you bring more cakes. Sounds like he can't get enough of them."

"I don't know what you put in those cakes, but now everybody's clamoring for a new appointment," Lars said delightedly when Medea gave him back the empty container the next morning. "I've never been so popular. I've got all these customers standing there with a mouthful of cake asking when they can see me again."

"You can also sleep with an apple in your left armpit and give it to the person you want. If she eats it, she'll love you forever."

"You're full of tricks." Lars chuckled. "But I'll stick to the cakes. Otherwise this place will be overrun. If you bring me another batch tomorrow, I'll pump some more for you."

From that day on, Medea brought the boy all the milk he could drink, and Lars quickly became the busiest manlady in the neighborhood. When the boy stopped needing milk, Medea took energy for light and heat in exchange for the cakes. Or food. Or a stove. Lars was always generous. As for what the convent would do if they kept him pensive for months, maybe even years, like they did with the people who wouldn't cooperate, Medea didn't know.

THE BOY WAS A SURPRISINGLY SOCIABLE CREATURE. MEDEA had thought males preferred to be alone, which was one of the reasons why she disapproved of their living conditions at the Center. She'd assumed it bothered them, being stuck cheek by jowl with other males all the time. Maybe it was because the boy was only seven. There was no telling when things might go wrong. She didn't know what they'd do once he started to turn dangerous—another reason why she kept the snake drops reassuringly at hand on the top shelf. If he suddenly showed signs of growing uncontrollable, the drops would put him to sleep in a matter of seconds.

"It won't kill him, will it?" Eldest had asked, looking uncertainly at Medea and the little bottle.

"Of course not," Medea had replied, offended. She was aware of what Eldest was insinuating, but didn't take the bait. She knew it wasn't her who'd killed the boy's mother, even if Eldest thought so.

Balancing the lunch tray on one hand, she fiddled with the lock on Eldest's door with the other. It was high up enough that the boy couldn't reach it. Lately, though, Eldest hadn't been able to figure out the bolt. That was why she banged on the floorboards instead. And the lock *had* become difficult to open. It was old, pieced together from the odd few working parts they'd found in the house's bathrooms. Medea had snuck into some of the other unoccupied, tumbledown houses in the area to see if there were better parts to be found, but had no luck. Either they'd been taken by collectors fond of unpleasant mementos from a bygone age, or they'd been broken off and destroyed during periods when many people didn't believe that sort of thing should even exist.

Medea agreed—locks had no place in the world. But when it came to males, they were needed.

At long last she managed to unlock it and open the door. Eldest was staring blankly into space, the blanket pulled up underneath her chin. She looked older than her hundred and thirty-six years.

It struck Medea that this was the first time she'd thought Eldest lived up to her name. Or the name she'd been given when the previous eldest died. Before that, Eldest had been called Oliver. Whenever the convent got a new eldest, it was hard at first to forget their former name, but now Medea never thought of her as anything but Eldest. Silence had also had another name when she arrived, and Medea must have been told what it was, but she couldn't recall.

Medea had likewise been encouraged to change her name when she joined the convent as a girl. But it had never felt right—Medea was simply who she was. It had been chosen for her by her mothers.

"You were so tiny when you were first born, but you seemed strong, so we had to give you a heroic name. Who was a greater hero than Medea? In ancient times she fought a tyrannical man and his sons—and won," they said. Medea loved her mothers, but she didn't love her name. She'd never seen what was so heroic about Medea's actions—yes, they may only have been sons, but she'd murdered her own children.

Yet, when she was given the chance to change her name, it felt false. And besides, no other options came to mind. The sisters at the convent had had plenty of ideas, some of them even good. For a while they'd tried calling her Medusa.

"It's a perfect fit, since you're so good with snakes," the sisters said. But Medea couldn't get used to anything but her own name, so in the end she asked them to call her Medea, like before.

The boy ran up to her stark naked when she came into the room. He took a drawing out of the raspberry bag and gave it to her.

"For me?"

He shook his head, making a tousle of his wispy white hair. Eldest used to keep it tidy, and complained when Medea cut out big tufts for her experiments. But it had been a long time since she'd brought it up, and a long time since she'd combed him. His hair was matted at the nape, like Eldest's.

"I see, you just want me to look at it?" she said and smiled at the boy. She actually liked him, and was surprised by how mild he was.

She looked at the drawing, which showed him and the only three people he'd met in his life. Eldest, with ribbons in her hair; Silence, mouthless; and herself, only half as tall as the others and with hair that tumbled to the floor. The rat snake was a stringy blob in the corner.

She gave him back the drawing, and he skipped toward Eldest, humming. The growth between his legs flopped side to side. He put his hand down and played with it a moment, then climbed onto the bed and held out the piece of paper to Eldest, who didn't take it.

Medea looked away. Until the boy she had never seen a penis, and she still considered it a deformity.

Her mothers had recognized her abilities early on, and had sent her to learn magic instead of giving her traditional schooling. That meant she had never taken body classes, and never passed the exam that allowed access to a male at one of the Centers. She'd seen Lars's silicone penis, which he liked to show off while he sat out on his terrace. But somehow that didn't count.

Not going to an ordinary school had also exempted Medea from obligatory masturbation. Most of the sisters at the convent had rolled their eyes at that sort of thing, although a couple of them believed it was a necessary part of getting familiar with your body and leading a healthier life.

Medea's limited knowledge of males and their appendages made it all the more intriguing to have the boy in the house. She had no shortage of experience with male snakes and male dogs, but this was different. Animals were easier to tame than people, yet there was a part of Medea that believed it could be done with human males as well. Despite centuries of rape, criminality, and warfare suggesting otherwise, there were examples like the horned god Pan, who was capable of controlling his masculine energy. Still, perhaps it took divine strength to overcome his testosterone—something the average human male definitely did not possess.

The boy was jumping up and down on the bed. His penis wagged back and forth as he sang one of Eldest's bird songs.

Unable to hide her disgust, Medea passed him the tunic, but instead of putting it on he threw it sulkily onto the floor and crawled under the duvet next to Eldest. Was this the first hint of testosterone's unpredictability beginning to emerge? After all, it was one thing to contemplate what might happen to her, Silence, and Eldest if they were found to be sheltering a male, but living with the threat of testosterone within the convent's four walls was another. Sooner or later, something was bound to go wrong.

WHEN MEDEA MOVED INTO THE CONVENT NEARLY FORTY years ago, twelve older sisters had been living there. The eldest had recently died, and Medea brought them back up to thirteen, which they preferred. She completed their number: thirteen was a sacred figure; it gave them strength when they danced in a ring.

The original thirteen sisters had been there since the beginning, when the convent was formed. Medea was the first newcomer to be let in. It was a big upheaval, a new member joining. More than eighty years had passed since the thirteen magic-wielders elected to move into the black patriarchal house with its straight walls and cornered windows. They'd wanted softer surroundings, of course—but softer surroundings didn't want them. The sisters called themselves wielders; everybody else called them witches. While deliberately excluding a group from a community wasn't allowed, something unfortunate always seemed to crop up at the last minute, preventing the wielders from settling their convent in one of the desirable round districts. Eventually they stumbled across the black house on the corner, still miraculously standing even though it had been decades since the previous occupants moved out. The exterior walls were covered in ivy and other foliage, which was trying doggedly to penetrate the brickwork. But the insulation—as well as decades of human resistance and ingenuity—had so far kept nature more or less at bay.

The garden, which ran all the way around the black house, was so overgrown they'd had to slash their way through, sawing away the branches around the front door to get inside. They'd had to wait until winter had smothered nature's flame before they could get the last plants to release their grip on the brickwork.

Some of the wielders were in their forties, others much younger. Eldest was the youngest, just sixteen. They were all daughters of the Evolution, full of enterprise and joy; they possessed none of the militant anger that had been the cornerstone of their grandmothers' and great-grandmothers' lives. The obstacles of past generations had been swept aside, and they could live as they saw fit. People tended to look down their nose at settlers in the patriarchal districts, but nobody forbade it. So, amid the empty houses, ruins, scarce loners, and strays, the women who called themselves sisters took over the house of angles in Frederiksberg and made it a home. House and neighborhood were both in dire need of care, but the sisters had plenty of it to give, and it wasn't long before the dark walls brightened, drawing in nightwalkers and other curious folk. Soon the roadside stall was busy.

They didn't rip up a single plant in the rest of the garden, but spent many years coaxing them to grow in more appropriate directions. They persuaded thistles, nettles, and thorny leaves to limit their range, or at least turn back from the areas earmarked for herbs, flowers, or bare ground, where animals and people sat dozing in patches of sun. Similar sisterhoods founded convents in other old parts of the city, but none of them flourished like the one in the black house. It was their convent that people from the round districts preferred to visit when they went sightseeing through the ugly places of the past. Not only was the stall at the Frederiksberg convent bursting with intriguing items designed to cure everything from heartache to unwanted pigeons, not only were its dark bricks and wild garden alluring, but it was also conveniently close to another dangerous and seductive attraction: the Street.

The Street long ago, at the dawn of the Evolution, was much like the Street today. But in those days there were also real men on the Street, competing for customers. They were heavily medicated, of course, to keep their testosterone in check, and had to resort to the same fake penises as the manladies, but they were still more popular, because they had an air of genuine danger. These were untamed creatures, capable of raping and killing on a whim. They were so dulled by the medication that they could barely lift the dummy appendages to use them, but their mere presence could still send some women into screaming orgasms, and the lines outside their doors were always long. Still, not many people protested when it was decided that keeping real men on the Street was too hazardous, and they were soon comforted by the knowledge that whenever the urge to have sex with a man arose, they could simply go to the spa at one of the Centers, where the safety of both males and humans was assured.

For a while after that, the Street went into a decline, but it recovered within a year or two. As long as the Street was unauthorized, and the manladies acted both condescending and vaguely threatening, it turned out that nobody cared all that much whether the fake penis concealed the genuine article or not.

By the time Medea moved into the convent a century later, the only young woman among aging sisters, she had no other convents to choose from. They had all been dissolved, either when the sisters had a falling-out or it became too difficult to stave off the natural deterioration of the buildings. The use of "witchcraft," as it was called, wasn't outlawed, but it certainly wasn't fashionable, nor was it presented to children and teenagers as a useful perspective on the world. It wasn't the practice of magic itself that was despised, of extracting medicines from animals, plants, and herbs, or the act of playing with telepathy, spirits, and such. No, what people frowned on was the witches' belief that a society in proper harmony required a balance between female and male. It was the witches' refusal to countenance what other religions had rushed to do: to kill off their male gods, or at least subordinate them; to render them exotic but harmless flavoring in both practical and theoretical theology. To turn their male deities into faintly amusing appendices to the female ones. The sisters' decision to worship their male gods on an equal footing with the female ones was unprecedented. It would have been easier to take a lenient view if the sisters had practiced in secret, but the witches from the black house—and, in earlier days, those from other convents too—insisted on demonstrating outside the Centers. Protesting against the way that men were kept. When pressed, it became clear that none of the sisters had any interest in defying their foremothers' beliefs and letting men loose on the streets, but they did feel that masculinity wasn't getting the respect which by nature it deserved. The males should at least be kept under better conditions behind those walls. Unfortunately, this meant that none of the sisters at the Frederiksberg convent were willing to visit the spa or the breeding unit at the Centers to use the men, and so they all remained childless.

Medea was fifteen when she moved in, because her mothers believed she ought to pursue her unique talents for snakes, herbs, and magical baking. She had arrived at the convent with a handwritten book of recipes, the golden cloak, an uncertain gaze, two grass snakes, a two-header, and Pythia, who was a baby then.

It was Eldest who, as the youngest—at ninety-six years old—had been tasked with making sure Medea settled in, so she was one of the sisters to whom Medea grew most attached. And it was a comfort that Eldest, then called Oliver, remained throughout the next few decades while the other sisters died of old age.

Apart from Medea, Silence was the only other new arrival. The day that Eldest dragged her in, only a handful of the old sisters were left. Several of Eldest's crows had begun mysteriously to vanish, and she had gone out into the slum to discover what was happening to them. She found no crows, but she did find Silence.

"She needs us. She doesn't have anybody else," she said, and put her in one of the late sisters' rooms. The others weren't enthusiastic. The current Eldest pointed out that they were struggling to feed everyone as it was. It wasn't just that they had fewer sisters to make things, or that many of their talents hadn't been passed on, but the craze for nightwalking had fizzled out. This meant far too few people happened across the stall.

Nightwalking, which had persisted for centuries after the Evolution, had finally gone out of fashion, and now hardly anyone cared to do what women of the past could not: go out at night on their own without fear of encountering a man.

Even though no one nowadays was afraid of being raped, assaulted, or murdered by a man, the thought of it while wandering around the slums had still titillated. It was like riding a roller coaster: you knew in your head it wasn't dangerous, but you still got butterflies in your stomach when it flipped you upside down. And when visitors neared the convent, there'd been an extra thrill in knowing they might come face-to-sinister-face with a witch in the dark. The sisters had laughed about that. One of them had even made a pointy hat, just to make the illusion more vivid. On those nights they did especially well at the stall.

Given the shortage of youthful energy at the convent, the other sisters agreed that Silence could move in. She didn't draw much attention to herself, but she didn't contribute anything either. True, she could coax any plant to grow, but she refused to pluck a single leaf off any bush or flower. *So what use is she?* Medea thought.

When Silence moved in twenty years ago, Medea had tried casting chatterspells to make her speak. She'd put jimsonweed seeds in her tea. But nothing seemed to take. At most it made her sway a little and go to bed early. Or she disappeared into the night with a tortured look, only to return the next day, frozen and damp-haired. Just as silent as before.

In those first years, Medea had complained to Eldest.

"Silence never helps with anything. She won't even gather

herbs and plants for me. She just comes home and expects everything to be taken care of for her."

"Unhappy people mostly think about themselves," Eldest said, and asked her to put a little more on Silence's plate next mealtime.

THROUGHOUT ALL MEDEA'S YEARS AT THE CONVENT, SHE had gone with the other sisters every Friday to protest outside the males' Center in Lolland. There were Centers across the country and everywhere in Europe—across most of the world, in fact, as far as Medea knew, but the one in Lolland was the closest to the convent, so that was where they always went. She had gone every Friday except the last. Eldest had had one of her bad days, calling for Medea several times in the night and demanding things all morning. When it came time for Medea to leave, she put on her outdoor clothes like always: hat, mittens, and shawl over the dog-skin. She packed the signs, both of them, as usual, even though now that Eldest was sick she was the only one demonstrating. These days she alternated them while shouting.

As she was about to leave, she got so dizzy with exhaustion that she had to lie down between the dogs, and she didn't get back up until most of the day was gone. Silence, who had been in the kitchen when she took her hat and shawl back off, frowned. The convent had never skipped a demonstration before. Medea threw up her arms in despair.

"You go, then!" she'd yelled at Silence, who of course did not reply. Silence soon lost interest anyway. She was going all around the house, searching. Lifting cushions and looking under piles. She'd been doing it for days. Eventually she sighed and went upstairs.

Medea had been feeling guilty all week. Thankfully, Eldest didn't seem to realize she hadn't gone to Lolland. She'd be so disappointed. So: today Medea *would* be going, and she would force Silence to come too. It was high time she took part in the work of the convent. Besides, Medea was planning to spend the night at Wicca's, and she wanted Silence to take the signs home. She felt warm inside just thinking about a night with Wicca. And faintly ashamed, for indulging in something of no use to anybody.

She fed the animals in a rush, making no attempt to get the dogs or birds to obey. She pushed them aside. Madam pecked at her angrily, and she jeered back, which made it look even more affronted.

Without waiting for Eldest to bang on the floorboards, she went upstairs with the tray.

Eldest was asleep. The boy glanced up at her alertly, then back down. He was fitting together the pieces of an old jigsaw puzzle.

"Well done," Medea said to him, and meant it. He continued to impress her. She'd never expected much more from him than from the crows, or the most single-minded of the snakes.

The boy froze, pointing at the end of the rat snake as it slithered through a hole in the wall. Medea shook her head indulgently.

"It's not dangerous," she said to him. Perhaps he wasn't that intelligent after all.

"We'll go once the sun reaches the gable," she called outside Silence's door. The dried sweet clover was a prickle in her nose. She knocked three times. Waited. Knocked again. Two dull taps in response.

Medea ran downstairs to the laboratory to pick up a thing or two to boost fertility. She'd give them to Wicca's white cobra, so it would be ready when she took it after the service on Saturday.

The corners of Silence's mouth drooped and her expression was surly as she dragged one of the signs through the slum. The cold stung everywhere they weren't wrapped up. Medea wore so many clothes underneath the dogskin she could barely move.

She hustled Silence impatiently onto the train at the platform, checked for the women in velour, then sat down, relieved.

"You sit over there," Medea said, as she sank into the soft, pleasantly shaped seat. Silence perched uncomfortably on the edge, gazing out the window as the hills rolled by. The trees were planted and pruned to suit their surroundings, and the curving flower boxes were lovely even in winter. Even the clouds seemed well-ordered in the sky. It was a stark contrast to the slum, where it felt as though an assortment of random items had been tossed into a pile and shaken.

Medea moved the signs aside when two women had difficulty getting past.

"Sorry," she said, lowering her eyes. Silence glared after them.

"Ow," Medea said, looking at her hand. She had gotten a splinter in her finger. The wood on the stake had split in several places, worn by time and weathered. The writing was so damaged that it was almost impossible to read what it said. Medea, who usually found this exasperating, didn't have the energy to care about it today. She just had to get the protest over with so she could get to Wicca's, who'd said she would cook them a nice meal. She couldn't remember the last time anyone had made her food. Not since the communal meals, when more of the sisters were alive. Now it was Medea who organized everything eaten at the convent.

The wind was blowing as they stepped off the train and walked the short stretch to the Center. They weren't the only ones disembarking. Several people in pale yellow uniforms, Center employees, got off and strolled chatting toward the entrance. They went up to the big gate and were let in. Medea took up her position by the wall.

"Come on," she told Silence. "Hold up your sign." Medea raised hers above her head.

"Men have feelings too," she shouted. The sign said the same thing.

"You don't have to shout, obviously," she said to Silence. On her sign was a picture of a naked man curled up in a small cage. A HUMAN BEING, it read in indistinct lettering. It was the most controversial of the signs, and Medea only used it when she felt strong enough to deal with patronizing comments and derisive laughter, from both the people in pale yellow and those visiting the Center men. Reluctantly picking up the sign, Silence trudged back and forth.

Medea and Silence were the only two protesters. It hadn't always been that way. When the sisters were alive, there were still women from other convents showing up. It wasn't unusual to see more than fifty of them, marching, shouting, and calling for better treatment of the men. Reminding everyone that masculine energy was simply another of nature's gifts. Gradually, though, as the other convents dissolved and the sisters of the Frederiksberg slum grew older and more frail, fewer and fewer of them gathered on the Fridays.

Recently, an elderly sister from another convent long since fallen into earth had turned up. She hadn't been a witch for years, but came to say goodbye.

"Demonstrating meant a lot to me," she told Medea. "This was where we really joined forces, across convents."

Now that her convent had gone, along with the little building in the Østerbro slum where she'd lived since, she was moving back to her childhood town in Jutland. There were the most beautiful round districts there, surrounded on all sides by open plains.

Medea had wondered where she would move if her convent was razed. She had no idea. Her mothers were still alive, but they had all gone their separate ways. Her childhood home was still standing, but strangers lived there now, and Medea could not move back. The convent was her only home. The snakes her only family.

Two women in pale yellow walked by, sneering at them. Silence shot them an angry look.

They marched back and forth for another half an hour, until they were pelted with rain and ran for cover under some of the big trees by the entrance. Medea sat down exhausted on the knobby ground. All she could think about was a hot bath at Wicca's, then a long night against her soft body.

"Why don't we call it a day?" she asked. Silence eyed her dubiously, then shrugged and plodded out into the downpour, toward the train. Medea pulled up the hood of her dogskin. Getting it wet hadn't done much to improve the smell. She ran after Silence, stomach churning both with anticipation at the prospect of a night to herself and with guilt. Eldest, the boy, the animals, the convent, the lovecakes, the women in velour—it all felt like a sinking ship. And she was the captain, going down with her vessel.

Tomorrow she would do better by everybody, she promised her conscience. If she could just have this one night, she'd work twice as hard tomorrow.

"There's food in the fridge for them," she said, as they flopped down into their seats. "And give Eldest an extra bit of rosemary in her porridge, she'll have a better day tomorrow. I'm getting off at Himlingeøje. I've got a few things to do, but I'll be back in a couple of hours." She stared hastily out the window. She had no intention of coming home that night. But Silence wouldn't know whether she was in the convent or not. If she wasn't roaming the slums at night, she was holed up in her room.

Silence nodded indifferently. When Medea got out, she didn't look up.

Medea hurried along the winding roads, and by the time she reached Wicca's roundhouse she was dripping wet.

She tried to shake the worst of the rainwater off her dogskin, then hung it on a branch outside the house. Just to be on the safe side; she didn't want its odor filling Wicca's room. She knocked on the window and was let inside.

She'd slept just as well as she did with Pythia. She and Wicca had made love and talked and made love again. She was used to Pythia sucking out her body heat at night to keep warm, so there was something euphoric about Wicca having enough for them both.

Wicca was asleep. Medea stroked one of her dark curls away from her face and behind her ear. She was so beautiful. A ray of sunshine broke through the gray clouds, falling across Wicca's cheek. Her skin glinted like a snake's. It must have been nearly eight. Medea knew she should be getting home, but she didn't want the night to be over so soon.

Wendy was asleep in the corner, thumb in mouth. Medea had seen Wicca pull it out several times.

"You're seven. You're too old to be sucking your thumb," she'd said. The boy did it too, and he was the same age. But, of course, she couldn't tell Wicca that, and Medea wasn't sure you could compare girls and boys of the same age anyway.

She grabbed her coat and put it on, so that she wouldn't lose any warmth as she crept over to the vivarium.

"Hello, love," she said, reaching down to the white cobra female. There was a golden shimmer to it, and it would have beautiful, strong young. Today it would be joining Wicca at the service. For the first time.

"You're going to do so well," she whispered to it as it wound around her hands and up into her hair. Its skin caressed her shoulders, sliding around her neck and down between her breasts. "Then after that you'll come back home and visit me."

As she placed it back in the vivarium, she realized she had to pee. She could either put her clothes back on, climb out of the window, and do it in a bush on the way home, or she could take her chances sneaking into the bathroom and hope she didn't bump into anybody. She opted for the latter. Wicca might wake up, and they could make love one more time before she returned to all her obligations.

She listened in the doorway for a moment, checking if the coast was clear. Then, cautiously, she padded along the corridors, reached the bathroom, and hurried inside.

"Oh, hey, it's you," said Eva. She was just getting out of the shower, and quickly wrapped a towel around herself.

"Sorry, should I wait?"

"I'm the one who should be apologizing. Kind of weird, I know, wanting to take a shower alone."

"I understand," Medea confided. "We're lucky we've got lots of bathrooms at home."

"Yeah, that's the slums for you."

"Maybe that's why you prefer to be alone too?"

"Yep, maybe," Eva said dismissively, tightening the towel around her body and starting to brush her hair. Her rat was on the edge of the sink, waiting.

Medea sat down on one of the toilets and peed.

"There's no more paper. Here, use one of these." Eva put a little stack of embroidered handkerchiefs next to Medea.

"Oh no, they're much too pretty for that."

"Those? I just do them to relax. I've got a closet full of them. I'm just glad they're coming in handy. Anyway, my mother would say they aren't pretty enough." Eva smiled and shook her head. "Only pretty enough to wipe your backside with."

Medea looked at the tiny embroidered flowers, and the leaves that whorled closely around them.

"I think they're lovely."

Eva left the bathroom without answering, rat perched on her shoulder.

Medea dabbed herself gingerly with the handkerchief. She couldn't bring herself to throw it away, so she put it in her pocket instead.

The sun was much too high in the sky by the time she set off running for the train an hour later. Her cheeks and heart were hot. She felt utterly clear-headed, cleansed by countless orgasms. She laughed to herself. Her, the woman who'd never even had a girlfriend before. Until now she'd only experienced orgasms alone. She'd never tried a Center man, nor considered one of the manladies, although she could probably have traded a session for a few lovecakes. She had accepted unthinkingly the idea that solo orgasms were all a body needed, although she knew there were some who believed a partner was required to achieve the good orgasms.

Now, having been with Wicca so many times, and especially after this last magical night, she wasn't so sure anymore that lone orgasms were enough. What she felt in her body at this moment she would never be able to produce on her own.

Perhaps it was like laughing, thought Medea. You can amuse yourself alone, chuckle quietly to yourself, but if you want the kind of over-the-top laughter where it's difficult to stop, where in the end your stomach cramps and afterward you feel that strange release inside your soul, you need to share the fun with someone else.

The road through the slum was icy after she got off the train, and it took half an hour longer than usual to get home. As she passed the Street, she kept a hopeful eye out for Lars. He wasn't there. Forgetting to watch where she put her feet, she slipped and fell, banging her head on an old cobblestone. She touched her forehead: a cut. Since she didn't have anything else, she fished the embroidered handkerchief out of her pocket and held it against the wound.

"Hey, little girl, you want a ride?" she heard one of the manladies say behind her.

"No thank you." Medea smiled. "By the way, I've not seen Lars in a while?"

The manlady sighed. "He's got himself thrown in with the pensives. I don't know how long they're keeping him. Apparently, he gave some bigwig a cake with a euphoriant in it, something to make her obsessed with him. That's what I heard. You should get home and clean that cut."

"Hopefully they'll let him out soon," Medea said. They wouldn't last long at the convent without Lars's goods in exchange.

"We're not complaining," the manlady said. "Without Lars, there's suddenly a lot more customers to go around."

Medea half ran back to the convent, blood dripping down her forehead into her eyes. She'd better hurry up and clean the wound with her herbs, or it might get infected. Besides, Eldest was probably enraged she'd not had breakfast yet. If she'd pounded on the floorboards hard enough, there was a slight chance Silence might have heard and brought them up a tray. Medea knew that was unlikely. She'd probably sidled off into the slums as fast as she could, since she'd been forced to join the protest the day before.

As soon as she opened the door to the convent, she could tell something was wrong. Madam was screeching, the crows were cawing, and the male dog barked desperately.

"What's the matter with you all?" she asked. She could feel the snakes heaving in the basement.

She went on up the stairs. Silence sat on them halfway up, staring at the wall. Her hair was damp, and she was clutching her throat. The little female dog was pressed up against her, howling miserably.

"Has something happened?" Medea asked anxiously.

Silence sat as though turned to stone. Flustered, Medea dropped the handkerchief she'd been pressing against her forehead, and it fell to the floor as she barged past Silence. She ran up the last couple of steps and down the narrow hallway, almost tripping over Eldest, who lay on her stomach with one leg bent beneath her and both arms outstretched. Her blue skirt was spread like angel's wings.

"Eldest," Medea screamed, grabbing her shoulders. She was ice-cold. Medea turned her over. Dead.

The boy.

Medea hurtled toward the room at the end of the hall. The door was wide open. She rushed inside and checked behind the bed, behind the wardrobe, underneath the blankets. He wasn't there.

Medea ran back to the staircase, where Silence was still motionless. She had picked up the embroidered handkerchief and was gazing at it in wonder.

"Where's the boy?" Medea yelled, shaking her.

The rat snake, which had been climbing the stairs, turned around and slithered noiselessly back down.

Silence cleared her throat and tried in vain to form a word with her lips, but all that came out was a rasp. Then she began to cry.

WICCA

WICCA STRETCHED LUXURIOUSLY. SHE MISSED MEDEA already, although she'd only jumped out of the window an hour ago.

She put her hand between her legs, then brought it back up over the covers and saw to her relief that there was blood on it. She'd gotten her period after all: she could participate in the service today at church. Finally. She'd been looking forward to showing off the white cobra to her mother for months, and it would have been infuriating to have to miss out because she couldn't bleed on time. She quickly canceled the menstruating priest she'd had on standby, one of several she'd had to ally herself with because her own cycle was so erratic. She could go anywhere from twenty-five days to thirty-five without bleeding, a nightmare for someone in her position. How would she ever be a reliable priest if the others couldn't count on her menstruating at the services? Of course, the other priests couldn't exactly be annoyed with her, but nobody took it for granted that she'd be able to take the shifts she was assigned.

So it was rare for her to be given one of the important festival days. The chances of her not bleeding were too great—better to depend on a priest with a regular menstrual cycle.

It was frustrating, because as someone of Walborg lineage, Wicca was automatically a draw for the church. And, frankly, if it hadn't been for her family connections, they might not have been so forgiving. But lineage or no lineage, her inconsistency meant that neither the congregation nor the priests had ever regarded her with the same affection as they did her mother, grandmother, great-grandmother, and the other descendants of Walborg.

Her mother, Waleria, had always been punctual. Not only did her periods arrive at the expected time, but she also bled for at least eight days, sometimes up to eleven. Always heavily and usefully. Which was also part of why she was the most popular menstruating priest at the church. The older ones, who could boast that they no longer bled, were obviously more important, but her mother was almost as feted.

Wicca's cycle wasn't merely unpredictable—she also bled for only three days at the most, and not very heavily at that. Sometimes there wasn't even enough to collect for church. It wasn't fair. Her body and her bearing were exactly like her mother's, and Wivi's and Wanana's, for that matter, her grandmother and great-grandmother. All of them were lush and soft, turning heads and drawing gazes.

"Your skin gleams," people said. Even her great-grandmother, one hundred and twenty years old, was like a shining star hovering across the church floor as she finished the service.

The W priests were widely known in Christian circles, both for their compelling looks and their capacity to bleed during their menstrual years. And, of course, for being correspondingly wise in later life, when they kept their blood to themselves.

According to myth, the church mother Walborg—the reason their bloodline was held in such esteem and high regard—had started her periods at the age of three. Walborg had lived through the very first years of the Evolution, seemingly an ordinary child. Her mothers were nonbelievers, and Walborg had never heard of the Mother. When the blood began, coming first in dribbles, then increasingly in gushes down her legs, she was terrified. She thought she was dying. But the Mother came to her in the guise of Jesus, and told her she had nothing to fear. She had been chosen to lead Christianity out of the patriarchal dead end where it had languished for so many hundreds of years.

Snakes came slithering from near and far to share their wisdom with Walborg and remind everyone that the original meaning of "menstruation" was "divinity." The snakes were glad they were once more being listened to, and not driven off with hatred and suspicion as those of a patriarchal mindset had done, fearing that the snakes' universal wisdom would reveal men for what they were.

Walborg's mothers were skeptical, but although Walborg was a small child, she never doubted that she was the chosen one, and as a young woman she became the first true priestess of the Mother's church. Hers was the most important voice during the transformative church congress of 2225, when Christianity was saved from seemingly inevitable doom.

Since it was obvious to anyone who met Walborg that she'd been touched by a divine power, she was able to save Christianity by returning it to its original form, to the way it was before the men of the patriarchy destroyed it.

Walborg lived to be over two hundred years old, and every daughter in her bloodline since had been an abundant bleeder. All except for Wicca. Her mother consoled her by saying it might still come, and she'd kept Wicca hoping for years. But why would it suddenly happen now, when she was nearly thirty and had already had her baby?

Wicca moved her arm onto the side where Medea had slept, hoping a little of her warmth would be left. But the sheet was cold.

Wendy was in bed, sleeping open-mouthed, exposing the gap where her tooth had been. She was a lovely child; it had just taken Wicca some time to realize it. To allow herself to love her. When Kali left, and all the plans they'd made together fell apart, she had been overwhelmed by grief. Instead of giving birth to little Wendy in a loving relationship, with Kali by her side, Wicca had shrieked her into life, deserted and lost. Her mother, grandmother, great-grandmother, and several others from the church had been at the delivery, of course; she wasn't alone. But it wasn't what she'd imagined when she got pregnant, her belly growing alongside Kali's, both of them gasping excitedly whenever they felt the baby kick. Although the others had sung her favorite hymns between contractions and hung beautiful garlands of fruit to please the Mother, Wicca had cried the whole time. The tears only stopped when she briefly fell asleep, exhausted.

"You're doing so well," her mother had said, in a voice that sounded too jaunty. After two days of labor, she hadn't left her side. "It won't be long now. When I had you, you slipped right out in the blink of an eye."

"Shut your goddamn mouth," Wicca had screeched, tearing off the snake stole in a rage and flinging it into the delivery room after her mother told her for the twentieth time how good she'd been at birthing Wicca. Everyone fell silent, horrified by the discarded stole and the blasphemy, especially during a moment as sacred as birth. Her mother quickly brushed it off, asking her great-grandmother to read some passages from the Bible aloud. "So we can all find succor in the Mother's love."

Wendy was born legs first, and Wicca tore all the way to her rectum. The pain, which made her scream louder than she'd thought possible, had a soothing effect, because in the moment there was nothing left in her to feel the burning loss of Kali. In a fog of pain she saw her fraying heart tugged out with the placenta, so when they showed her daughter to her she felt nothing. Wicca shook her head and turned away as the doctors went to work, putting the pieces of her belly back in place. The delivery had taken place without anesthetic, the best way to ensure the healthiest child, but the rest she didn't feel, and by the next day she didn't need pain relief anymore. It was Eva who had pulled some strings and got Wicca the best obstetricians, trying not to make an already bad situation worse.

"At least you'll know you're in the best hands, medically speaking," Eva had said, giving her one of her hard squeezes and wiping away the constant flood of tears from Wicca's cheeks with an embroidered handkerchief. Embroidering handkerchiefs was Eva's tedious hobby.

"It helps me relax," she said. The mere thought of those prim little flowers and all the curlicues was enough to stress Wicca out. But Eva kept piles of them by her bed, near the toilet, in the kitchen. She used them once, then threw them out. After the birth, Eva had begun to leave them in strategic locations around the house, wherever Wicca cried the most. Wicca had even found a couple of them on the slope behind the house, tucked under a rock beside the bench. She'd noticed them when she went up there one day to get away from her crying child, and from all the things she didn't feel for her newborn baby.

THE SNAKE WAS RESTLESS IN THE VIVARIUM. USUALLY THE mere sound of it made Wicca feel guilty, but since Medea had been there, she knew it was content and had everything a snake could need.

Wicca was aware that as a priest of Walborg's bloodline, she was supposed to be good with snakes. All the other W women were. The truth, though, was that she didn't really like them. Not seeing them, not holding them. The only reason she could handle them at all was because she'd grown up with them. But the odor of the snake in her bedroom bothered her every time she came inside and shut the door.

People said that of all the priests currently working, her mother was the best snake-handler. They came from parishes all across the country, asking for advice or wanting to buy snakes. When Wicca's first cobra died, she had been sympathetic.

"It was probably just from bad stock," she'd reassured Wicca, who had received it as a confirmation present. "I'll get you a strong one, one from the same pedigree as mine. This was just a trial cobra. We know it can be hard at first. Keep your chin up—it helps if you've got a good one." Waleria herself had never lost a snake to anything but age.

A new one hadn't helped. The snake slowly languished and died; it must have been lying there for a couple of days before Wicca realized. It was desiccated around the mouth, one eye had fallen out, and its scales sloughed off as she picked it up hopefully, trying to shake some life into it.

She hadn't dared confess to her mother, and with Eva's help

she got a new cobra that looked exactly like the old one. Eva wasn't happy about going behind Waleria's back, and wouldn't tell her where she'd gotten it. She brought it home one Tuesday after Wicca had begged her for help. "Just this one time," Eva said. "You know I've got a soft spot for you. Don't take advantage of it."

If her mother had looked more closely, she'd have realized Wicca was getting new snakes all the time. Twenty-three of them, in total. The back garden at Himlingeøje was crammed with buried snake skeletons. They were supposed to be laid to rest in consecrated ground, of course, but it was too risky to bury them at the church with the other sacred snakes, so instead she performed her own little funeral rites under cover of darkness. And prayed that the Mother would forgive her.

Eva, after procuring ten of them, had refused to help anymore, so to hide her incompetence from her mother Wicca resorted to unauthorized dealers, and the snakes she got were runts.

Most of them didn't survive more than a month or two, and their bite was so weak that its intoxicating effect only lasted a few seconds during the ceremonies. If it had any effect at all. Too many times she had to pretend to be in a trance. No one in the congregation seemed to notice. Nobody looked at her askance. Probably it never occurred to them that a priest could be dishonest. Not that she didn't feel guilty—she apologized contritely to the Mother, to Mary, Magdalene, and Agatha, to the whole lot of them. More than once she'd wondered if this was why Kali had left. If she was being punished for faking her trances and burying her snakes in unconsecrated ground. Mostly, the thoughts came when she lay awake at night and couldn't sleep. They got worse year after year. The thoughts had always been troublesome, but after Kali left they were like torture, and there were times she cried as hard as Wendy during the colicky phases she went through as an infant. In daytime, when her mind was clearer, she knew the Mother didn't work that way. That punishment and revenge weren't in her repertoire.

Wicca got out of bed and sighed contentedly. Gently she stroked the leaves of her red coleus, which radiated the sexual energy of the night before. She bent down and inspected the plant. Yes, there was a new shoot. The first since Kali. Its leaves had become visibly redder in the past few months, ever since she'd met Medea, and the plants by the bed were benefitting once again from the energy of her orgasms. The ones she achieved through masturbation alone didn't do her or the plants much good. She needed a partner. But what could she do, when she couldn't visit the spa at the Center because of her mother's edict, and she didn't want to go to the Street because she was afraid of running into Lars and Kali?

Wicca wasn't good with snakes and she wasn't good at bleeding, but orgasms? Those she had mastered from the moment her groin woke up, in early puberty. She got perfect grades in Body at school, and not because she'd worked particularly hard. She knew instinctively what to do to achieve ecstasy on the highest level of the scale.

The only time in Wicca's life when her houseplants hadn't had glossy leaves and new shoots was in the years after Kali. Until now. Even the plants in the vivarium looked more vital this morning. There was a fizz in her body since last night. Satisfied, she put on her red bathrobe and draped the stole over it. She opened the door carefully, trying not to wake Wendy, and slipped out into the hall.

In the bathroom, Eva was putting on lipstick.

"Good morning," said Wicca, sitting down on the toilet and taking out a medium-sized blood collector.

If it had been anyone but Eva in the room, she'd have concealed the fact that she only needed the medium. Or she would have put in one that dried her out and felt uncomfortable until she could change it. But it was different with Eva. Although they had their disagreements about the Easter ritual, Eva wasn't the type to make you feel small. She never bragged or showed off. And unlike many others, she didn't make a big deal about her periods, or the status that it brought her to be nearly at the age when she'd stop bleeding.

"Good morning," Eva answered. The rat waited patiently on the windowsill. Eva adjusted her top so that it fit perfectly over her breasts. She had nice breasts, despite the fact that she was nearly fifty and never used support. Then again, she'd never used them to feed a baby.

"I love babies," Eva said, if anybody brought up having children. "I've just never felt the need to carry one, and anyway, the rest of you'll be having enough of them for me to love and play with when I feel like it."

Which she did. All the children in the house liked Eva best, including Wendy. Wicca was under no illusions about which of them Wendy preferred, Eva or her own mother.

"Visitor last night?" Eva asked, smiling with her freshly painted lips. "I was lucky enough to bump into your little witch girl here earlier."

Wicca nodded, washing her hands at the sink. "Yes, she's very sweet."

"I can see she makes you happy. So I guess it doesn't really matter that she's a bit, you know . . . right?" Eva gave her arm a squeeze as she walked past.

"You look gorgeous," Wicca told her. "Is all this in honor of that new doctor at the Center?"

Eva sighed. "I'm afraid Nanna turned out not to be quite what I'd hoped. I wouldn't even call us friends anymore."

"Oh, but you two were so smitten with each other when she came over for dinner?"

"Life—what can I say?" Eva smiled, throwing a last critical glance at her makeup. Wicca could hear her footsteps all the way down the hall and into the kitchen.

Wicca could see, obviously, that Medea was a funny little thing, with her too-long hair and short stature. She smelled odd, and then there was all the witch stuff. Not exactly meet-the-friends-and-family material. She was dreading introducing her—especially to her mother. After meeting Medea, Waleria might even start wishing Kali back, and she hadn't had many nice things to say about her. Not just because she was an amazon; Waleria was never keen on anybody who didn't worship the Mother and Jesus. She never said so outright, but it was obvious she considered non-Christians to be second-class.

Of all the people Wicca knew, her mother and Medea were the most skilled with snakes, but even that probably wasn't enough to make Waleria drop her defenses and have a conversation with Medea on an equal footing. It was too bad, she thought. Medea really had a way with those snakes. They worshiped her.

Wicca wasn't fond of Medea's paganism, either, but she was the first person since Kali to make her feel alive. That mattered more, she thought, and she was sure the Mother would agree. The fact that her own mother wouldn't was something she'd have to look past. Or try to.

Despite how badly she needed the orgasms, after Kali she hadn't been able to bear the feel of another body. Medea was the first to tempt her like the old days.

After seven years without a partnered orgasm, Wicca had been getting headaches, insomnia, aching joints, and days of depression. Kali's loss was like a splinter, bothering her whenever she happened to tread on it, but with Medea in her life, with the energies flowing once again, everything had turned brighter and more bearable. Now she dared to imagine there might be a future.

It was Lars who'd told her about Medea. Many years ago, when she and Kali were still together. Lars had been Kali's preferred man when they went to the Street. Wicca switched between several, depending on her mood. Or on who was available. She wasn't fussy—as long as she got something between her legs.

Kali stuck to Lars, and they didn't always have sex. At the Center, Kali sometimes trained up to ten men a day, so she didn't always feel like more sex, but she didn't mind a trip to the Street for a chat with Lars. Looking back, Wicca realized she had no idea if Kali and Lars were ever intimate at all, or if their relationship was purely platonic.

Lars nearly always had a kid hanging around, drinking greedily from his breast. They weren't his—he made a living nursing them. There were always women who, for various reasons, preferred an alternative solution to the publicly available options.

"It keeps my milk coming in, and I can also offer the service to ladies who like to play with that sort of thing in bed," Lars said. There was always a sour smell where he lived, the scent of milk-damp rags and breast supports hung out to dry. Still, there was something cozy and reassuring about his house. Or whatever you'd call it. It was an old supermarket on the bottom of a corner building, converted somewhat slapdash with half-height walls and wobbling partitions. In a few spots, floral carpets had been hung up and used as screens, as well as old bricks Lars had gathered from the more dilapidated buildings down the road. It was always warm inside, unlike many of the other houses, which didn't have as much energy to spend on heat.

"I have my contacts," Lars said, whenever anybody asked him how he did it. Even so, he only used lanterns and other types of flame when it was dark. "No reason to go wasting energy," he said.

There were limits to how good one's contacts could be, even as a manlady. And it was more important to keep the tiny breastfed babies warm than to see clearly.

"Actually, in my business, it's not the worst thing if people are a little blurry," he said, grinning. "But of course that doesn't apply to you, gorgeous," he said to Kali. Wicca had no doubt he meant it. Kali, with her white hair and green cat's eyes, was the most beautiful woman she'd ever seen.

When Wicca returned from her own adventures with one of the men and knocked at Lars's door, she usually found them deep in conversation. They loved to debate—about anything and everything.

"Back in the Stone Age they had it figured out. Men only had symbolic value then. Otherwise we wouldn't have sent them out to hunt, where they could so easily die. The women were too important to risk, so they stayed safe at home" was one of the discussions Wicca had been thrust into, and she didn't have a clue how to contribute. Then there was that time they'd argued about whether it was proof of men's lower basic intelligence that they hadn't seen the Evolution coming.

"If half the population—i.e., women—lose interest in sex, which in practical terms means they don't want to reproduce, it's a sign that society is sick," Kali said. "I mean, can you imagine women today not wanting to have sex?" They both laughed.

No matter the volume or the topic of discussion, Lars always called Kali "my best friend" when they said goodbye, so it seemed somehow inappropriate that she paid him by the hour for sex even though they'd only sat and talked.

"I can't not pay him," Kali said whenever Wicca questioned it. "He sells his time, and it's not his fault I've had enough orgasms for one day. That I'd rather use my head instead."

Lars had the biggest silicone penis on the street. He enjoyed swinging it around, proud of both its size and the beauty of the work that had gone into it.

"Where did you get it done?" Wicca asked him one day. Sewn-on penises weren't strictly forbidden, but they weren't entirely legal either. Wicca struggled to imagine a doctor agreeing to help.

Lars winked at her cryptically. "As I said, I have my contacts."

"Did it hurt?"

"At first it was difficult to get the skin to stretch all the way around, but time and age are your friend." Lars paced back and forth in front of them, allowing them to admire it hanging heavily between his legs.

Wicca leaned forward, studying it more closely. "You must have a pretty skilled seamstress. Those stitches are a minor work of art."

One day, on a visit to the Street, Wicca's mind had kept wandering from the manlady whose door she'd knocked at. Another one of her snakes had died, and she'd complained about her predicament to Lars.

"My mother's going to kill me if she finds out," she said despairingly. "Nobody at church will sell me snakes under the table anymore, and the ones I buy from ordinary traders keep dying. They're sick before they even get to me, I think."

"There's a funny little snake lady living in the black house on the corner," Lars told her. "You can't miss it—all the other walls still standing are white, it's the only black one. She digs up roots in my back garden. No idea what she uses them for. She's nuts, of course, but I've heard a lot of people say she's preternaturally good at rearing snakes. I have clients who buy them from her for research. Apparently, the place smells weird and it's so dirty it seems inconceivable that human beings can actually live there, but the snakes are exceptionally high quality."

Lars had told her the snake lady believed she could do magic.

"She casts incantations over the roots and chants to the moon," he said. "And she wanders around with this big overgrown wolfdog that never listens to her. Come to think of it, it's probably more the dog that wanders around with her."

They'd laughed at his stories. Afterward, Wicca had forgotten all about the witch and her snakes. She'd gone and confessed to her mother, who had procured her another one—though not without a deep sigh, various injunctions about how to look after a cobra, and disapproving looks at the next ceremonies.

In the years after Kali went missing, Wicca, lost in a haze of depression, had managed to kill so many of her snakes that it was impossible to admit it to her mother. When eventually the day came that there weren't even enough ailing snakes for her to buy one, she remembered the story about the strange little witch.

It was much too hot the day she set out on the arduous trek through the slums to find the black house. It ended up being a long walk, because she was intent on giving the Street a wide berth. She had no idea if Kali was still seeing Lars, but the thought of possibly bumping into her and coming face-to-face with her betrayal brought tears to her eyes even now, seven years later.

As she neared the black house, a bird with an orange beak began to circle above her. It wore a blue bow around its neck and settled on a branch above the door, where it scowled at her malevolently.

That thing looks ridiculous, she thought, before it sent a dollop of bird poo in her direction.

"You asshole," she yelled, but that only made the bird dive straight toward her. She screamed and flailed at it, and it disappeared through an open window into the house. Wicca hesitated for a moment at the doorway, but decided that she'd never been afraid of birds before and wasn't about to start today. Still, she glanced around cautiously before she stepped inside. The bird was nowhere to be seen, but she could hear several others gabbling somewhere in the house.

Her first impression of Medea wasn't promising. The place

reeked of animal feces, poor ventilation, and mold, plus whatever Medea was stirring at the kitchen table.

"Come with me," said the greasy little woman, whose unkempt, gray-streaked hair fell in knots to her knees. Wicca had never seen such a creature before. From behind she had looked like a child, with long, ugly locks, standing on tiptoes to stir the bowl.

Two large, unappealing dogs lay in the corner, watching her. They could have used a bath as well. Wicca was careful not to touch anything. You never knew what infections you might pick up in these old patriarchal villas. At the top of the basement steps sat a glowering bust of the Devil, and for a second Wicca wondered if she was being led down into Hell. Offering up a quick prayer to the Mother for protection, she followed Medea down the stairs. There she was asked to wait, because Medea wanted to change. It seemed odd, but then again, most things in this house were odd.

When Medea emerged from the anteroom in a long golden cloak, her hair in braids, she seemed so different that Wicca was struck dumb. Everything about the tiny woman had changed—her appearance, her aura. Somehow it made all the grime irrelevant. Wicca, to her astonishment, felt herself swell between her legs.

Medea took her in to see the snakes and introduced her to the different kinds, but since Wicca's eyes were focused on her face, her hands, her lips, she didn't hear much of what she said. Luckily, she wasn't the first Christian priest to buy a snake from Medea, and she came home with an unusually elegant white cobra. It would cow the whole church into stunned silence, once it grew big enough to take part in a service.

WICCA SAT OPPOSITE EVA IN THE KITCHEN.

"Coffee?"

Wicca nodded, also taking a piece of the bread Eva had set out. One of the teenagers in the house sauntered in and took a slice. She walked off without deigning to look at them.

"Whoa, hold up," Eva said. The girl turned, gave Eva a hug, and strolled drowsily away.

She passed Wendy, who came skipping down the corridor with her stuffed snake.

"Hey, you're up! Come here, sweetheart." Wicca held out her arms. "Did you sleep well?"

Wendy walked straight past her and up to Eva, clambering onto her lap. She gave her a kiss, then the rat on her shoulder got one too. Eva glanced apologetically at Wicca, who took a sip of coffee. If she were honest, she preferred not to have a squirming child on her lap.

Wicca pulled the dark gray clerical gown over her hips and zipped it up at the back. She adjusted her breasts so that they fit perfectly in the curve. The white ruff had just been cleaned, and it shone almost as brightly as her skin. Her snake-green stole, like the other priestesses', was decorated with crosses, but Wicca and her family also had a large yellow *W* emblazoned on both sides.

She tried to drape the stole so that it didn't cover too much of her chest. She was always proud to wear the yellow mark, which showed that her and her foremothers were descended in a direct lineage from Walborg. Plus, the yellow at least perked up all the gloomy gray a bit. It felt wrong not to be wearing red, and she tried to make up for it with lipstick.

Wicca took a step back to admire what she saw in the mirror. It wasn't bad, although dark tones didn't suit her. The other priests in the parish wore black robes, but Wicca had been bold enough to have some made in charcoal gray. There wasn't much spirit in it, but anything was better than jet black.

In pictures from Walborg's day, before the momentous church congress, the priests had worn vestments in all the colors of the rainbow, and collars in more shapes than the now-obligatory ruff. Wicca wished they were still free to knock themselves out. If it were up to her, they'd wear long brightly colored silk gowns in soft fabrics that clung to the body and draped across the floor. That would be perfect for worship, and make a nice contrast to the snakes around their necks. Did the Mother really prefer being bored to death by women in black? It made no sense.

She understood, of course, that certain things were best kept traditional, given that there were other, more important symbols they'd had to change in order to preserve Christianity. There had to be some elements of continuity amid all the upheaval. The robes and the ruffs were easy to keep, although arguably the black-and-white vestments represented patriarchal tyranny more than anything else.

"All it's missing is a swastika or a Mars symbol on the back, then we'll really be paying tribute to the past," Wicca had remarked ironically as an adolescent. Her mother sadly refused to be baited, merely explaining once again that it was a small price to pay for Christianity surviving the Evolution. She was right, of course. It would be silly to jeopardize everything Walborg and the other church mothers had fought so hard to achieve over something so frivolous. The mere fact that they had salvaged the faith when it was hanging by a thin thread was a miracle. When things had begun to move quickly, and male dominion over society finally gave way, nobody had been interested in preserving a faith built around a male god, his son, twelve male disciples, and even a holy spirit with a masculine pronoun.

It didn't help that the Bible explicitly commanded women to be silent at assemblies. Or that Christians, in the name of God, had subjugated and oppressed women in the cruelest ways, even—at worst—burning them at the stake, justifying their actions with their crosses held aloft. But all of that had hinged on a terrible misinterpretation of Christianity. Everybody knew that now.

Originally, human beings had believed not in some trumped-up Father but in the one true Mother.

During the Evolution, when at last the patriarchy was forced to release its grip on power, texts and other discoveries that proved Christianity had been misinterpreted finally emerged from the hiding places of the past. It didn't take long to see through the smoke screen put up by the patriarchy around the true faith in the Mother. Out came the voluptuous goddess figurines, the swollen genitals and curving shapes. Ancient scrolls were found, texts that spoke of the divine Mother, her son Jesus, and the religious stories as they had really been told.

What made it easier was that men had been unimaginative enough to name their first man Adam. That was the name of the first human in the Mother's creation story too: Adamee. Adam, in the feminine form. It wasn't a particularly ingenious cover-up, because the mythological creatures in the false Christian tales were the same ones the Mother had used. The patriarchs had simply given the original female names a masculine ending instead. Often, the result made the stories illogical. A male god conceiving a son breaks all the laws of nature. Where's he supposed to get him from? Whereas a Mother having a son—nobody questions that.

So, with a few corrections, Christianity post-Evolution regained a solid foothold. The Mother was back at the helm, along with her only begotten son, Jesus, who was reborn and died in tribute to the cyclical beginning and end of all things.

In a distant past, snakes were the Mother's greatest mouthpiece. They whispered her divine instructions to the priestesses, who helped the congregation understand the origin of life and the Mother's purpose. The priestesses kept the snakes in the temples, tending and nurturing them, worshiping them as the sacred beasts they were.

In honor of the Mother and of fertility, priestesses in those days made love to men on their altars. No man refused an invitation to the temple. To be permitted sex with a priestess was to be granted a share in the divine. With the Mother's assistance, the men who were invited there impregnated the priestesses. The daughters inherited their mothers' titles, their riches, and privileged social status.

Evidence showed that in ancient times there had been thousands of temples built in the Mother's honor. The weekly ceremonies were held under the trees in the temple gardens, where they shared the apples of the trees and other fruit, pretending it was the Mother's flesh and blood. They sang as they made miniatures of the goddess, figurines with heavy breasts and swollen labia, and anointed them with holy menstrual blood.

Everybody knew that in a woman's monthly blood there was the wisdom of the ancient days. It was to be welcomed each month with respect and reverence, and when a woman reached the years when she no longer menstruated, she was exalted as a sage. She retained the wisdom now within herself, and understood things men and younger women did not.

One of the most important ceremonies in the Mother's church was the Easter ritual—the annual death and rebirth of the son. He came into the world each spring with the budding flowers, grew over the course of summer, became the Mother's lover in the fall, and in winter died, only to be born again along with the new shoots on the trees, to grow anew and die once more with the passing of the year. Men were carefully selected to take part in the ritual. Symbolically, of course. The Mother's religion was not barbaric, and they did not kill the men used in the ceremonies or in their lovemaking. A few early writings suggested that at most they'd been castrated, to make sure the sliver of the divine transferred to them from the priestesses was not passed on to laywomen, who might not know how to wield its power.

Life went on in harmony for thousands of years, until men came from the north and looked with greed and envy on the wealth possessed by the Mother and her temples, on her loyal followers and material goods. Contrary to what one might think, their motive in destroying the Mother's faith and inventing the Christian Father was not religious. They didn't object to the open lovemaking and hedonistic way of life. No, what they wanted was power. They wanted men to be the ones in charge. They wanted sons to inherit from fathers—and not, as it then stood, for all the wealth to go to daughters.

But greed is a difficult tool with which to sway the masses, so instead they used religion to sow fear and doubt among the people. They waged war on nature's own laws of creation. It wasn't a female who'd first made life, they said, but a male god. They shaped a whole new religion around defiance of the Mother.

In practical terms, this meant burning down as many of the Mother's temples as they could. If they found a goddess figurine flecked with menstrual blood, they crushed it under their heel. If they came across a fruit tree, they felled it on the spot. If they had to write the Mother's name, they deliberately misspelled it, so that instead it came to mean "shame." They changed words like "prophetess" to "prostitute," and marked as masculine anything that had previously had a feminine ring.

But they were also cleverer than that. They didn't just destroy material things and tamper with language. The men knew it would take more. To really change a habit, to instill in the people greater respect for the masculine and make them scorn the blessings of the Mother, they had to whip up so much fear in people that they wouldn't dare to break the male god's rules.

Snakes, as mentioned, were the Mother's greatest mouthpiece, and her direct conduit with the priestesses. So men rushed to demonize them. They weren't sacred creatures of wisdom and prophecy, men said. They were evil, a conduit to the Devil. Anything a snake might whisper to a woman was manipulative, subversive to humankind. Those who listened, either to a snake or to a woman who had taken its advice, and who believed what they had heard, were to blame for the downfall of humanity.

To keep other men away from the beautiful, naked priestesses, they announced that nudity was not tolerated by the new god. The same applied to making love.

And so the most natural and necessary thing on Earth, a woman and a man coming together to create life, was forbidden in the new faith; it was made dirty. Where they had once lived in natural contact with their urges, people who enjoyed sex were now supposed to feel disgusted with themselves and pray to the male god for forgiveness when they felt the desire to have sex with another person. The alternative was to burn in Hell.

But resisting a beautiful naked woman offering a moment's pleasure in a temple garden was easier said than done. The men found it too difficult to obey. So, to spare them, it was decided that if a man and a woman had sex, the shame and guilt were the woman's. If he took her against her will, that too was her responsibility, because she'd tempted him. To draw women away from the freedom of the temples, it was necessary to frighten them as well. They were made to believe that if they had sexual desires, the male god would call down a great collective punishment on humanity and on their innocent children. Therefore, women had to be virgins until they were married. If they acted like whores, as free women were now being called, their entire family would suffer for it. It became a mortal sin to have sex with anyone except your husband.

One thing men couldn't stop, something they feared to the point of hysteria, was menstruation. Everybody knew it was a magical event, capable of draining a man of his strength and mental energies. It was a potential landmine underneath the new, masculine religion. So men were encouraged to stay away from women on their periods, and women were forbidden to take part in religious activities or even speak to men on the days they were bleeding. The older women, the particularly wise ones who no longer bled, were now marketed as being in league with the Devil, which would eventually lead to the stereotype of the ugly, wart-nosed old witch: lonely, embarrassing, and unpleasant. Nobody was allowed to listen to her.

The Mother's creation story, in all its simplicity, celebrated the emergence of life and fertility. In this account, man and woman were made simultaneously out of clay, and both mattered.

Male Christianity grew different branches over the centuries, and they made up various narratives of creation. All of them, however, had in common the desire to rule through fear. And all insisted that it was the man, Adam, who was the ultimate and true human being. God had fashioned him first, then woman—out of Adam's rib.

They spread lies about snakes and declared that eating fruit underneath trees, as the Mother's disciples did, was directly responsible for their expulsion from Paradise.

Men were capable, you had to give them that. Century after century, they managed to keep women in an iron grip with their made-up tales, allowing them only the role of the all-sacrificing maternal madonna or the cheap whore who could be treated as badly as they liked. The real lives lived by women, lives of spirit, vigor, and feminine strength—those had no place in their version of Christendom.

When the church mothers read the original texts, they could only shake their heads at the things men had come up with. Not least the notion of a motherless male god.

"It's not a supernatural phenomenon, it's an unnatural phenomenon. Nothing else in nature supports this kind of thinking. Never in the history of the world has there been an example of a life that began anywhere but in its mother's womb," Walborg said in the speech that brought about a sea change at the church congress.

"To deny motherhood is to deny women. This denial of women is the only original thought the Christian patriarchs ever had—everything else they stole from the original faith in the Mother. The trinity, the son, the resurrection. All of that existed already. The only thing that didn't exist—and the only thing that will not exist in the future—is misogyny, and the theft of our sacred religion and tempestuous sexuality by men."

Wicca knew that part of the speech by heart. She recited it to herself before she had to perform a ceremony at church. She must have done more than a hundred services by now, but she never stopped being nervous. Especially when her mother was there. Today she was more nervous still, because she was bringing the white cobra for the first time. It was long enough now to hang around her neck, its jaws large enough to deliver a bite, passing on the stimulant she needed in order to comprehend the divine words it whispered to her.

WICCA HAD HER FIRST SNAKEBITE AT THIRTEEN, JUST like her mother, grandmother, and the other priestesses in the generations before hers. Thirteen was the age when, in addition to regular schoolwork, you began gradually training to enter the ministry, if you wanted. But as a descendent of Walborg, you did want to be a priestess: it was impossible to imagine anything else. For Wicca, and for the rest of her family.

The first cobra that bit Wicca had venom so weak she was supposed to barely feel it. That was how they got you used to the intoxication, until in the end you could extract all its benefits and let the Mother speak through you. Although the venom was weak, Wicca's arm swelled up. Her upper arm doubled in size, and she struggled to breathe. It passed within a few hours, but she had felt unwell for days.

"Your body is just unusually sensitive," her mother said, "but you'll get used to it. And once you learn to handle it, your susceptibility could mean you become the greatest priestess of our age."

"Did it happen to you too?" Wicca had asked, drooping over a bucket. The venom had made her nauseous.

Waleria had smiled and shaken her head. "I barely noticed my first bite. I got all the way up to snake seven—the one they don't give you until the third year—before I felt anything at all."

"Maybe I'm just not meant to be a priestess," Wicca had cried, hacking up bile until her throat stung.

"Nonsense, you were created to be the Mother's mouthpiece. You're a descendent of Walborg, and my daughter—don't you ever forget that."

Wicca had been brave and let herself be bitten by the cobra every week. And it was equally disastrous every time. She was sixteen before they decided to try her on one with more powerful venom than the starter snake, but Wicca had instinctively withdrawn her arm as the snake theologian went to put the cobra on.

"Don't be scared, it's just a little bite," the theologian said, pouring her a glass of juice and setting it in front of Wicca. "Here, the sugar helps if you feel sick."

She'd had to call in an assistant to hold Wicca's arm so that the snake could get a proper latch. Wicca screamed as it hooked on. Then she lost consciousness and slid out of the chair. When she came to, her ears were ringing and her vision was blurred. Thoughts raced up toward the clouds, forming patterns she'd never imagined had existed. Afterward she threw up all over the theologian, who was bending over her with a worried frown.

"Aren't you Walborg's bloodline?" she had asked, putting pressure on the spot where the cobra had bitten. "A dose like this shouldn't produce any noticeable effect, especially since you've already passed snake level one, but why don't we try again next week. Let's hope we have more luck."

Next time, it happened again. The only change over the following year was that she got used to the discomfort and learned to live with the nausea. Over the last few years, ever since Eva had been giving her the anti-nausea meds, things had improved. But she was still nowhere near capable of handling the cobras her mother and the other priestesses let bite them.

Medea's new white cobra was still young, so she wasn't worried about tolerating the bite. Mostly she was looking forward to seeing her mother's stupefied face when she, Wicca, came strolling in with a rare white cobra. None of the other priests in the parish of Brønshøj had one like it.

She picked up the golden box with the red silk and placed

it into the vivarium. Her mother's cobras slithered in without being prompted, but Wicca's never had. The white cobra was no exception.

"Come on," she said irritably, poking at it with the cross.

It hissed at her. Wicca sighed, gripped its head, and managed to stuff the rest of it into the box. It rasped again, and didn't look at all like the triumph it was supposed to be at church.

SHE SAT DOWN ON THE BED, ABRUPTLY TIRED AT THE thought of Brønshøj and the church. What if it didn't go as she expected? What if she disappointed everyone, again? She often thought that if only they'd focused on the lovemaking bit of the Mother's original faith instead of the snakes, the bit where the priestesses honored the Mother by practicing divine sex in church, she would have had the chance to shine.

Body was the only class she'd ever been much good at, and the only one she'd ever been interested in. The first module, which they were taught at twelve, consisted of theoretical masturbation. At times it got a little boring.

"You are your own first sexual experience, so make sure it's a good one," the theory teacher began. Being a self-professed masturbator, she didn't hesitate to add, "Don't expect orgasms with a partner to ever be as good as the ones you have alone. And if a penis is involved, you can forget about it, frankly. Under the patriarchy, a lot of women pretended to orgasm with the male so he'd let her go to sleep in peace. You bear that in mind, should you ever find yourself wandering into a Center one day, thinking it might be fun to encase a penis. You're not going to get much out of it. There's nothing wrong with you—it's just the old-fashioned notion of the importance of male genitalia for our physical well-being, which has been exaggerated and romanticized. There are always a few misguided souls still touting it."

The next part of the class, practical masturbation, was more exciting, but still one of the more tedious elements of Body. That said, in the seven years between Kali leaving and meeting Medea, Wicca had sometimes wished she'd listened better and been more diligent with the exercises they were given as homework.

To make sure students had all the tools they needed to be human, it was also recommended that they take Fundamentals of Partner Orgasm. These things were good to know, if you ever wanted to get into an intimate situation. Moreover, that was the exam that gave access to the Centers and sex with a male—although only a small part of the semester related to men. The focus was squarely on having sex with another human.

The tug-of-war between these two groups, the onanists and the vaginists, flared at regular intervals into fierce debate, both in the public sphere and in the home. Was it possible to be satisfied with masturbation and achieve the same pleasure alone—or was a partner required to obtain the maximum possible effect? The vaginists believed that an orgasm produced solely through clitoral stimulation was nothing but a surface ripple compared to what the body could attain through the proper pressure in the vagina by someone other than oneself. After all, just as you can't make yourself laugh, you can't stimulate yourself to release enough active chemicals for an effective orgasm either.

One thing they did agree on, and one thing only: a penis was never required in order to reach orgasm.

From time to time, a third group—the penisists—would start bleating about how penises gave the best orgasms. But they always turned out to be advertising for the Centers on the sly, and when the claims were investigated more closely, there was never any scientific evidence that the penis did anything in particular for women.

The Christian church and the W lineage had no preference either way. As long as you were orgasming regularly, the Mother was happy. There was nothing in scripture about the best way to climax. It was up to Wicca whether or not she wanted to take the advanced class. Her mother was more concerned about snake training. As long as Wicca wasn't neglecting that, she could do as she liked. So Wicca threw herself into the later modules with unaccustomed zeal. She found even the units on the chemistry of orgasm fascinating. She was one of the top students in her year group, the teacher's pet, because she always came so well prepared. She did her coursework on *The Successful Partner Orgasm*, demonstrating through careful calculations which chemical reactions could be initiated in the body by an orgasm in which the erogenous zones were stimulated by another individual. The goal was to reach a plane of consciousness where you no longer cared how you looked, how you behaved, or what sounds and words you uttered. A point where the lizard brain took over and the person became pure body. It was from this point that dopamine exploded outward at climax, suffusing a woman's whole being with a euphoria that brought creativity, better color perception, and clarity of thought. Then oxytocin made the same trip around the body, causing the satisfied female body to bond with her sexual partner.

"Here we have part of the explanation for why the patriarchy was able to survive for so many hundreds of years," the chemistry teacher had explained. "It was lucky for women that more and more of them lost interest in sex with their male partners—and it was also nature's last-ditch attempt to save the species. Once they were no longer blinded by oxytocin, they could suddenly see men for what they really were, without the intoxicating effects of falling in love or the desire for mutual connection. The chemistry of orgasm is powerful stuff, which is why you must never forget to take your shot of antidote, if you do choose to visit a Center. Of course, when you're with partners other than the Center men, all you have to do is enjoy it. Just bond with whoever you have feelings for."

One reason why so many women lost their desire for men was that the males themselves had too much faith in their genitals' ability to give pleasure. For several centuries, their increasingly self-centered behavior in bed was a catastrophe for women, because if you set off the initial chemical reactions without also providing the explosion of orgasm, it has the opposite effect. Instead of energy and joy, women felt anger and helplessness. This triggered a series of psychological problems, such as stress, depression, and anxiety.

Wicca's thorough understanding of oxytocin also served her well when she gave birth to Wendy. Grief over the loss of Kali had prevented her from bonding with her newborn. Her milk didn't come in. So she asked Eva to bring back a dose of oxytocin from the Center in Lolland, the ones they used for the males when they wanted them to bond with the women they were satisfying. Wicca took two sniffs and milk began to dribble from her breasts.

"It's an old housewives' trick, from before the Evolution," Eva said. "But you and your body will be able to produce it soon, I'm sure—this darling little blob is just irresistible." She stroked baby Wendy's bald head affectionately.

Being in touch with her own body and passing the practical and theoretical exams still wasn't enough to permit access to the Centers. Wicca also had to understand the male body in order to be admitted.

"Experience has shown us that if they're not well prepared, most people get a shock when they see their first male. They may view him as a freak, and that can spoil the pleasure he's there to give," the teacher explained. "Fortunately, the male body is not as complicated as the female body. Although men do have their own body parts, in many ways they're a simplified version of women's."

By this point, only a third of the original class was left. Of those who had not stopped after masturbation, half dropped out before the final module. Neither they nor their mothers could imagine ever visiting a Center, and although most scientists recommended natural conception, because it produced the strongest offspring, they preferred to get pregnant through artificial insemination. Many people found the idea of a male body off-putting, and they didn't want their young daughters frightened by the pictures of naked men. In any case, there was always the option of taking the course later on, at one of the Centers' continuing education facilities, once they were older and perhaps more ready to face the devalued segment of the human species. But Wicca couldn't wait to pass the exam, so despite the nausea and the swollen snakebites she sat in the front row, eager not to miss a thing.

"I know many of you are worried about your first encounter with a penis," the teacher began one of her classes, "but you should try to look at it as an overgrown clitoris. It also has a hood you can pull back, and in many ways it functions similarly. It swells when the man becomes aroused, just as you do. This swelling of the penis makes it easier to encase and easier to use in the way you want. However, the penis is not as sensitive as the clitoris. Whereas in women, all the nerve endings are gathered in a single point, in the penis they are spread across the whole engorged head. Which is practical when you're running all over the place with your genitals flopping around outside your body. Just another example of how the female design is more fit for purpose than men. They do have orgasms, by the way, like women do, but they can only achieve one type. It's over for them quickly and it simply shoots straight out of their genitals; they don't feel it in their whole body, like we do. It's a moment of ejaculation, then they're done. They also can't reap any of the benefits of orgasm—it's just a discharge of energy for them. They get tired and sleepy afterward. Oh, and don't worry about the swelling—they're given medication so it happens when you need it."

Fifteen-year-old Wicca wrote it all down in her notebook. She spent hours practicing on models, as well as anything else that resembled a penis. Knowing she was only one exam away from being allowed to visit the Center in Lolland, she studied every spare second. And although most people were at least a year or two older before they made their debut, she felt ready.

She passed on her first try, one of the youngest ever at her school to do so.

THE NIGHT BEFORE WICCA WENT TO LOLLAND FOR THE first time, she was so keyed up she couldn't sleep. She'd practiced encasement until the soft walls of her genitals were worn, and she'd had to take a break for a few days, just to be sure she got the most out of her visit to the Center. She had studied the male body so intently that she felt as though she knew it as well as her own, watching all the simulations of erections she could find and visiting places that had tame animals, which she stroked to get used to the feel of hairy skin under her hands.

She had been given a list of the various turn-ons to choose from. But she was too inexperienced to know if she preferred the hairy ones or the outdoorsy types, deep voices, muscles, dark or fair hair, or which of the wide array of skin tones she would like.

Wicca had only just moved into the roundhouse where Eva lived. There was no way to extend her mother's roundhouse, and Wicca and her mother were too cramped in the two small rooms available. On that they agreed. Her mother felt comfortable with Wicca moving in at Eva's, where a room was newly vacant after the death of an older resident, because as a young woman she had helped rescue Eva from the slum. Apparently, Eva had been at death's door, but the church and the Ws hadn't just helped her get back on her feet, they'd seen to it that she got an education.

"I can't take *all* the credit for the fact that she's a doctor today, of course, but I can say she wouldn't have become one without me," Wicca's mother liked to boast.

Eva was nearly twenty years older than fifteen-year-old Wicca, but they were still close friends. Eva, more experienced, offered

Wicca guidance when she needed it. She'd lived in the Christian roundhouse when Wicca was a child and had been like an older sister to her and a daughter to Waleria. She stayed for years, only moving out when she got a job as a doctor at the Lolland Center. Initially she was assigned to the breeding unit there, where they focused on achieving the strongest genetic conception. Later she transferred to the young males, with whom she felt she had a good rapport. The ones who weren't yet sexually mature. Wicca considered her an expert on men and was always peppering her with questions. Eva answered as best she could.

"I don't really have anything to do with the men in use at the spa, I'm just responsible for rearing them," Eva said. "But I do know I'd recommend taking the beginner's program. It gives you a taste of what the spa can offer. A toned-down version, so you don't get scared off if what you try isn't really for you."

"I don't feel like a beginner," Wicca had said. She thought it should count for something that she'd gotten the best grades in the class.

"There's no rush. You've got time to try everything," Eva said, ruffling her hair. "You need to leave something for when you're ninety-five, remember."

"Which is your favorite turn-on?" Wicca asked.

"Oh, you know, I spend so much time around them," Eva said. "It's like cake—if you bake it yourself, you don't really want to eat it. Hey, pass me the coffee, will you?" She poured some coffee onto a plate for the rat, which scrabbled down her arm, sat on the edge of her hand, and lapped it up.

Wicca went with Eva to Lolland the next morning, much more nervous than she'd imagined she would be.

"Relax, they're just men," said Eva, unable to hold back her amusement. "They won't hurt you."

"If they're not dangerous, why can't they be loose among the rest of us?" said Wicca, chewing on a nailbed.

"Those were the old days. And yes, men left to their own devices do kill, rape, and steal, but it's not like that anymore." Eva laughed. "The man you'll meet today has been tamed, medicated, and chipped. We have full control, so all you have to do is lean back and enjoy it."

Wicca was uneasy both about the men she was going to meet and whether she would be unable to perform, in equal measure. Now was the time to show why she was the best student in her Body class. Tomorrow she had another snake lesson, when she'd feel inept and afterward be nauseous for days.

As they passed through the yellow gate, she caught herself wanting to grab Eva's hand—but that would seem far too childish. The space around them was bustling with people in pale yellow clothes, chatting and laughing. They had just gotten to work and were telling one another things that had happened yesterday as well as planning the day ahead. Several of them came up to exchange a few words with Eva. She was clearly popular with more than just the children at the house.

"I'll show you to the baths, then I'd better go and see to the juvenile males. But I've spoken to Diana, and she's agreed to take good care of you today, since you're family."

Diana, a beautiful woman with big red hair, showed Wicca around the facility.

"We have all the scents and all the soaps you could possibly want. And showerheads that'll douche you till you're on cloud nine. The only limits here are set by your desires, not by us. You can spend as long in the baths as you like, but since you're here to try out a male, I'd suggest no more than an hour. Unless you'd like a massage, or some other kind of relief first?"

"No," said Wicca, "an hour is fine." She hadn't come to laze around in a scented bath. Although the slight delay was welcome, now that her encounter with a male was fast approaching.

"Right. First, we need to choose you a man," said Diana, once Wicca stood swaddled in cashmere, dark hair in waves down her back.

"The starter pack includes ten sessions, and I'd recommend a different choice each time you come—that way you'll get a sense of what we can offer you. Looking at the men is one thing, of course, but you also need to smell them. That's more important if you ever decide to have a child, but it's a good idea to train your nose anyway. It knows better than the eye. No matter how precisely we quantify everything, we can't pick you as good a match as your sense of smell can. It knows who complements your immune system best, so you'll have the strongest offspring. Often that turns out to be the ones who also give you the best orgasms. You'll probably gravitate toward one of the younger ones, and that's something you should play with further down the line, but I'd recommend starting with a slightly older model. One who doesn't look like he's got many goes left. For one thing, he'll be well trained, partly by the exercise riders and partly by all the women he's serviced during his lifetime, which will mean a better experience for you. Plus, there'll be no surprises, no sudden movements. It'll be a smooth and steady ride to satisfaction. It's a good way to figure out your needs and get to know your body."

Wicca chose a blond middle-aged specimen with nice eyes, moderately hairy.

"Good choice," said Diana, "he's a Chris. You can never go wrong with one of those. A reliable, all-around type."

Wicca was shown into the lovemaking area of the spa, a room scented with the same fragrance she'd chosen for her bath, pleasantly lit, and with a big soft bed in the middle, all of it in an agreeable shade of cream.

"Don't expect too much of yourself. Remember, it's your first time. You've got a hundred years or more ahead of you to be adventurous," said Diana.

The Chris was led in. He was naked, fit-looking but not obviously strong. His chest was covered in blond fuzz, with scattered patches across the rest of him. He looked at her with friendly eyes and an obliging smile. Wicca smiled nervously back. She glanced down at his member, which hung limply between his legs.

"Are you ready?" asked Diana.

Wicca nodded.

Diana signaled to one of the handlers, who took out a syringe and stuck it into his penis.

"Obviously we'd prefer things to be as natural as possible, but it's a perennial problem with virility in captivity. We're currently trialing a version of the medication used to produce the erections that's made from a hundred percent natural sugars. Soon we'll be trying the same thing with the chip in his neck, which allows us to monitor any upticks in aggression during lovemaking." Diana laughed briefly. "Look at me trying to impress you just because you're Eva's sister. Why don't I just let you get on with what you came here for."

Wicca swallowed once or twice, unable to take her eyes off the Chris's now stiff member.

"At his age that'll last fifteen minutes, so he'll need another shot if you're not finished. Enjoy him, and remember, we're keeping an eye on his movements and intentions, so nothing can happen to you. Have fun." Diana left the room.

As it turned out, she was right. A Chris was all she needed. In no more than ten minutes she had achieved her first orgasm with a man. His penis was a thrilling sensation. He was in good shape, and knew tricks with his hands that had never even crossed her young mind. Afterward, they lay beside each other. She curled up against him, and he stroked her hair. Kissed her gently on the forehead. She felt like lying there forever, safe and loved. As they gazed into each other's eyes, she was sure he felt the same way, and when they kissed her body came alive with joy. To think that life could be like this. And then, they both fell asleep.

Wicca awoke to find Diana rubbing her neck. She sat bolt upright.

"Where's my Chris?" she asked. He wasn't there.

"You liked him?" Diana smiled. "With a stamp of approval from you he'll get a nice meal tonight and a day off tomorrow. In the meantime, I think we'd better hurry up and give you something to stop the oxytocin making you too attached to lovely Chris." Diana shook her head, grinning, and took out a syringe. "Bonding hormone. Powerful stuff, especially for someone young, like you."

Wicca was giddy with delight when she left the Center that day. The flowers on the path back to the roundhouses were more fragrant than ever before, and the shades of purple where the path broke off were so sharp against the sky that she was dazzled. She felt like hugging everybody in the house and taking a bite of every dish set out on the table that night. Everything she put in her mouth tasted wonderful.

Barely a week later she was back at the Center. She chose a Chris that time too, and was not disappointed. An hour later, dizzy and ecstatic, she found herself back outside the yellow gate.

She didn't understand why anyone would choose not to do this.

The next five times, she made the same selection. When, on the sixth visit, she pointed again at one of the Chrises, Diana looked unsure.

"Don't you think you should try something different today? Best not to stick to just one type. How about a Lloyd? They're better equipped, without being vulgar, and they've got particularly sensitive hands."

The Lloyd was good too. And the two gentle AnneLouises with softer penises she tried after that. She made her way through various colors, penis sizes, and regions of the world; through bald ones, long-haired ones, angry ones, and ones with pointed tongues, rough tongues, and forked tongues; one whose voice had never broken and others that made a low grunt when they ejaculated.

Wicca visited the Center in Lolland at least once a week. It was a bright spot in her days, the thing she pictured during the hours she was training with the snake, lying sick after a bite, or reading the old texts, which were beautiful and straight from the Mother's mouth and yet so hard to focus on for stretches at a time.

All was well until her mother and grandmother got an idea that called an abrupt halt to Wicca's use of the Center men. It started when her mother decided the Easter ritual at church needed a few improvements. They no longer wanted to use a symbolic effigy but a live male, as in the early days of the Mother's church.

"Imagine what a big draw this will make the Brønshøj church," her mother said.

"Nobody's going to die, of course," she reassured Wicca when they told her about it.

"But castration might be on the table," her grandmother added.

At the original Easter ritual, a young man had been led up to the priestess, who had sex with him on the altar. Scripture suggested everything from strewing flowers beneath his feet wherever he went to cutting off his penis. One text decreed that he be put to death, but it was a papyrus scroll from one of the more rabid communities, so they didn't take what was written there too literally.

"I'm not sure if one of us should make love to him. Maybe just go through the motions on top of him, the way we do nowadays with the dummy," her grandmother said.

"First things first—we've got to get hold of a man, then we'll figure out how we want to use him afterward."

"Wicca, why don't you talk to Eva, see if we can borrow a male? You're on better terms with her these days than I am," her mother said, giving a curt laugh so as not to sound bitter. She bent her head toward the ailing snake Wicca had at the time. Wrinkling her nose, she gave it some fresh water.

Eva said no.

Waleria came over again, this time when she knew Eva would be home. "Maybe she'll say yes to me. I'm the one who rescued her, after all," she murmured to Wicca in the hall.

"We're not going to hurt him," she tried to persuade Eva. "You can have him back right after the ceremony."

Eva shook her head. "Look, this would require safety measures that simply aren't feasible in a church."

"Nonsense," Waleria said. "We're used to handling venomous snakes. How much more dangerous can one man be? You can send Center staff with him to keep him in line."

"Men are too dangerous to set loose," Eva insisted.

"We could buy him—that way he's our responsibility, not yours," Waleria said.

"He can live in the back rooms at the church, there's space behind the snakes," her grandmother suggested.

But Eva was not to be swayed. She refused to even ask the management. Testosterone in its pure form, the kind men had, was too dangerous to be allowed at large in the community. Period.

"You could put in a good word for us, it's the least you can do," Waleria said resentfully. "If it wasn't for us, you wouldn't even have that job."

"I will always be grateful that you helped me when I needed it,"

Eva replied, suppressing her irritation. "And I've never interfered with your religion, but let me remind you that when the Centers were built all those centuries ago, and the first generations of men were housed there, they put up a giant effigy of your Jesus character by the exit. Nails through his palms, blood oozing down his face, weeping eyes turned upward to the sky. They hung him up to sow fear, and as a warning to the men, so they'd never forget what the world outside did to males that broke the rules. I'm not sure the generations of males that exist today would understand the symbolism, and I don't think it's fair to take them to a church and show them something so terrifying."

Mother and Grandmother flew into a rage. They screamed and shouted in the Himlingeøje kitchen, calling Eva every name in the book, and from that day on, both of them boycotted the Centers.

"There's no way we can support something so blinkered and unspiritual," they agreed.

They insisted that Wicca and the rest of the congregation do the same—unless they were planning to conceive a child and needed a man to breed with.

Wicca had been taken hostage during the showdown, although she was mostly thinking about Kali, whom she'd met for the first time the day before, on her way out of the Center.

"I promise I'll never go there again," she said absently. All she could think about was when she'd get her next chance to see Kali, and, most importantly, when she could have sex with her. Compared to her, the males at the Center seemed abruptly not to matter.

SHE FELL HEAD OVER HEELS FOR KALI THE FIRST TIME THEY met. No, it was worse than that. This was no mindless crush, no possessing madness that exploded into stars, suns, moons, orgasms, and fickle till-death-do-us-part fantasies, only to burn out as swiftly as it had begun. It was not the kind of infatuation she'd felt before, where she'd meet some captivating woman and let herself bask in oxytocin's transient blessings.

No, from the moment she saw Kali standing there in tight black leather, one breast large and one breast bound, white hair ruffled and a dazzling smile ringed with scarlet lips, Wicca had loved her. Kali had charmed herself deep into Wicca's heart, and she never found her way back out.

They met at one of the Center's post-processing areas one Friday afternoon. Kali, who had just come from training one of the males, smelled of feces. The amazons had a separate area where they could wash and otherwise tidy themselves after work, but Kali had been on her way out of the Center when she noticed a smear of excrement on her sleeve, so she'd ducked into one of the visitors' areas closer to the exit to wash it off. Wicca, who had spent an enjoyable afternoon making love to three Carstens—specialists in vaginal ejaculation—had gone to rinse off before she went home with Eva, who was always at work. Except on Tuesdays. She would never explain what she did that day. "A woman has to be allowed her secrets, but don't worry, you know how boring my hobbies are. Embroidery, and not much else," Eva always said when Wicca got curious.

"Damn, I've got a bit on the hem as well," Kali swore, peeling off her leather dress to rinse it under the faucet. Wicca gazed spellbound at the long legs, high-waisted deep red panties, and black support garment, which was laced magnificently at the back and pulled tight across her left breast. It was the kind the amazons wore. Wicca knew they bound one breast in imitation of the female warriors of Greek mythology, who had cut one off in order to better their skills with a bow. Modern-day amazons kept their breasts, but wore clothing to make one appear large and full while the other lay as flat to the body as possible. Kali told her later that she was naturally endowed with one large and one small breast, which was why she'd been drawn to the amazons in the first place. With a chest like hers, she had to be a natural-born amazon, she'd thought.

Wicca observed her out of the corner of her eye. She'd seen amazons before, like everybody else, at the Center and on the streets. Usually in groups. Nobody could help staring after them as they strode past, graceful and authoritative, black-clad and red-lipped. Never looking to the side, never making contact with ordinary folk. They had eyes only for each other and for the road ahead. Wicca, then, was not expecting a conversation with the amazon by the sink and was caught off guard when Kali spoke.

"Hey, can you help me get some more soap out? Don't want to touch anything else, I'll just end up smearing shit over everything." Kali gave a loud, genuine laugh, and Wicca couldn't help but join in.

"You'll have to excuse the stench." She held the dress under the soap dispenser. "But I just so happen to be the Center's premiere scat-based exercise rider." She did a little curtsy, which looked so silly in conjunction with the words that Wicca laughed again.

"Wow," she replied, unable to come up with anything better.

"Not that people were exactly lining up for the job. But then again, there aren't many males to be trained, because the demand is low."

Wicca nodded. She'd never considered a Jeppe, the ones trained for scat. It wasn't that she found the thought repulsive, there was simply so much else on offer that seemed more appealing.

"My job's probably grosser than training men for bondage, vacuums, suffocation, feet, electricity, and all that other stuff. Less messy, less smelly. But on the plus side I do get off earlier," she said, scrubbing her sleeve clean. "Kali," she added, hiding her hands behind her back. "I don't imagine you want to shake." She laughed.

"Wicca," Wicca said. "And I'm not that delicate."

They left together.

"You taking the train north?" Kali asked, and Wicca said yes, even though she'd agreed to meet Eva. She left her a message so she wouldn't wait around, then hurried after Kali, who was walking down the path with an authority she seemed to take for granted. Wicca caught up with her at the yellow gate, where they were let out. Outside, a handful of bedraggled protesters were shouting slogans, something about improving the men's living conditions, giving them more activities and bigger exercise yards.

"If they knew how much I got shit on, they'd be out there demanding better conditions for me." Kali laughed, taking Wicca's arm.

They had talked all the way across Zealand. Whispering what others weren't meant to hear, laughing when one of them said something funny, and holding hands at earnest moments. The trip wasn't even an hour, but it felt like a lifetime. Wicca was flying high when she got off the train at Himlingeøje, having agreed to meet Kali the very next day. On the date they picked up where they'd left off. The conversation flowed, easy and unforced, as they went on a walk in the hills. By the time they reached the foot of the third, Wicca took Kali's hand. From that moment on, it was the two of them. They belonged together like no one else they knew.

Wicca's mother was definitely not pleased.

"Is she a believer?"

Wicca couldn't say that she was. Kali believed in her own abilities, and she believed that life wanted what was best for her. Wicca had never been more at ease than in her company, not even at the moments when she was sure she was in genuine contact with the Mother.

They could talk about anything. Even when they disagreed, they never fought. Kali was a vaginist, of course, a position Wicca's own experience had led her to share. But she also believed that in many respects the penisists had it right. The ones who were convinced a serviceable orgasm required a penis.

"You're just afraid you'll be out of a job," Wicca teased. But Kali was unshakeable.

"Nature created the penis to be the perfect implement for a woman's genitals. It flexes without being too hard or soft when you encase it and push down. At the moment it ejaculates, it spurts pure energy into the woman, energy she can absorb. You can't do that with fingers or a silicone copy. You need a real penis to get those benefits."

"Maybe," Wicca said, and kissed her. She thought the argument was too radical, but didn't want to spoil the mood between them.

The leaves on Wicca's houseplants were glossy, and the color of the flowers intensified each time they bloomed. And although her snakes continued to sicken, they didn't seem to be dying as quickly as before.

At first, she didn't care that she couldn't visit the Center anymore. She had Kali, that was plenty, and it never occurred to her to be with a male. But within a year her body began to cry out for a man, and she saw no choice but to seek one out. She didn't dare defy her mother and grandmother by going to the Center, so she suggested to Kali that they visit the Street. Wicca had never used it before, although she'd been there as a kid, giggling with her friends on nightwalks into the slum. It was the closest you could get to male proximity without taking the final exam in Body.

Kali had tagged along without enthusiasm. She'd spent all day in Lolland, training up a new young Jeppe. He was unusually virile but also struggled to control the sphincter muscles in his anus, so they had to pause several times to temper his exuberance with injections. She was exhausted.

"It's not a man I need, or a manlady, for that matter," she said, but came along anyway, for Wicca's sake. "To look, then you can have a few goes."

Lars was out on his terrace, nursing a baby as they walked down the Street.

"Hey, you're one of those amazon warriors," he said, looking Kali up and down.

"Yes, I am," said Kali proudly.

"We never see your kind here on the Street, and we see pretty much everything else."

"We get enough of men during the day, I guess." Kali laughed.

"So what are you doing here, then?" Lars put the child to the other breast.

"My partner has a need that's got to be met. I'm just along for entertainment purposes."

"All right, well, then sit down and entertain me. I've got two more little ones to feed when they wake up."

That was the start of Kali's friendship with Lars. While Wicca trawled the houses end to end, trying to pick the manlady she liked best, Kali was with Lars. Sometimes she had to wait on the terrace, if he had a client. But it rarely took more than twenty minutes, and definitely not more than forty-five.

"I'm good at my job," said Lars. "No reason to spend an hour on something that can be wrapped up in half. Most women orgasm in less than four minutes, if you know what you're doing."

Wicca visited many different manladies on the Street, but unlike Kali she never befriended any of them. Probably none of them had given her a second thought when she stopped coming, after Kali walked out.

In her darkest hours she'd imagined Lars and Kali were together. That it had always been him she loved, not Wicca. But Kali had never shown that type of interest in Lars.

The convent was the nearest she'd come to the Street since Kali's disappearance seven years earlier. It was only around the corner. She'd taken pains to choose a route she and Kali never would have gone—the mere thought of coming face-to-face with her again made her want to cry. It was impossible to picture herself getting through an encounter like that without breaking down and begging Kali to love her like before, and she could do without that humiliation.

HER MOTHER WAS STANDING WITH HER BACK TURNED, draping the curtain in front of her snake, when Wicca brought her box into the church. They still had a few minutes before the congregation came flocking in. Wicca felt butterflies in her stomach at the thought of how her mother would react when she saw the white cobra.

"Aha, so you're here after all?" her mother said without turning around. "I thought you were using another substitute today."

Wicca swallowed her irritation.

"Why would I do that?" she said, unfolding the legs of the box that contained the white cobra as she felt anticipation build. She moved it closer to the altar and chinked the curtain aside so her mother would catch sight of the snake.

"And how is your cobra?" her mother said. She didn't take her eyes off her own snake's cage. The curtain hung in perfect pleats, like always, although that didn't stop her from adjusting the folds.

"Fine," said Wicca with a sigh. "I've got a new one."

"You always do," her mother said, spraying dashes of gold onto her cheeks. "You look different." She scrutinized Wicca. "You're not angry, like you normally are."

Wicca nudged a wider gap into the silk curtain, although the snakes were supposed to be kept hidden until the ceremony began. Usually she was trying to hide her drooping snake. Now she wanted her mother and everybody else to see it.

"Did you meet someone? Oh, here comes Grandma."

Wicca's great-grandmother had, as ever, arrived at the last minute. She hadn't menstruated in decades, and that conferred more than a few privileges. As the oldest serving priestess, her snake was the most important. It lived at the church, where they employed an attendant solely to care for its needs—and to be present if it received wisdom from the Mother that it wished to share outside the services. It was the oldest snake they had, and thus the one that spoke most clearly. If the cobras delivered conflicting messages, it was her great-grandmother's they listened to.

The congregation reached out their hands to touch her great-grandmother, to share in her strength and status. She seemed to float up the aisle with not a glance to either side, allowing her fingertips to graze the outstretched hands. Reaching the altar, she nodded briefly to her grandchild and great-grandchild, and although Wicca had now flouted the rules by pulling the curtain so far back that the white snake was in clear view, neither her mother nor her great-grandmother had noticed. The verger slunk past with a dish that overflowed with slices of apple. There were no apples left in the orchard outside the church in Brønshøj, so at this time of year they had to import them from warmer places.

The chatter in the pews swelled as the dishes of fruit were passed around. The people were quick to laughter and full of cheerful anticipation, knowing they would soon come in contact with the Mother. Many of them hugged and nestled against the women next to them, caressing each other's hair and faces. Some held hands, whispering sweet things into the ears of those who sat closest.

"Have you found yourself a girlfriend?" her mother asked. Wicca drew the curtain even farther back.

"Hello, Great-grandmother," she said, watching her expectantly, but her eyes were already closed, and her breaths echoed the movements of the snake.

As the bells chimed, the three priestesses drew back the

curtains, then opened the doors to let out their snakes. Every woman in the congregation placed her right arm around her waist and the left crosswise over her chest, hand on shoulder, as they had prayed to the Mother from the very first day.

Out of the corner of her eye, Wicca watched to see if her great-grandmother or mother would notice her cobra, but they didn't open their eyes so much as a crack. Nor did she hear the gasp she'd imagined would run through the assembly when she took it out. Peeved, she draped the cobra around her neck. She turned in sync with her mother and great-grandmother, and all three raised an arm, took hold of the snake's head, put its jaws to their throats above the ruff, and waited for it to bite down. Then the whole church burst into song.

The bite was so painful that Wicca couldn't suppress a grimace. The congregation swayed back and forth with her mother and great-grandmother, but Wicca had to stand still. She was overwhelmingly dizzy. After years spent pretending that her snakes' weak bites had an effect, she was totally unprepared for the nausea that rolled up from the fathoms of her belly. Breakfast and coffee gushed out of her mouth in a warm brown swell. She tried to put her hand up, tried to stop what was coming, but all she could do was throw her head back as she felt the next surge sweep up her esophagus, out of her mouth, and down her chin.

But then, the miracle. A tender sensation, spreading like an orgasm. It began in her feet and rippled up through her knees, thighs, and on into her groin, oh, the groin, then out and through the opening and back, up into her breasts, out of the nipples and her shoulders and through each sense: nose, ears, eyes, mouth. She could taste the Mother's love. She splayed her fingers, wanting to share the sensation and its luminous energy with the congregation, and her mind opened upward to the Mother. The snake glided down her right arm and vanished into the Mother's mouth, came out through one eye and crawled into the other. Her whole body was shivering with love. Joy fizzed in every cell. The euphoria of her night with Medea rushed through her, and she laughed out loud. The song of the assembly swirled up to the church roof and slipped out through the cracks. As she shut her eyes she saw the Mother smile, open her arms, and cradle her in an embrace. Colors broke through her eyelids, purple, yellow, red, arranging themselves like the lines of a poem, one after another. Life was verse to be sung. Her genitals quivered, and the Mother bade her sit astride the altar's edge, rocking gently back and forth, almost to climax, until she was interrupted when Waleria came and stood before her.

She could see her mother's mouth open, she could hear that words were coming out, but the noises made no sense until they shaped themselves into a wondrous song. Her great-grandmother stood behind her flapping her arms, but Wicca laughed aloud, because her eyes were moving around on her face. She set off at a run, jumped, and then she flew: over the pews and congregation, up to Jesus by the altar, above the statue of Agatha, the martyr whose breasts had been cut off because she loved only the Mother and refused to believe in the Father.

Agatha, whose face had always been a picture of suffering in her martyrdom, relaxed her stony expression into a broad grin and took Wicca's hands. Together they danced around Jesus, faster and faster, as Wicca's clothing crumbled in the air. She laughed until there was no more breath left in her. She tripped over something near the altar, but was caught by the snake, which led her on a creeping path beneath the church pews, up the walls, and in through Jesus's left ear. They came out through his penis, which had always been hidden under a loincloth, but now hung free and fleshy to his knees. Wicca recognized desire between her legs. How typical of Jesus to have a big penis. She leapt off the snake and crawled back to him on all fours. She'd not been near a real penis since making Wendy at the Center. She reached out for it eagerly, but just as she took hold, she was tugged hard in the other direction. A sharp pain jolted through her rib, radiating down into her thighs and feet. Someone was hammering nails through them. Were they about to hang her next to Jesus? She shrieked in terror. Then both her body and her mind shut down.

When she came to she was lying on a cot in the back room of the church. She was naked, covered with a blanket, and so nauseous she didn't know how it could be borne. She tried to get up, but found that she was tied down, a cord around her chest and legs.

Someone was speaking, moving things around inside the church. She writhed her arms free and untied her legs. Still dazed, she stood up and wrapped herself in the blanket. Approaching footsteps. Should she hide? The nausea made her stomach cramp, and she doubled over in pain. What had happened to her rib? Supporting herself on the table by the bed, she moaned faintly.

"She's gotten loose," the verger cried. Wicca recognized her mother's tread across the room. She stepped right up to her daughter and laid a hand on her shoulder, gazing at her watchfully. Wicca stared dully back.

"Can you hear me?" her mother asked loudly, a deep furrow between her brows.

"Of course I can hear you," Wicca said, in a voice more gravelly than she'd expected. She cleared her throat. The verger gave her a glass of water.

Her mother put her face very close to hers and studied it.

"Stop it." Wicca pushed her irritably away, but her hand struck only air, and she toppled backward onto the mattress.

"You spoke to the Devil instead of the Mother," Waleria said.

"I've heard of it happening, but I've never seen it before. Do you remember anything at all?"

Wicca shook her head and gazed in bewilderment at the frightened-looking verger, who stood in the doorway.

"Come and see," her mother said, helping her to stand. Wicca tottered into the main hall of the church.

"What happened?" she asked incredulously. The altar was coated entirely in white dust. Her charcoal-gray robes hung over one of the pews, torn to shreds. The snake-green stole of which she was so proud was ripped clear across the yellow *W*.

Several of the colored panes in the oval windows had been shattered, and the plinth where Agatha used to stand was empty. Scanning the church, Wicca caught sight of Agatha's head on one of the pews. The rest of her statue had been swept into a pile on the floor. Jesus appeared to be untouched, except for some scratch marks on his crotch. In the corner lay the white cobra, in two parts. Dead.

"You went crazy," her mother said. "Smashed up the whole church. And who's Medea? You kept screaming for her."

"You bought a cobra from a witch in the slum?" Her mother was furious. Shouting. "Have you completely lost your mind? Goodness knows you've given me enough to worry about, but I never thought you'd be this stupid. You're supposed to be a responsible priest of W lineage. Well, neither the church nor the congregation will want you back after this, you can be sure of that."

Wicca took her mother's dressing-down with her head bowed. Every word worsened the feeling that she wasn't good enough. The fact that she'd thought her mother would be impressed only made it sting more. At long last, her great-grandmother came up and laid a conciliatory hand on Wicca's arm.

"I think she understands it was a stupid thing to do," she said. Her mother had to go and sit on one of the pews, red-faced with rage.

"Where is everybody?" Wicca put on the clothes her great-grandmother gave her, still woozy from the snakebite.

"The congregation fled in terror when we couldn't stop you."

"Do you really think I'll never be a priest again?"

"We'll have to see about that," her great-grandmother said. "It would be best if you didn't come here for a while. Probably a good idea to take a break from your mother too."

Wicca felt dizzy, but was beginning to think clearly enough to understand that the snake Medea had sold her was a conduit to the Devil. That cursed little witch. It was probably no coincidence that she had a bust of the Devil sitting in the convent stairwell. Wicca felt a brewing rage.

"Go home and get some rest," her great-grandmother said. Wicca nodded, knowing that as sick as she felt, she wasn't going home. She was going to Medea's, to give her a piece of her mind. And, for the sake of the Mother, to kill every diabolical serpent Medea was rearing in that basement.

"I'm going to make this right," she told her mother as she passed her in the church. Waleria held up a dismissive hand and looked the other way. Wicca strode doggedly out of the church and along the path through the orchard. Her vision was blurred with tears of shame, so she didn't see the white-clad pensive who was raking fallen leaves. She smacked straight into her, and they both grabbed each other to stay upright.

"Sorry," Wicca said, before she instinctively took a step back, uneasy at having touched a pensive.

The pensive lowered her eyes and clasped her hands before her, the way they were supposed to when encountering regular people. Wicca was about to walk on when she realized who she was looking at.

"Lars?" she said, in shock.

Lars didn't reply. As a pensive, he wasn't allowed to.

"Don't you recognize me? It's Wicca, Kali's girlfriend?"

Lars was still looking down at the ground.

"Ex-girlfriend," she corrected.

There was nothing out of the ordinary about one of the man-ladies being thought-quarantined. The Street was already on the fringes of acceptability, and it never took much for someone to decide its residents ought to be given an opportunity to find themselves. The length of a person's sentence varied, but all pensives had to meditate at least five times a day, were not allowed to speak to other people, and had to spend their term tending to green plants. Many districts therefore gathered the pensives into greenhouses, where they lived until their souls were judged peaceful enough to rejoin the community.

This was the third time Lars had been pronounced pensive. In the past he'd gone straight back to the Street and picked up where he'd left off.

Wicca generally shunned the pensives when she bumped into them. There was a reason, after all, why they had to live withdrawn from everybody else. They weren't the sort she wanted to associate with. Even if, as a Christian, she was supposed to do the opposite, to help those in need.

Lars stared blankly at his rake. Picking up the bag of brown leaves, he clearly wanted to move on.

"Have you been tidying up the church orchard?" Wicca asked, trying to stall him. Lars darted a swift glance at her before looking away, but it was long enough that Wicca could tell he recognized her.

"Do you still live on the Street?"

Lars bit his lip. He was clearly uncomfortable with the situation, which was hardly surprising. If he got caught doing anything he wasn't supposed to, he could have his term extended.

"Kali and I broke up . . ." Wicca began. "I haven't seen her in ages."

Lars picked up the bag, then edged past Wicca and walked off along the path.

"I was wondering if she ever drops by the Street?"

Lars disappeared around the corner, without turning back. Wicca closed her eyes for a moment. *Don't think about Kali, don't think about Kali, don't think about Kali*, she recited, as nausea clutched her stomach and sent up a shot of bile, which she hacked up underneath a leafless apple tree.

WICCA HAD NEVER GIVEN MUCH THOUGHT TO HAVING A child. The women in her family generally had one each, when they turned twenty-five. It was what the church mother Walborg had done; now it was expected of everybody in the W line. It was a sacred custom, and breaking it was looked on with disfavor; you had to have at least one child. Those who enjoyed pregnancy and birth had more. A priest at one of the other churches had ten. With so many children sharing your blood, you were also unlikely to be asked to carry the pregnancy to term, if you were unlucky enough to be expecting a male.

Wicca's mother, grandmother, and great-grandmother had all become mothers at the age of twenty-five. Wicca reached twenty-six and then twenty-seven without observing the tradition. Her grandmother and great-grandmother had prayed for her. It was the first time Wicca hadn't done what her mother and the church expected of her, but she knew she was on borrowed time. At some point she would have to carry on the bloodline.

So when Kali started talking about wanting a child, she didn't dismiss it out of hand, although there was no urge inside her to procreate.

She and Kali knew every inch of each other's bodies. They could spend whole days exploring. Taking each other hard, stroking gently, kissing, licking, sucking. They bit and tore. Wicca would never get enough of Kali, she knew that. And she needed nothing more. At long last she was happy, with a person so extraordinary that she knew she'd never be able to love anybody else as much. Why spoil it all with a baby?

They'd begun discussing it one night after Wicca's mother had dropped by. She had left without saying goodbye, to make sure Wicca understood her relationship with Kali was unsuitable.

"You know, I think she might actually accept my relationship with a non-believing amazon, just about, if I gave the bloodline a child," Wicca had remarked, shaking her head.

"Why don't we?" Kali had surprised her by saying. "I've wanted a child for a long time."

"You have?"

"Yes. A little girl who steals my leather clothes and paints her face with my lipstick—can't you just see it?"

"She'll be gorgeous because she's made from you," Wicca said, pulling Kali close.

They hadn't spoken any more about it that day, but a few weeks later, Kali brought it up again.

"We could have one each, at the same time. I could move in here, if the others don't mind. We could be an old-fashioned family."

"What about the amazons?" Wicca asked.

"I'll go back afterward, when I feel ready."

Wicca had been taken with the idea. Of being bonded yet more intimately with Kali, perhaps, more than with the child itself. It showed how much she loved her. If it would guarantee the permanence of Kali's love, she was even willing to grow a child inside her. She bought Kali a big green emerald ring, the color of her eyes, and one evening she got down on one knee and sang to her. Kali laughed.

"You're such a romantic." She put on the ring and gazed at it. Brushed away a tear. "You've almost made one out of me as well."

That night they made love fiercely, and long.

Straightaway they began to synchronize their cycles. Kali was so engrossed in the project that she found it hard to concentrate on work.

"Me! I've always loved males, and now I'm tired just thinking about what I've got to make them do. All I want is to tap them of semen and bring it home to us."

They'd decided to apply to use the same male. It wasn't a done deal, by any means—it depended on the composition of their genetic material. Eva said she'd put in a good word for them.

"But I can't make any promises. It's all down to the graphs and statistics. They've tightened up the rules in the last year or two, since there was that outbreak of hip dysplasia among the males. It's more important than ever to optimize the right genetic material so that we don't end up replicating all the defects people had under the patriarchy. You can't imagine the sorts of hereditary diseases that afflicted people before the Evolution—there was one they called cancer, and a whole host of other maladies. You only lived to be ninety years old, half as long as we live today—and that's if you were lucky," Eva told them. "Anyway, with a bit of good fortune, you won't be required to birth a male. That's only a tiny fraction of cases."

"We could go abroad, somewhere they're happier to bend the rules, and choose the same male, or be artificially inseminated?" Kali suggested. But Eva was against it.

"I wouldn't advise that. The body knows best, and while there's a lot we can do as doctors, nature is wiser. It always creates the strongest version of a human."

They began with a stroke of luck, when they were granted permission to use the same male. Wicca went down to the Center the day after Kali had been impregnated by the one they'd both thought smelled good. He was a Pär. Scandinavian in appearance, with large hands and a dazzling smile. Moreover, it was his debut as a breeding male, which Eva said they should view as a big plus. Wicca was happy to be back and hoped it would take several tries before it worked. But no—sadly they both got pregnant on their first attempt, although they could hardly believe it. Sometimes this type of thing took years.

They toasted to their new life together and to the children germinating in their respective wombs.

"I can stay in your room, no problem," Kali said, "at least for the first couple of years. I own nothing but my clothes, a few pairs of shoes, and my makeup."

"Or we could find a roundhouse with a few spare rooms that's willing to take us both, and the kids?" Wicca said, worried it might be too crowded.

"The two of us can do anything, as long as we're together," Kali said. "I could live in the tiniest room in the world, as long as you're there too."

Wicca thought back to that moment often, so often that she wasn't sure now whether Kali had actually said it. Or if she'd wanted it so badly that her memory had tricked her into believing it.

One month after they'd toasted their new life, their luck ran out. At eight weeks it was possible to tell whether the fetus had malformed into a male, and Kali, it turned out, was expecting a boy. The test also showed that because of her genetic makeup, she would be required to contribute to the 11 percent of males who were kept available so that the human race could reproduce without inbreeding. If she wanted a child, she would have to deliver a boy to society first.

They cried all day when they got the news. Kali threw up several times, leaving Wicca alone and stricken in their room, ridden with guilt because the creeping thing that now dwelled inside her would turn into a baby, while Kali, who was really the one who'd wanted to carry a child, couldn't have one until she'd delivered a boy.

After a night of tears, they agreed it was a setback, but not a disaster. Kali would just have to skip a turn. They'd known the rules, like everybody else. Women who wanted to be pregnant might be required to give birth to a boy. Of course, the runts were winnowed out early on, and if you were from a branch that birthed lots of children, like the W line, then it was unlikely you'd be asked to carry a male pregnancy to term. Kali, however, was the only child of an elderly biological mother who also had no siblings, a woman who had left immediately after the birth and had no more children. Kali would help diversify the gene pool.

"We'll bring up my child as though she were yours as well. We can say she's yours?" Wicca consoled her.

"Maybe it's a good thing we're only having one infant at a time," Kali replied, putting on a brave face.

All was well for several months. They gratefully accepted all the coaching they could get, trying to help Kali through the process. A small number of women carrying males developed a false maternal attachment, believing that they loved the male in their belly and wanted to keep him. A kind of madness that possessed the pregnant mind. Kali could only shake her head at the thought.

"I feel nothing but disgust for what's inside me, and I can't wait to get it out so I can have a baby," she said, both to Wicca and their coach.

Women unfortunate enough to be required to birth a male for the sake of social preservation were amply compensated. Cash, but also massages, baths, and other forms of pampering. But Kali wasn't interested in any of that. She threw up multiple times a day and couldn't bear to be touched, not even by Wicca. She had to take an indefinite leave from her job as an exercise rider at the Center, and instead spent her time reading up on pregnancy and childbirth.

"So I'll be ready for the day when my turn comes," she said. She sat up, stifling a burp as she tried not to vomit.

"I can't imagine going through this nightmare a second time to have a child," Kali said, starting to cry. "Maybe I should give up on having my own and settle for yours."

"Not mine," Wicca said, putting her arm around her. "Ours!"

Kali's belly grew faster than Wicca's, or maybe it was because Wicca was already round, so it didn't show on her the way it did on Kali's angled body. The tight leather dresses were uncomfortable enough as it was, so she'd been to the amazon tailor to get a few made with room for her growing middle. She had no intention, at least, of abandoning the style just because she was donating a male.

Kali had lost interest in sex the minute she fell pregnant, and even when the nausea subsided, the desire did not return. Wicca, on the other hand, needed it more than she ever had. She frequented the Street at least once a week, and sometimes three or four times. Kali always came with her, making arrangements with Lars in advance so she could sit with him while she waited.

"I'm like a new person after I've spoken to Lars. He clears my mind," she said.

"All you do is talk?" asked Wicca, jealous.

Kali laughed. "If I wanted to express myself physically, you'd be the first person I'd turn to, you know that," she said, and Wicca felt reassured. But she was still jealous. Jealous because Kali didn't feel her mind was cleared talking to Wicca, only to Lars. She tried to make excuses for herself, saying it was the hormones, but that didn't help.

"What do you talk about?" she asked again and again, doing her best not to sound suspicious.

"Oh, everything under the sun. Today we talked about what it's like for Lars, living as a man."

"But he isn't a man."

"No, you're right," Kali said amiably. "Could you help me out of my dress? My bound breast has grown, and trying to squash it down only makes it unbearably painful as the day goes on."

They were both nine months pregnant, and the births were only days away. Wicca had slept the sleep of the dead that night and hadn't heard Kali get out of bed. She wondered where she was when she woke up, but assumed she must be in the shower or making breakfast. She lay there hoping Kali was making pancakes. Whereas Kali had become increasingly gaunt as the pregnancy wore on, never quite getting over the nausea, Wicca pounced on everything, practically foaming at the mouth. It was as though her taste buds, senses, and general appetite for life had been multiplied a hundredfold. If it hadn't been for the child at the end of it, she'd happily keep getting pregnant forever.

The letter—or rather, the hastily scribbled note—lay on the bedside table. She found it only after she'd been all around the house, searching for Kali.

> Sorry, but I can't do this after all. I hope with all my heart that you and your child have the happiest possible life. You deserve it.
>
> I will always love you both.
>
> Kali

Wicca stared for a long time at the scrap of paper. Shock spread slowly, from the inside out. She raced into the kitchen, where Eva was embroidering.

"Have you seen Kali?"

"You look terrible," Eva said, putting down the needle.

Wicca handed her the letter in silence.

Eva clapped a hand to her mouth. "She must have lost her mind. Do you know where she could have gone?"

Wicca was breathing heavily, clutching her stomach. "I think I'm going into labor." She sat down on a chair, snarling into the pain of the first contraction. "Where is Kali?" she screamed.

More than two weeks went by before she had the strength to leave the house in Himlingeøje. She left baby Wendy with Eva, who had mostly been the one taking care of her anyway.

Wicca's lower abdomen was still heavy by the time she eventually reached the Street. From a distance she spotted Lars outside his house, nursing a red-haired baby. It drank greedily from his breasts. Kali was nowhere to be seen. For a moment she was gripped by the thought that this was Kali's baby he was feeding, but then she realized it was much too big. She felt like running up to Lars and pleading with him to tell her where Kali was, but couldn't bring herself to do it. If Kali didn't want to be found, Lars wasn't likely to tell her. She turned around in tears and went home to the child she hoped she would come to love.

WICCA SWALLOWED ONCE OR TWICE TO FORCE DOWN THE nausea from the memory of the church service. She tried to focus on how Medea had tricked her, had sold her a snake that was the Devil's spawn. Wrath lent her new energy.

How naive she'd been, how blinded by the orgasms. Medea might even have bewitched her. Placed amulets, skeletal remains, herbs, and other hexcraft inside the roundhouse. She had given her a stone, but Wicca, foolish as she was, had merely thought it sweet.

"To help you feel more rejuvenated in the morning," Medea had said, spit-polishing it so that it shone brilliantly. Fucking witch scum. Then there were the sprigs of herb she'd said would help with Wendy's nightmares. She might even have done Wendy permanent damage? Her mother was right. She'd been unbelievably stupid.

Wicca dropped into her seat on the train and felt her stomach churn. Her esophagus burned, like the tears behind her eyes. Not only had Medea duped her, but she'd been humiliated in front of the entire congregation. Assuming she had any congregation left.

Tears ran down her cheeks, and a couple of the older passengers eyed her approvingly. They were from a generation where tears brought status.

Wicca turned away from them.

To think that Medea had chosen her to be the victim of her perversities simply because she was easy prey, the weakest animal, the one the wolf picks for the hunt. That evil little bitch. Wicca's vision went black, and she had to lean back in her seat and take a few deep breaths. The one good thing about possibly being excommunicated by the parish was that she'd never have to endure another snakebite.

The road through the slum was unpleasant as always. It took Wicca an hour to reach Medea's house. There were lights on in all the windows of the convent, which surprised her, because Medea had mentioned several times that they had limited supplies of energy for heat and power. The bird with the ribbon around its neck was screeching on the other side of the windowpane. Wicca had a shock when she made eye contact with it, and it opened the hasps on the window and flew out. It began to circle above her, crying. That's how it sounded. Like a shrill keen, two long howls and a gasp.

"Get away from me, you devil," Wicca screamed at the bird, which dove into an attack. She flailed at it, but missed.

Once she killed the snakes, she'd kill that fucking bird as well.

Shielding her face with her arms, she sprinted up to the front door, which to her astonishment was locked. The bird plunged closer, catching her with one wing. She screamed and pounded on the door.

"Medea," she shouted, "let me in."

Wicca kept hammering as the bird cried loudly into her face. By the time Medea finally opened the door she was terrified, and tumbled inside.

Medea looked at her, eyes wild. She had lacerations on her cheeks and an open cut on her forehead. Her long hair was streaked with mud.

"Have you seen a child?" she whispered hoarsely.

SILENCE

SILENCE PUT A HAND TO HER THROAT. IT STILL FELT strange. She'd let out a raucous wail when she'd found Eldest dead on the floor. Frightened herself with the sound. Then she'd tried to call for the boy, but her voice would do nothing but croak, and the words were unfamiliar shapes in her mouth. They were the first she'd tried to say in more than thirty years. Since she was fourteen.

In the beginning, for some time after she'd gone mute, she occasionally found herself humming to a plant, but only when she was alone. Until even that became more pleasurable than she felt she deserved. Instead she started whispering the tunes. It came out in a gruff rasp, nothing really that would do the plants much good. So she stopped.

Madam was flapping overhead. Silence, sitting underneath the birdcages in the front room, got up and did a few jumping jacks on the spot, hoping to scare the miserable thing away. It was always trying to eat the berries on her berry bushes and nipping at the flower buds, which she coaxed into sprouting even under the wretchedest conditions. She was so used to playing the scarecrow when Madam and the crows were nearby that she forgot there weren't actually any plants in the room. Although not a day went by when she didn't wish the crows were somewhere far away, she still felt guilty occasionally about eating so many of them before Eldest took her in. Eldest loved those birds.

The living room was the birds', so Silence hardly ever went in. But she did now. That awful W priest who'd gotten her claws into Medea six months ago, the one she knew Medea had visited several times, was yelling in the kitchen. It was bad enough that

Eldest was dead and the boy was gone—Silence couldn't cope with being bawled at by a Christian too. From the moment she'd caught sight of the W on the priest's stole last summer, she knew she was bad news. The W clan was best avoided.

"That bird is cuckoo," Wicca was shouting in the kitchen. "You should have it put down before it pecks someone's eyes out."

"Cuckoo," Madam repeated, now rocking furiously in its cage.

"What are you doing here?" Medea's voice cracked halfway through. "Did you see anybody in velour out on the road? Somebody with a child?"

Silence could hear Medea running from window to window, hoping the boy would miraculously reappear. It was cold outside. And he had already vanished by the time she'd returned from the slum that morning. She had no idea if he'd only just gone missing, or if he'd been out so long he must have frozen to death by now. They'd searched the house from top to bottom, searched the garden, the nearby ruins, the Street, and Medea had even gone to check the caves in the tower at the old town hall, where it was said that many people hid to evade thought-quarantine.

Silence would stay in the front room until the W priest left, then she'd keep looking. She picked up Eldest's floor cushion to see if her pruning shears had ended up underneath it. They'd been missing for two weeks. She was sure she'd been carrying them on her, because she always did; then abruptly they were gone. They were long and sharp and perfect for cutting precisely where a leaf needed to be removed in order to encourage the rest of the plant to grow. She had been given them by her mothers as a child. The shears were the only thing she took with her when she ran away from Aarhus.

She rested her forehead against her knees. Tried to puzzle out where the boy might be hiding.

The dogs were barking, perplexed by all the agitation in the convent.

"This place is a madhouse," Wicca shouted. "Get those dogs away from me."

Silence heard Medea shoo the dogs away and couldn't help but smile. The dogs never did as Medea told them, although she tried patiently day after day. It was always funny watching her try to drag them off, because the hulking dogs looked so much bigger than Medea.

The little female dog came slinking into the front room, tail wagging, and sat down next to her. She put a reassuring hand on its head.

"And you sold me a snake that's in league with the Devil! You've ruined everything for me!" Wicca screamed.

Medea's restless pacing ceased.

"The Devil?" she said. "I have nothing to do with the Devil. He's a Christian invention, the poor thing—you'll have to take responsibility for him yourself."

"You've got a bust of him by the stairs. I should have known the first time I was here. You *are* a witch."

Those last words were spat out in contempt. Silence knew exactly what Wicca's face looked like right now. Mouth twisted, eyes full of malevolence. The way you'd picture the Devil. Wera had been the same, that afternoon at the church in Aarhus. There was no doubting they were of the same bloodline.

"That's not the Devil," Medea defended herself. "That's the horned god Pan. He never harmed a fly. You need to leave. Eldest is dead, and I have to feed the dogs." Medea's voice shook. "Did you bring the white cobra? I promise you'll have it back as soon as possible." There were tears in her voice. It irritated Silence. Medea was much too sensitive, and therefore too naive. Typical of her to get herself snarled up in the W clan's web. Silence had been seduced by them too, but in her defense, she'd been only twelve years old. Medea was in her fifties. She ought to know better.

"Where are you going?" Medea cried. Silence heard a commotion, and her curiosity got the better of her: she crept out and peered into the kitchen.

"Your devil snakes have got to die," Wicca screamed, trying to fight her way into the basement. "In the name of the Mother, the Son, and the Holy Ghost."

The male dog growled, Madam screeched, and Medea seemed suddenly possessed. Despite her puny size, she dragged Wicca out into the hall, flung the door open, and threw her out.

Silence was impressed.

Wicca howled outside the house. "Your filthy white cobra is dead, just so you know. I killed one of your devil serpents, at least."

Silence couldn't tell if she was laughing or sobbing outside. Only that she must be leaving, because the sound was fading.

"She killed it." Medea was pale. "How am I going to make more youngstock now?" She clutched her head. "How am I going to save Pythia?" She moved toward the basement stairs, but stopped short. Went back to the front door, then turned and stood in the middle of the kitchen. "The boy," she said. "I've got to find the boy. I've got to tap the boy! He's my only hope." Medea rushed to the cupboard, took out a pot, filled it with water, and put it on to boil. Then she headed down to the basement. Madam flew out of her cage and over Silence, who thrashed her arms reflexively above her head. It opened the window, then fluttered out and up the street. Before long, they could hear Wicca shrieking again. Madam, at least, was not beguiled by the W clan's treacherous charms, Silence thought with satisfaction. Then the pain of Eldest's death and the missing boy set in again.

They'd picked up Eldest's lifeless body and carried her to the bed. Medea had murmured something to protect her soul and body until they could lay her in the earth. Then they'd left the dead woman and hurried out to search for the boy. In vain.

Medea came up from the basement wearing the gold cloak and carrying a snake in her hand.

"It's the wrong one," she muttered, "but what else am I supposed to do . . ."

An odd smell soon began to emerge from the kitchen. Medea was on her stool, vigorously stirring the pot, speaking invocations and making gestures Silence had not seen before. She went up to the stove. In the pot there was a snake, floating around with herbs and other greenery. She looked quizzically at Medea.

"Look, we can't find him." Medea was crying. "If he's outdoors, then it won't be long before he dies of cold. I need him for Pythia. If someone finds him, they'll take him. And if they find out we've been hiding him, they'll make us pensive for the rest of our lives!" Medea looked at her in fear. Silence shrugged. Punishment wasn't what troubled her. What troubled her was that she couldn't live with another boy's life on her conscience.

"It's supposed to be an adder, really. Boiled adder water would give me the sight, and I'd be able to see where he is. But I don't have any adders, Pythia ate the last one the other week." Tears of frustration dripped down Medea's cheeks. "Dammit." She sniffled. "I'm trying a grass snake instead, but I don't know if it'll have the same effect, or any effect at all."

Silence went into the garden. She didn't much care for Medea's snakes and had only been into the basement once. That was enough. Then, of course, she'd helped carry the boy's mother down to Pythia. The sight of it hadn't made her any less uncomfortable sharing a house with so many snakes. She could live with the brown rat snakes prowling around the corners, but had been careful to seal her own room so they couldn't get in.

She looked behind the winter-bare berry bushes. Maybe the boy had gone outside, then come back and didn't know how to get in. He had never been outside before. She sat down in the middle of the garden and listened. All she could hear was

Madam, jabbering somewhere up by the Street. She hoped it was still tormenting Wicca. Silence shuddered. With a sigh she went indoors, the tears stuck in her throat. She wouldn't mind being pensive for the rest of her life, so long as someone found him safe in the cold.

In the kitchen, Medea blew on the snake soup and lapped up a spoonful. She winced as she burned her tongue. Then she put down the bowl, held out two branches, and began the recitations.

"Mother of the winds, let these rowan twigs point me in the direction of the boy." Medea repeated the words three times. Silence sat expectantly on the corner stool, ruffling the female dog's fur. It was the only one of the dogs she could stand. The male's pelt was too oily, and it drooled too much. But the little female was gentle; it understood what she wanted, even though she never spoke to it.

Medea looked at the two branches, which hung listless on either side. Evidently they had no intention of revealing the boy's whereabouts.

"Oh, a grass snake doesn't work, it's *got* to be an adder," Medea wailed, but nonetheless she gulped down more of the soup and tried the incantation one more time.

Silence went back into the garden. She could sense there was something happening. Unlike all the other sisters at the convent, she had no supernatural abilities, nor wished for them. But when you don't speak, you learn to listen to the world. In the cold garden there was a faint whistle in the trees, but above the wind, several houses down, she could hear Madam imitating tears. The sound was coming nearer, carried with the beat of its wings. Madam circled overhead. Beak wide, it let out two long howls and a gasp. Just as the boy had done when he was small, if he was hungry, and now, as an older child, when he was very sad. Silence went back into the kitchen and quickly grabbed her poncho, trying to make eye contact with Medea, who was now drinking the soup directly from the pot. Most of it spilled down her front and puddled on the floor, where the male dog guzzled it up. Silence gave up trying to bring her along and hurried out onto the road. Madam sat swaying in a chestnut tree. It flew in the direction of the Street, as Silence chased after it. The little female dog caught up with her halfway. Together they continued up the road until they reached the Street, where Madam abruptly disappeared from sight. Silence could hear it crying, but the bird wasn't in the first alleyway she went down. She glanced inquiringly at the female, which trotted back out and farther down the Street. Madam appeared, crying heartrendingly. Behind the noises of the bird, Silence could hear the boy's, which were so like Madam's sobs that they were indistinguishable.

She turned back toward the female, which immediately put its nose down and scurried away, muzzle to the ground. It paused once or twice, but in the end it slipped into the garden where Medea dug up loveroots. Silence didn't have great faith in those roots, but to Medea they were magical. Which was impossible. A root at the end of its useful life could in a pinch be used to make tea, but for the most part she disliked the thought of consuming plants. Silence preferred to eat only meat.

Wicca stood in the back garden, staring in alarm at the blanket in the corner. The green one Medea used to protect her knees from the cold when she was digging in the soil.

"In the name of the Mother, the Son, and the Holy Ghost." Wicca's voice was trembling. She had her right arm around her waist and the left diagonally across her chest. Madam, perched on the blanket, let out a long victorious scream.

"It's a male," Wicca whispered tensely. "I saw him myself. He's naked and he has a thing between his legs. He looked right at me."

Silence pushed her aside and removed the blanket, and the sobbing boy reached up his arms toward her. His lips were blue, his movements stiff with cold. She picked him up, but he was too frozen to cling on to her neck. His weight was too much for her slight body, and he slipped back down. Clenching her teeth, she tried one more time, but couldn't lift him.

"We've got to go and get somebody," Wicca said hysterically. "Eva can help. She's a doctor and she works with the young males and—"

Silence looked at her angrily. Wicca broke off.

Get Medea, Silence thought at the female dog, which set off at full tilt, haring out of the back garden and down the road. Silence removed her poncho and put it on the boy. She drew him onto her lap and rocked him gently. He nestled up to her, teeth chattering.

"You know him?"

Silence nodded.

Wicca stepped cautiously nearer. Crouching down, she touched his white hair. The boy stared at her in fear.

"I knew somebody once with hair as white as his. She had green eyes too."

The boy was shivering with fever as Medea scooped him up. Her strength always astonished Silence. She carried him out of the back garden, across the Street and to the convent, the raspberry bag dangling at her side. Softly she sang one of her witch's rhymes, probably to console him. It sounded eerie. It always did when Medea chanted, Silence thought. Often as she sang she'd turn the whites of her eyes and gesture with her arms, trying to rouse one thing or another in the natural world. Things Silence wasn't sure even existed. And if they did exist, against all logic, it was better to let them lie.

"Put my coat around him." Wicca had taken off her jacket and was striding after them. She tucked it clumsily over the boy.

"We'll deal with this," Medea said, giving her the coat. "You can go home."

She trudged on thin-lipped, absorbed in stepping around the

slippery spots in the road. Wicca was still behind them when they reached the convent. She opened the door and held it for Medea.

In the front room, Medea laid the boy down on the couch underneath the birdcages. "Please just let him pull through, so I can tap him," she said to herself.

Wicca drew her warm red jacket over him again. She felt his forehead.

"He's burning up," she said. "We have to get Eva."

"No!" Medea said quickly.

"If he doesn't get the right treatment he could die. I know it's only a male, but he's still a living creature!"

"She can't come," Medea whined. Again, she irritated Silence. Couldn't she threaten Wicca with witchcraft? Say she'd curse her with eternal itching, rotten teeth, or make her lose all her hair if she went tattling? Or that Wicca's Devil, of whom she was clearly afraid, would come after her if anybody found out the boy was living at the convent?

Wicca sat down on the couch, by the boy's feet. "He needs a doctor."

"I have herbs that are better than anything a doctor can offer, and they won't disrupt his hormones, either," Medea said, before turning back to Silence. "Keep an eye on her."

Silence nodded. She sat down across from Wicca, staring darkly at her. Of course they couldn't trust a priest. She would betray them the first chance she got. They thought only of themselves and of their church.

Wicca bent over the boy, stroking some of his damp white hair back from his forehead.

"How old is he?" she asked. "Is he eight?"

Silence crossed her arms.

"Is he ten?" Wicca guessed. "He looks about the same age as my daughter, Wendy. She turned seven six months ago. But I don't know if boys grow the same way children do."

Medea set a tray of jars filled with herbs and some hot water on the table by the couch.

"Where did this boy come from, Medea?"

"I'm giving him something to bring his fever down," she said, mixing the items on the tray.

"What are they?"

"Herbs. And a drop or two from the basement."

"If your hocus-pocus hasn't worked in an hour, I'm getting Eva."

Gingerly Medea parted the boy's lips and let a few drops of something Silence was sure was snake venom fall into his mouth. The boy moaned weakly. Silence bit her cheek. She hoped Medea and her potions weren't about to take the boy's life now as well.

"Where did this boy come from, Medea?" Wicca had raised her voice, and Medea sighed.

WICCA HAD SAID NOTHING FOR AN HOUR. SHE WAS STARing at the leather dress, cut to ribbons, and the black boots the boy's mother had been wearing. She ran her fingers delicately over the leather, then brushed away her tears. Medea had also found the green ring the woman had been wearing, which she'd taken off so it didn't end up in Pythia's stomach. She placed it in front of Wicca, who looked at it as though it were an old friend she hadn't seen in a long time.

"I gave it to her when we decided to have children together," she said. Tears dripped from her chin. Wicca kissed the ring.

Medea set a cup of tea in front of her.

"And she died in childbirth?" Wicca's bottom lip trembled.

Medea shot Silence a glance. "She was in a bad way when she got here, already in labor, and the baby was coming. We did everything we could to save her, but there wasn't time to call anybody before she died. Everything happened so fast."

"But why didn't you do it afterward? Where is she now?"

Medea hesitated. "She's buried under the chestnut tree in the front garden. Where the sisters are buried, and where Eldest will be laid to rest when the frost thaws. Just by the roses. We gave her a beautiful burial, sent her out of this world with love."

Silence looked away.

"Love?" Wicca took an angry sip of tea.

"We were in shock, we weren't thinking clearly. Also, we felt sorry for the boy, the idea of him . . . You know we don't like the Centers very much."

"I know that," said Wicca vehemently, "but it's one thing to believe that men should have more legroom in their pens and another one entirely to keep a live boy within your own four walls. It's indefensible." Then she leapt up in a fury, clutching the leather dress and ring tightly. "You're insane," she shouted. "What would you do if he killed one of you? Or when he becomes so obsessed with his penis that he rapes you? Anyway, he's Kali's boy. I'll have him picked up this afternoon. You're both looking at years as pensives!" She took a few steps toward the door, staggered, then came back and sat on one of the chairs in the kitchen. "I just need to sit down for a minute first."

"Why don't you lie down?" Medea asked solicitously, picking up a rug that she spread on the floor beside the dogs.

"Do you have a pillow too?" Wicca sniveled.

A few moments later she was lying on their kitchen floor, snoring loudly. The little female dog and the male settled down close to her. Soon they were asleep as well.

"I gave her a sedative in the tea," Medea said apologetically. "Seemed like she needed it."

Silence, thinking of the boy's mother, eyed Medea dubiously.

"Don't worry, she'll wake up in a few hours." Medea took the cup and rinsed it well in the sink. "I promise. Three hours. Ten at the most."

THE BOY'S TEMPERATURE HAD DROPPED. MEDEA, CURLED up at the other end of the couch, laid a hand on his forehead every quarter hour.

"I was starting to worry I'd have to take him down to the oak trees and drag him naked through the oval opening."

Silence looked at her wearily. She had no doubt Medea would drag the boy out into the winter if she thought it necessary.

"I just need Wicca to sleep for another few hours, just until the boy's temperature is low enough for me to tap him. If the Center's going to take him, I need as much raw material for Pythia as I can get."

Silence had no idea what she was talking about. She got up off the floor where she'd been sitting, stepped over Wicca in the kitchen, and went upstairs to Eldest.

It was ice-cold in the bedroom. The window stood open to the winter cold. Silence rolled herself up in two duvets. She was still freezing and wished she could shut the window, but for Eldest's sake she didn't. At this temperature, they could stave off putrefaction.

It was Eldest who had found her in the slum, after Silence had decided at long last she wanted to die. She wasn't from the area. Or from the slum. She'd grown up near Aarhus, in Risskov, living with her mothers in one of the large old patriarchal villas on the water. Just beside the Drop.

Few visitors came to her childhood home, because although the view was beautiful, the Drop wasn't a place people wanted to stay or swim. That was where Ane had been found, at the beginning of the Evolution. She was the last girl in Denmark to be raped, and she had been lying at the water's edge with her clothes in pieces. Torn up, inside and out. It looked like a wild animal had gotten hold of her. But it was a man, Ane's neighbor, unable to control his urges. She was found lying on her stomach. When they turned her over, her eyes were wide open, with such a sorrowful look that everyone who saw her instantly began to cry. As they carried the dead girl out of the water, tears trickled down her cheeks. They didn't stop, even after she was dry and long since brought ashore. Ane wept in her coffin all throughout her funeral, and everybody else wept with her.

They named the place where Ane was found the Drop, and they planted three weeping willows that were never to be cut or kept in any way in check. The trees became a symbol of the new, wild-growing age, when the sisters who had dragged themselves through past century after century were mourned. Hamstrung by conditions worse than men's in the labor market, in cultural life, financially, and sexually. No longer would a woman be forced into something, forbidden something, or be required to give something she didn't wish to give. Which was why it was not forbidden to live in the patriarchal districts—although nobody could stop others from frowning on the practice, or wondering why somebody might choose to live in the old houses.

"The suffering of the past is in the bricks," they said, and most were eager to see the villas swallowed up by nature quickly. It was part of the healing process to let the waterholes, lakes, and marshes emerge out of the past and slowly wash away the age of men, which had inflicted so much trauma.

The recurring question was whether it was even possible to live in the old houses without being affected by the misery of the past. Could thoughts and emotions move at will in rooms made up of angles? Weren't they constantly bumping up against a wall or a corner that hindered free movement? It was an assault to force a person into a square. Nature created nothing square-shaped. Flowers, leaves, treetops, lakes, and hills, all were curved and sinuate. Even brooks and streams, which sought the direct and straightest path down a mountain, were winding.

Silence's mothers were a collective of workers who built dwelling places. They had viewed the patriarchal villa by the Drop as an interesting challenge and moved in to see if they could make the old house bend to them instead of the other way around. They feminized corners and walls. Inset arched windows where they could.

Her mothers did not think there was any reason to let nature take materials that could be reused. Better to adapt what already existed to a more modern outlook. They often built from stone and iron found in the dilapidated slums, which lent an exotic quality to the new homes they were hired to construct. Still, the materials always had to be disclosed in the construction report, to make the new inhabitants aware there was a bygone era in the walls.

It wasn't that the mothers were opposed to the round districts. Far from it. Their collective was known for its beautiful ovoid roofs, which, like eggs, were optimally structured. They all wore the same thin silver chains around their throats, to remind themselves and others that when the decision is left up to nature and gravity, the strongest shape is the oval arc.

"There's no reason to fight what nature wants, to use rulers and right angles" was their motto. "Take the curve of the silver chain, turn it upside down, and build. You won't find a better roof."

In the part of Risskov situated farther from the water, the old houses weren't built as solidly and had crumbled one by one. They perished with their flat roofs on top of their foundations, or scattered across a piece of earth that slowly consumed any and all reminders that there had ever been families living there with fathers at their head.

NATURE CLEANING UP, read colorful signs along the edge of the slum, to alert people that they were entering an area of decay.

Its residents were loners, misfits, former pensives, adventurers, and others with an alternative worldview. They kept individual houses going, rebuilt when they collapsed, patched where the weather had torn holes or the plants were trying to get in. But the vast majority of houses vanished over the years, abandoned to ruin, as a reminder of everything that could never be permitted to return.

Silence's family consisted of five mothers and five siblings. She had her own room with round windows that overlooked the water. She loved the sea, especially her own sea outside the windows. She loved it before she was old enough to understand the story of Ane and the Drop. When she was old enough, she loved it anyway. Her mothers tried to keep her away from the water, and not only because they didn't want her swimming in the rape victim's sea. They were also afraid that she would drown.

The problem was that Silence—who wasn't known as Silence yet, but Benja, because she was the house's last-born child and thus named Benjamin—couldn't keep away from the shore.

Her first memories were of being in the water. The joyful sense of calm that spread from the inside out as the water closed around her, and she could hear nothing but her own beating heart. She pestered them to put her in water long before she could talk, her mothers said. Sometimes she wailed for hours until they got a tub, filled it up, and sat her in it. You could keep her occupied all morning that way, but the sea was best. She learned to swim at the same time as she learned to walk, and when she ran off as a toddler, they'd always find her stumbling toward the beach.

The water made her feel weightless, as though she didn't exist. The longing to be floating on her back, just her nose above the waterline, would overcome her sometimes from the moment she woke.

Her mothers insisted that one of them always had to accompany her if she wanted to swim. And if she absolutely *had* to swim at the Drop, then it had to be a short distance away, hidden in a little bay, so that she wouldn't bother the mourners or the curious tourists who came to see the willows growing wild. But the magic of the place waned with each century that passed since Ane's sad fate, and Benja could usually swim in peace when she slipped out and went to the shore near the house.

Even before she started school, she'd be fidgety and irritable if she didn't get down to the water for a few days in a row, biting her fingernails into small frayed moons and gnawing on her bottom lip until the skin started peeling off in flakes.

Her mothers took her to the water as often as they could, but they were all at points in their lives where they wanted to make a difference in other ways, so they rarely had the time. None of them was her biological mother. She was the result of a new resident's spontaneous desire to have a child. The woman had also worked with buildings, and like the others she had been drawn by the forbidden corners of the house and the desire to make curves out of something angular.

It wasn't a happy time, the year the woman lived there. She didn't share the mothers' views on masturbation, which led to many heated discussions. In some of them she even went so far as to declare herself a penisist. When, after giving birth, she decided motherhood didn't feel right to her either, she gave her birth daughter to the others and left. That wasn't a problem for Benja, or for them. They thrived in each other's company, and there were mothers enough in the house. The only thing was, she was fifteen years younger than the youngest of her other siblings. The toddler phase was over, her sisters were too old to bother much about her, and her mothers probably felt they were done with small children. So Benja was often left to her own devices, and to her craving for the water. The impulse was so strong that she usually had to give in, even if it meant lying to her mothers.

She always felt terrible when she lied. But if she had to choose between feeling guilty or the calming effect of the water, she chose to float a little way away from the Drop, which couldn't be seen from the house, and live with the guilt. One more trip to the water and the guilt was gone anyway.

When she wasn't in the sea, she was wandering around in the slum. She had to do something while she was waiting for her hair to dry after a swim.

The first time she was scared, because her mothers thought the slums were dangerous as well. Benja wasn't allowed to walk the overgrown roads and around the old ruins, where the gardens had returned at last to marshland and little pools, to what they'd been before the patriarchy drained the area.

At first, she only ventured to the outskirts. Peeped cautiously through the tall hedges. After that she grew braver, inching farther into the undergrowth, crawling over a few old roofs and tossing leaves into a pond.

"I don't go anywhere near the slum or the water," she told her mothers. "I look at trees and plants at the edge of the ruined city." To persuade her mothers that the lie was true, she made drawings of plants on the fringes of the slum.

They weren't very nice drawings, but because she felt the plants were speaking to her, they were so detailed that the mothers shared approving nods. She was a special child, they said, sensitive and wise. But when they thought she wasn't listening, she heard them say her character alarmed them. It was a problem that she preferred her own company to the group's, and that she fell into reveries, sometimes for half an hour at a stretch, if she was near water or plants.

"Who knows what's going on inside her head," they said to each other. "Who knows if there's anything going on at all?"

When she was difficult to reach it was because she was trying to conjure the feeling of water. There could be nothing better. Or she was attempting to make contact with a plant she could see through the arched living-room window.

When it was impossible for her to get away from the house, she sat in the crown of one of the old trees in the garden. But they were so tamed by her mothers' attempts to keep an orderly garden that they didn't dare speak to her. That was why she preferred the slum's green wildness, which bowled her over sometimes with its smells, stories, and untrammeled colors. Outside the slum, scents and colors were carefully arranged, patterned to induce a certain mood in passersby. The slum had a life of its own.

Thankfully, her mothers rarely asked to see a drawing when she came home. They only asked if she'd had a nice time. Still, Benja always had one on her, just in case. If nobody asked, she could use it the next time she'd been in the water or hanging out in the slum. Her record was nine weeks without having to draw a new one.

When Silence looked back on her childhood, at least until she turned twelve—when she met Wera the priest, and not long after that made friends with Chaplin—she didn't see much difference between that time and the life she lived at the convent now. She went days without speaking, lost in her own thoughts and her own company. And that of the plants. She didn't think of solitude and silence as anything special, until she made it a conscious choice.

At school she was expected to talk, of course, but if she was lucky she could get through a whole day in peace. Teachers and students alike had given up on prying more than a few sentences out of her at a time.

Wera was the first person to insist on speaking with her. And the only one who really listened when Benja talked about the plants she conversed with.

"They don't say anything in words, but I understand how they feel, and what they need," Benja said, and Wera nodded.

"I get that," she said. "It's the Mother speaking to you through the leaves."

Benja didn't know anything about the Mother, and thought the plants could speak perfectly well for themselves, but it was so nice to be with Wera that she didn't contradict her.

Wera was in her midtwenties. Her skin was dark, gleaming in the places where the sun struck it. She was taller than Benja's mothers and broader in the shoulders and hips. Her black hair was always scraped back into a high ponytail that coiled down her back in long, thick curls.

Benja met her in the slum one winter's afternoon, when it was so cold she had to tuck her wet hair under a hat. It took ages to dry. That there was ice on the ponds in the slum and sometimes sheets on the water in the sea didn't stop her from swimming every day. The only thing that changed with the seasons was how long she spent in the water. At that time she wasn't yet venturing too far into the slum. She was afraid of getting lost, after darkness began to fall. Three or four rows of ruins deep, she'd go that far. So long as she could see the way out, she felt safe.

Benja was sitting on a log, throwing pebbles at a gable wall that protruded out of the ground. The light was fading and she'd taken off her hat, hoping her hair would look dry by the time she got home.

"Hello," she heard a voice say suddenly behind her. Benja quickly jammed her hat back on.

"Hello," she answered, startled, turning around.

"My name's Wera," Wera said. "What's yours?"

"Benjamin," Benja replied, stuffing her wet hair back underneath the hat.

"Do you mind if I sit down?"

Benja made room, ill at ease with company. She glanced sidelong at the long green garment hanging around Wera's neck. Wera followed her gaze and swished the stole.

"I'm a priest at the Church of Agatha. Bad habit, always wearing this," she said and laughed. "Do you live here in the slum?"

Benja shook her head.

"I live down by the water." She pointed in the direction of the Drop. She didn't like telling people where she lived. They mostly thought the place was vile.

"It's beautiful there," Wera said. "Would you like an apple?" She rummaged in her bag and took out a red apple. It looked crisp.

"No thank you."

"Oh, come on, I can't eat them all on my own. They're from

the church orchard—I cultured the species myself. They're winter apples, the last to ripen in the fall. My species isn't ripe until November—nobody else has apples that are good to eat that late."

Benja thought she'd be left in peace more quickly if she took the apple. In any case, she was curious.

"Cultured?" she asked, and took a bite. It tasted more bitter than expected.

"Why don't we head out now? It's getting dark. I've got to jump on the train just over there."

They walked side by side out of the slum. Benja's hair itched under her hat.

"I live in a round district by one of the newer lakes."

"Okay," Benja said.

"See you," called Wera, as they parted.

"Any luck this week?" Their Body teacher's eyes were fixed on Benja. The whole class stared at her.

"Yes," Benja lied, clearing her throat. Her voice was husky: she hadn't spoken a word since saying goodbye to her mothers that morning.

"And?"

"What you said last time. The colors got clearer and stuff."

The teacher regarded her skeptically.

"It's not as though you're going to die without good orgasms in your life. In the old days, most women lived without them, but they failed to thrive. They missed out on the natural energy it gives us."

Benja sighed. The abiding threat of past adversities. It was exhausting when adults refused to live in the present, to acknowledge that times were different now. They weren't oppressed by the patriarchy anymore. Imagining a woman who didn't treat her body properly was silly. Benja's mothers spent at least an hour a day ensuring that their orgasms released tension and dark thoughts. The same way they took care of themselves by exercising, getting massages, brushing their teeth, and surrounding themselves with the right fragrances.

"In the old days, women spent far too much time talking things through, with professionals and with friends," the teacher went on. "They reached out endlessly, but they never got the release they desired. They should have been reaching down. Giving their minds the break they needed to be a well-functioning human being. A moment of trance. For several centuries it was fashionable to meditate, to sit cross-legged and concentrate on the breath. If you were skilled and—crucially—persistent, if you practiced for years, you might be lucky enough to enter into a trance. Not many people succeeded. It would have been better if they'd spent that time getting to know their bodies, because an orgasm sends you directly into the same transcendental state. Your whole mind travels briefly to another dimension, and returns in a new and better condition. The chemical reactions that happen in your body as the orgasm cleanses you are a source of genuine joy."

Benja looked out the window, imagining the release of lying on her back, bobbing in the water, letting it cover her ears so that all sound ceased. She doubted any orgasm could be as intense an experience as that.

It wasn't long before she saw Wera again. Benja was sitting at the edge of the slum while she waited for her hair to dry.

Wera started waving when she was still far off.

Benja waved back.

"This is nice," said Wera.

This time they sat for longer. And Benja had to admit, she enjoyed talking to Wera. She wasn't indifferent like the girls in her class, and she was freer in her thinking than the grown-ups Benja knew.

"Do you get bored at school?"

"We're doing Body right now, and it's pretty boring."

"I remember it being boring too, but I've got to say, it's come in handy once or twice since I've grown up." Wera laughed. "I still think plants are way more thrilling." She took out the bag of apples.

"Here." She gave one to Benja. This time, Benja didn't hesitate to take it.

They met a couple of times a week. Wera was in the slum a lot.

"To see if anyone needs help," she said. "Right now nobody really does, so I get to hang out with you instead." She kept cookies and sweet drinks in her bag, in case she met someone who needed sustenance. They shared them on a log or a heap of stones.

Her mothers were pleased she'd found a good friend in Wera, but laughed at the fact she was religious.

"They do good work for the people who've chosen to live in the slum, the pensives and so on, people who are struggling," they agreed. "She's from that special, fancy bloodline, isn't she?" Her mothers chuckled again and shook their heads.

One day in early spring, Wera and Benja attended Wera's church, which was situated in a part of the city-center slum where Benja had never been before. It felt like a long way from home. They took the train as far as they could, and the rest of the way they drove in the church's vehicle, which lurched noisily across the rubble. Benja had never ridden in anything like it before, and she clung squealing and laughing to the belt that strapped her in.

"Welcome to the Church of Agatha's apple orchard," Wera said proudly as they arrived, and she showed Benja around the church's garden, where they each picked an apple. They sat down on a bench and took a bite.

"These are the first batch to ripen," Wera said through a mouthful of apple. "They're a bit sour, so we can't use them for the ceremony yet."

"What's that down there?" asked Benja, pointing at two large domes at the foot of the orchard, which arced up into the sky like two swelling breasts.

"Those are the greenhouses, the old botanical gardens where the pensives live. There are lots of plants for them to practice on. It's very pretty in there, although they're not always the best at looking after the plants. They've got the biggest water lilies in the world. Or the biggest I can imagine, anyway. Water lilies can support more than a hundred and thirty pounds. They could easily carry your weight, for instance. I used to float on them when I was a kid, and the church took me down there to learn how to talk to the pensives and help them with their plants. I've taken plenty of cuttings over the years. From crown-of-thorns, paradise lilies, snake plants. I use them to decorate the church. You should come see them one day."

Benja had stopped listening. She was daydreaming of floating on a leaf on the water. It was as though the two things that she loved the most had merged.

"I'd love to go and float on the water lilies," she said.

"I wish you could, but apart from their supervisor and people from the church, nobody's allowed too close to the pensives. Children especially. But I'll take you down to see the water-plants on our lake, when they bloom. You can't float on them, but they're the most beautiful sight."

THE SPRING SUN HAD BEEN WARM FOR A FEW DAYS BY THE time Benja and Wera sat on the jetty by the round district. The lake was filled with aquatic plants. Wera was right. It really was beautiful.

"Aren't they lovely?" Wera said, pointing at the pink flowers springing up all across the surface of the lake. Benja nodded. She had said a brief hello to Wera's sisterpriests, as they called each other. They weren't so different from the sisters she met later at the convent, who believed so strongly in a common cause that they would die for it—a cause most people thought silly and saw no reason to fight for. But, unlike in the pecking order of old, when there was little understanding of the human mind's persistent need to explore, nothing these days was prohibited. Everyone was welcome to believe and practice in whatever way they liked, so long as it didn't affect anyone else. New minority faiths sprang up all the time, exalting the strangest creatures as sacred, only to wind down a few years later when the faith turned out to be yet another religious dead end.

Benja shut her eyes and inhaled through her nose. The plants smelled sweet.

"*Elodea canadensis* is its formal name," Wera told her. She lay on her stomach and stretched, trying to reach one of them with her fingertips. Benja lay down beside her. The plants swayed in the wind.

"See how they stretch, each one opening into a tiny flower?"

"They're lovely," Benja said.

"They do it hoping to catch some of the male plant's pollen."

"Oh," Benja said, and she could feel the longing deep inside the plant's heart.

"There's just one problem," Wera said, edging farther forward so she could touch a leaf. "There aren't any male plants of their species."

"Here at the lake, you mean?"

"No, in the whole of Denmark. Scandinavia. Europe."

"Why not?" asked Benja sadly.

"They aren't native to Denmark. They were brought here by patriarchal aquarium enthusiasts several hundred years ago. Wanting to exploit the plant, I guess."

"That's terrible." Benja felt sorry for the plant seeking futilely to be pollinated.

"Not at all," Wera said, snapping off a flower. Benja sensed its pain. "What do they need males for? Look out at the water! They're everywhere, they're one of the hardest plants to get rid of. They can go on cloning themselves indefinitely and at lightning speed. That's why the other name for them is *waterweed*."

"I still think it's a shame," said Benja quietly. If Wera hadn't been there, she would have jumped into the lake and let them shroud her in their grief. Wera gave her a hug.

"A woman's weakest spot is that she has too much empathy," she said. They stood up and Wera hooked her arm through Benja's. They walked arm in arm along the bridge and onto the path. "Bid your empathy welcome, dance with it, laugh at it, cry with it, but never follow it. That way is impassable. If you choose it, you will end up like our foremothers. Nobody wants that."

Benja inhaled deeply. No, of course she didn't want that. She turned and looked back at the waterweed's useless spring dance and held her breath until she could no longer feel any pity.

In April Benja didn't see much of Wera. She was busy preparing for and celebrating the Easter ritual at the church. After that she went to Zealand to buy a new cobra. There was a priest at Brønshøj who reared exceptionally good snakes. So Benja, bored, began to wander farther into the slum, killing time.

She zigzagged along the lumpen asphalt roads, talking to flowers, trees, bushes, and leaves. At one corner hung an old wooden board. It said MINT LANE, in crooked letters. The sign pointed down the path she was walking. A single house stood upright, while the rest of the track was nearly obscured by debris and vegetation. She walked on, noticing in astonishment the names of the paths that branched off. Lanes named after anemone, chamomile, juniper, thyme, rosehip—all plants and flowers she had spoken to. The handmade signs were hung up in trees or balanced on piles of rocks. The names were nothing like the aggressive, patriarchal ones she'd learned were common in the slums, back when the straight roads had names and were lined with social structures detrimental to women.

She smelled the sweet clover before she saw the house. And before she read the sign. SWEET CLOVER LANE had been carved into the wood in jagged lettering. The garden beyond it was bursting with sweet peas. The house was well maintained and sagged only along one side. The facade was covered in old house numbers, some rusty, some painted directly on, others scored into the old wood, half and quarter figures, jumbled together higgledy-piggledy.

The garden was overgrown, but tended enough to suggest

someone had been living there not long ago. The trees hadn't yet begun to nibble at the walls, and the berry bushes were still giving each other room to grow, although the sweet clover was doing its best to take command. For now, the white sweet peas owned no more than the front garden. She was paralyzed with delight at the quantities of sweet clover, each delicate flower atop its long stem eager to tell her a story.

She could tell from the overgrown path to the front door that nobody had gone up to the house that spring. Benja stepped carefully onto the property. Insects whirred up out of the clover. Moving around to the other side of the house, she tried to peer in through the windows, but they were too scratched and dirty. Bees were flying in and out of some old hives a short stretch away from a pond at the bottom of the garden. Benja stood amid the horde of sweet clover and breathed in through her nose.

A loud noise made her jump. She ducked down among the tall plants. When the sound rang out again, she got up and ran as fast as she could, until she was safely on the right side of the hedge around the slum.

A woman was walking into the slum with a basket. Probably on her way to pick something from the wild-growing gardens. She gave a friendly nod to Benja, who returned the greeting out of breath.

The very next day, Benja snuck back to the sweet clover house. She made sure not to put her feet in the same places as the day before, so the plants wouldn't be trodden down. After letting herself be wrapped in the scent of sweet clover and drawing a new sketch of the flowers, in case she got home late, she crept over to the house, up the front steps, and to the door. She tried it. It was sticking. She had to shove hard before it gave way.

"Hello?" she said nervously, hoping nobody would answer. She crept inside. In the living room there was an ancient couch, two metal chairs, and a square table. A candlestick on the table with the wick burned half down. A sink and a kitchen bench. Benja ran her fingertips along its perpendicular edges. The tabletop was higher than she was used to, the corners tapering to a point, and the graying walls were forbidding. It was the kind of layout she had only seen in old history books.

She brushed the dust off her dress. In the other room there was an old-fashioned metal bed. Going back into the living room, she sat down on the couch. A brown stain had spread across the green upholstery. She put her nose to it. It smelled at once bitter and sweet.

The same noise as the day before came trumpeting suddenly across the gardens. Benja dropped instinctively to the floor and scrabbled over to the window. She rubbed the glass to see out. Diagonally across from her, in the garden, stood a girl about her age. Maybe a little older. In her hand she held a horn. She blew it again.

"Stop that," someone shouted from the house behind her, which looked as though it once had been two stories, but now had been reduced to one. The top floor had collapsed onto the lower like a battered hat.

The girl put the horn to her mouth and gave it a final blast before wandering lazily into the house. Benja sat there for a long time, hoping she'd come out again.

THE FIRST TIME SILENCE SAW ELDEST, SHE DID NOT YET have gray hair. And there were still nine sisters left to die before she could be called "Eldest." Gradually, though, her hair began to lose its color at the sides, and she squinted when she had to look at things, because she didn't want to have her vision repaired.

"As long as I can see my birds, there's no cause to meddle with my eyes," she said. The other sisters shook their heads, because while there were many things about society they wanted no part of, it was foolish to struggle on with bad eyesight when it took little more than a round trip on the train to fix it.

"And if the day ever comes when I can no longer tell my birds from a rat, the birds will surely find me," Eldest went on, feeding a few seeds to the crow that always sat on her head. It only moved when Madam came and demanded its perch.

Now Eldest was cold and stiff, her hair thinned, eyes vacant, hands clutching lifelessly at the dried sweet clover Silence had placed on her breast. Her fingers wouldn't straighten, no matter how much Silence tried to position them gently around the stem.

The early sun had found some lone chinks in the grimy window. A few rays fell across Eldest's blue eyes, giving them a barren glow.

Medea had closed Eldest's eyes when they laid her on the bed, but one had sprung open. It made her look ridiculous, Silence thought, and with difficulty she managed to open the other one too.

Medea was busy downstairs in the kitchen. One of the dogs

barked. It had to be the male. It was never satisfied. Perhaps Wicca had already woken up. Madam cawed rancorously.

Couldn't you have taken Madam with you? Silence thought, stroking Eldest's hair. The scalp was cool under the scant wisps.

Wrapping herself in the duvet, she discovered a bloodstain she'd left on the back. Her cycle often ended with a short epilogue, and she didn't always catch it. She turned the duvet around so that Medea wouldn't notice the mark. Since Medea had stopped bleeding, she was scrupulous about wringing Silence for every drop, which she used in her baking. *Exhausting,* Silence thought; she preferred to lie weightless in the water and forget she had a body.

She went downstairs with the duvet. In the kitchen, Wicca was slumped drowsily against the wall, her gaze sluggish. She was barely conscious. The female dog was panting heavily in her face.

Silence looked questioningly at Medea.

"There might have been something pacifying in her morning tea as well. Just a little."

Silence bit anxiously at a nail. She knew Medea had dulling drops in the boy's room, in case he got dangerous. And that too much of it would kill a person. Like the boy's mother. On days when the desire not to live was in the ascendant, Silence had stood holding the bottle in her hand. The last seven years, as Eldest grew more and more strange, it was mostly the boy who'd made her want to live. She went to look at him. He was still sleeping on the couch.

"He seems stable, but the fever's too high for me to tap him, so I've given him dried yarrow. That ought to cool him down," Medea said.

Silence blew softly on his warm brow and gently ran a hand over his fair hair.

His mother had had the same white hair and green eyes. It

was why Silence had noticed her, up by the Street, where she'd stood knocking on the door of the house that used to be a supermarket. Silence had been to the lake and was on her way home. The woman's belly was a heavy bulge obtruding from her thin body, and she was crying as she pummeled on the door.

"Lars, let me in," she shouted.

The door had not opened. One of the manladies had yelled at her to shut up, that she was scaring off the customers. She was the only one on the Street. The woman staggered away down the road. Silence crept after her, hiding behind a tree when the woman tripped, fell, and screamed, hands clutched protectively over her belly. Silence leaned too far out, and the woman caught sight of her.

"Help me," she cried, holding out a hand to Silence. "It's coming. I'm in labor."

The woman got up and stumbled toward Silence, who was backing away toward the convent. She dropped to her knees, screaming in pain. Silence hurried away, and was just about to slip through the front door when she realized the woman had followed her, so instead she went on past the convent and hid behind a tree. The woman was panting, supporting herself on a caved-in roof at the corner of the road.

"I'm in labor," she cried out in an agonized voice.

No one heard, so she struggled on. The light in the convent kitchen drew her to the front door. With the last of her strength, she knocked.

"Is anybody there?" she cried. Silence chewed off a sliver of nail behind the tree as Eldest opened the door and let the woman in. She remained hidden for a few more minutes, looking around cautiously. No, nobody had seen the woman go inside the house.

* * *

It sounded as if Medea's herbs had worked the way they were supposed to. The fever had dropped again. The boy opened his eyes, discovered Silence, and smiled. She took his hand. The female dog came and sat with them, whining soundlessly. It was only Silence who could hear it.

It was odd how much the female liked her company. She'd never wanted a dog. Not even as a child. Her mothers had been more than willing to give her one, even two, or what about a cat, a tortoise? They felt guilty, leaving her so much to herself. She didn't even want a mouse. But maybe a greenhouse, she'd asked.

She received one as an eighth birthday present. Along with the shears, which were still her most treasured possession. When she could find them. They had never gone missing before.

She spent hours after school planting seeds, coaxing up the shoots, then bedding them out. Soon their whole garden was spilling over. When, at the age of twelve, she discovered the sweet clover house in the spring months, she brought seeds and other small plants from the garden near the Drop. Soon the bees were buzzing as merrily and plentifully as they must have done under the previous owner. She spent the month without Wera fixing up the house. Stealing in without anybody noticing, keeping an eye out in case the girl from Mint Lane showed up again. When she took a break from cleaning or planting in the garden, she spied on the house from the window. She had tried to polish the glass, but it was damaged, cracked in several places and clumsily taped over, which restricted her view. The only sign that somebody was living there was that the laundry hung to dry outside the house kept changing. Today it was a green dress fluttering in the wind. Yesterday it had been four pairs of underwear.

She had scrubbed at the stain on the couch with a bar of soap. But neither the odor nor the dark spot went away. Benja sniffed it several times, trying to figure out what it might be so that she could use the right cleaning agents to remove it.

Then one day there she was in the doorway, the girl with the horn, just as Benja was yet again trying to get the stain off the couch. Startled, she jumped down under the table in a ludicrous attempt to hide.

"That was where she died," the girl said, pointing at the stain. There was a rat climbing up and down her arm. She came inside without asking permission. Her hair was long and straight. She had on several layers of clothing, at least two pairs of jeans and a skirt on top.

"She was lying there for ages, but Mama said not to tell anybody, because then we might get blamed. We just left her, even after she began to stink." The girl pronounced some of the words in a funny, singing accent.

Benja shrank instinctively away from the couch, thinking of all the times she had lain there with her nose in the stain. Now she knew what the smell was. It was death.

"They were singing when they carried her away. And someone put a white flower on the stain. Made the whole room smell like piss. After a day or two that was gone as well. Are you going to live here?"

Benja shook her head. "I'm just making it cozy."

"My name's Chaplin," said the girl, taking a seat on one of the other chairs. The rat ran down her leg and scurried off along the baseboard, but returned at her whistle.

"Benjamin, or Benja, people call me."

"What would you like me to call you?"

"Just Benja," Benja mumbled.

"How old are you?"

"Twelve."

"Ha, then I'm older than you, I'm thirteen," said Chaplin, crossing her legs on the table. She was lanky, at least four inches taller than Benja, and now that she saw her up close she'd have assumed she was two or three years older.

"I'm not allowed out, really, my mama pitches a fit over the littlest things, but luckily she's started working at the hospital, so I can sneak out," Chaplin said, getting to her feet. She put the rat in her pocket. "You coming over here tomorrow too?"

"Maybe." It felt like her secret place had been invaded. Still, there was something about the girl that put her in a good mood.

"You're not here every day, but I like it when you are." Chaplin grinned, then was gone as suddenly as she'd arrived.

Benja skipped her swim the next day and went straight to the sweet clover house after school, hoping and fearing that the girl would come over again. She had brought a clean blanket from home, which she laid over the stain on the couch. Afterward she sat for ages in the chair, waiting. Peering out of the window. There was no one to be seen anywhere. She went out to the plants in the garden, but couldn't concentrate on talking to them because she was constantly keeping an ear out for footsteps. A couple of women walked past with their baskets. Benja ducked. One of them stopped at the sweet clover house and pointed in, but was called away by the other one, who'd found some spring blooms in an old flower bed. Benja hurried indoors.

She stayed until twilight, then she ran through the streets of the slum, getting home just in time for dinner with her mothers. She was more disappointed than relieved that there had been no visit.

When Wera got back, Benja told her about the sweet clover house. She regretted it even before she was finished talking, but there was something about Wera that made her want to tell her everything. Wera knew about the house already anyway.

"An old lady lived there. I tried to check in on her occasionally, but she didn't want visitors, me or anybody else from the church. When she died, we were the ones who carried her out of the house. She'd been in there a while—by then she was in a pretty sorry state." Wera took a sip of the tea she had poured for them both. "Maybe you can invite me one day?"

Wera had sworn not to tell anybody Benja was using the house.

"It's nice to have a place where you can be undisturbed," she said. "That's how I feel at church, and in the orchard. Somewhere I can be alone with my thoughts and feelings. Will you be at the service this Sunday, by the way?"

Benja didn't really want to go to church, but her mothers said it was a good idea to see what Wera did, since they were spending so much time together.

"They're not bad people, just because they dance around a man on a cross. People do all kinds of weird stuff to pass the time."

"But it's in the middle of the city-center slum," Benja said, trying to defend herself.

"Well, maybe we'll come too."

Chaplin didn't come on Friday, or on Saturday. Benja waited all day. She was only gone for the hour she went down to Wera's lake, to pick up a few shoots of the pining waterweed, which she planned to put in her own pond in the back garden.

On Sunday, she and two of her mothers went to the Church of Agatha in the slum.

They were the first to arrive. Her mothers had overestimated how long it would take to "fight" their way through the streets, as they called it. They sat down on one of the wooden benches, which had been repaired in so many places it was difficult to say whether there was any of the original left at all.

"It's so creepy the way they've got that big statue of a man in the middle of the room," one of her mothers whispered.

"It's disgusting," the other one replied. "You can tell they've tried to make him look kindly. Almost makes it worse."

"Why did we even have to come?" said Benja irritably. What if today was the day Chaplin returned to the sweet clover house?

Wera waved to her from the side of the church. She had on a long black robe, and of course the snakeskin stole with the *W*. Around her neck she wore a funny white collar.

Benja went over to her.

"Come and see my new cobra," Wera said, leading her behind the altar. "Isn't it lovely? It's the one I picked up in Zealand."

"Aren't they dangerous?" Benja lingered a few yards back from the snake's cage.

"They only bite when we want them to."

Benja looked at her uncertainly. Wera laughed at her expression.

"We're having one of our smaller Jesus statues restored, do you want to see? At least he won't bite. He's from way back in the 2150s. One of the few to survive when they smashed up the churches during the Evolution."

"Why are his hands bleeding?"

"He's sacrificed every Easter," Wera said. "But don't worry, he's resurrected. Like how plants go dormant for the winter then pop back up fresh in the spring. It's nature's way."

"I don't get why you have a man here; isn't that kind of . . . wrong?"

Wera smiled. "We'd probably be more popular if we'd phased him out, but he's part of the Mother and therefore part of the natural order. The Mother created men too, penises and flaws and all. Without the son and the lover there would be no crops, no fruit in the orchards, no children in their mother's bellies.

We can't have them running around willy-nilly, of course, but we should accept that they exist, because they're a part of the Mother's realm."

Benja nodded distractedly. It was hard to stay focused when Wera started going on about the Mother. She liked it better when they talked about plants.

"We'll be starting soon, so you'd better go and sit with your mothers."

Benja took a piece of apple from the dish being passed around among the benches. She hid it in the palm of her hand. People were chatting and laughing, hugging each other, some of them kissing. Benja jumped when the organ started playing. She looked up, not understanding where the noise was coming from. The congregation stopped talking and laughing as the three priestesses went to stand before the altar, carrying their snakes. Wera was one of them.

The church server welcomed the assembly. "In a moment, one of our priestesses will be speaking in tongues, channeling the Mother, so let us open our hearts to receive the Mother's message."

"Amen," the congregation sang.

Wera and the two other priestesses took the heads of their snakes and pressed them to their necks. Wera closed her eyes, bending back in pleasure as the snake bit down. She swayed, opened her eyes, and stepped forward. The other two priestesses took a step back, giving her the altar.

"Welcome, my children," Wera intoned, in a voice that didn't sound like hers. She passed her snake to the server, who took it away. "I am here to speak to you through this human being."

Benja shut her eyes and imagined lying on her back in the water near the Drop. Small waves lapping at her face. She held her breath, inhaling only when the water briefly stilled. One of her mothers yawned loudly.

At long last Wera was finished. Benja opened her eyes and saw Wera's head loll onto her chest. She gurgled. The server bustled over with a glass of water. She put her arm under Wera's, propping her up. Slowly Wera came to and stared wonderingly out across the congregation, which at the urging of the other priestesses began to sing a hymn about the Garden of Eden.

Benja looked at the slice of apple in her hand. It was already brown around the edges. She didn't really like eating fruit from the trees after all, she thought, and let it drop to the floor of the church. She nudged it under the bench with her foot.

"YOU WEREN'T HERE YESTERDAY!"

Benja turned around. She could hear Chaplin, but not see her.

"I waited all day."

She glanced up. Chaplin was sitting in the birch tree in the middle of the garden. The rat scampered down the trunk and over Benja's feet. She took a step backward. The rat made her uneasy.

"It won't hurt you."

"How did you get up there?"

"Climbed like a monkey," Chaplin said, hopping down. One of the two pairs of jeans she was wearing slipped halfway down. She yanked them back up and followed Benja into the sweet clover house, where she threw herself into one of the chairs.

"Did you come straight from school?"

"Yes." Benja sighed. "They let us out, finally."

"I've never been to school." Chaplin bit her fingernail.

"Why not?"

"We move a lot. And my mama thinks it's a bad idea. But I can read and write. My mama teaches me all the stuff you learn in school. Maybe even more, she says."

"You're so lucky," Benja said. The thought of never having to sit in another classroom, never having to worry someone might ask her a question, sounded fantastic.

"Did you get the dead-person stain out?" Chaplin lifted up the blanket Benja had put over it. The stain was still there. "Guess nobody really gets the better of death. But at least she left her mark on the world." Chaplin laughed.

Benja didn't know what to say to that. She picked up her bag; she still had a few waterweed shoots in it.

"Come on," she said, heading out to the pond in the back garden.

The rat went with them.

"Risskov used to be dry, and now there's water everywhere—isn't that funny?" Chaplin said. "I have some old maps at home. That's how I know what the roads are called. I was the one who put up the signs," she said proudly. "I can bring my maps and show you."

"Where did you get them?"

"Oh, I've lived in a lot of strange places."

Benja gazed at her admiringly.

"Like I lived in a secret underground passageway, near the old university. You know where that is?"

Benja shook her head.

"There's no windows, everything's at right angles, nothing's softened." Chaplin was whispering. "And you climb out of a hole in the ground because the stairs are broken."

"Weren't you scared?"

"Nah, not at all," Chaplin said. "But I missed the sun sometimes."

Benja carefully took the plants out of her bag and let them drift away across the pond. It was too late for planting out now, really, but she hoped they'd be all right. She wanted to give them a chance, since she'd been irresponsible enough to take them out of the big lake.

"Look," Benja said, pointing at some of the ones from the day before, which had already put down roots. "The way they're stretching out like that, they're hoping they'll get sprinkled with some male pollen."

Chaplin seemed unimpressed.

"But they won't be, because there are no males." Benja closed her eyes, because it was sad.

"There," said Chaplin, scattering them with a handful of soil, "now they've got a bit of dust to keep them happy."

"But it's not the same," Benja said, dismayed. "They want pollen from their own males."

Chaplin leapt to her feet. "Wait here, I've got something to show you."

She soon came running back, carrying the horn she'd blown the first times Benja saw her. Before that, she'd only seen one like it in pictures at school.

"It's called a trumpet. I polished it myself."

Chaplin blew as hard as she could. The trumpet's squeal carried across the gardens.

"My mother would flip if she heard me, but she's not home." Chaplin rubbed the trumpet with her sleeve. "I like the sound, but she says I can't make any noise with it. The patriarchs played things like this when they went marching in rows."

"Can I try?" Benja asked, feeling brave. She touched the horn warily, as though the past might be catching. She put it to her mouth and blew. A hiss passed through the instrument.

"You have to pinch your lips together," Chaplin said. She tried to squash Benja's lips into the right shape, and they both ended up laughing. Benja couldn't remember ever having laughed so much. She could feel it in her belly still, long after Chaplin had run home in time to be there when her mother got back from work.

"And she was up in the tree, I just couldn't figure out where the voice was coming from." Benja was laughing, blurting out all the things she'd decided not to tell Wera.

"Does she live in the slum?"

"Yeah, right across from the house where you helped carry out the dead woman. She keeps a rat as a pet. It's so cute."

"I'll never understand why some people choose to live in the old districts. And with a child. I've never actually heard of that before."

"Plus she used to live in an underground passage," Benja boasted.

"Underground?"

"Yeah, near the university."

"Hmmm." Wera looked grave. "I heard rumors there was a child living in the underground passageway between the old university and the library, but I didn't believe them. I thought only whack jobs lived down there."

"She's totally normal," Benja said indignantly. She hadn't slept all night, because she couldn't stop thinking about Chaplin.

"Does she go to the same school as you?"

"No, not yet, or . . ." Benja hesitated. "Her mother teaches her. But she'll be starting school soon."

Wera frowned.

"It was such a lovely service the other day—so interesting," Benja said, trying to change the subject.

"Thank you, I did have a particularly good connection to the Mother. You never know if it's going to work out . . ."

Benja waited an hour at the house before Chaplin finally arrived. They hadn't agreed to meet, but Benja was hoping so fervently she'd show up that she couldn't imagine Chaplin wouldn't come.

"Had to wait for my mama to fall asleep. I was getting worried she might not, even though she was up most of the night reading old books."

"I couldn't sleep either," Benja said. "I was thinking about going down to the beach for a swim last night. Want to go? I know a secret place nobody else uses."

It was a hot day, and the only reason she wasn't already bobbing at the water's edge was because she didn't want to miss Chaplin's visit.

"Eww, you swim at the beach?" Chaplin looked at her in disgust. "I'd never do that."

"Never?" Chaplin's stare made her feel small.

"It's gross. Isn't that right?" she said, turning to the rat and giving it a smooch.

"The plants we put there have opened," Benja said, clenching her teeth so she wouldn't cry. How could Chaplin hate something she loved so much? Did it mean they couldn't be friends after all? "Maybe the dust you sprinkled over them helped?"

"Of course it helped," Chaplin said, poking her with a laugh. "I'm like the fairy godmother for aquatic plants, didn't you know? I fly around at night, pollinating all the flowers." Chaplin spread her arms wide and ran off, flapping. She flew away across the garden.

Benja ran after her, relieved and laughing loudly.

THEY SAT DANGLING THEIR LEGS IN THE FOUNTAIN AT THE marketplace, not far from Wera's round district. They'd spent the morning studying Chaplin's maps, which were all several hundred years old. Many of them had been taped together, because the paper had crumbled along the folds. The funniest one was the map of Aarhus from the old days. They'd tried to figure out precisely where they were just then, but it was hard to tell. Most things had vanished into the earth, and new ones had been put on top. None of the original roads remained.

Benja had gotten them cups of ice cream. Chaplin ate it with her eyes half closed.

"That tastes so good," she said, smacking her lips.

"You must not eat a lot of ice cream!" Benja laughed. She felt like plunging into the fountain and letting the water engulf her.

Chaplin shook her head. "My mama never buys it. And I don't really get out of the slum much. Poor me—I've got to settle for eating berries and midges."

"You could make midge ice cream." Benja laughed, following a group of passing amazons with her eyes. They strutted haughtily across the square, all of them with screens over their eyes, tight leather dresses, and scarlet lips. They didn't speak to anybody. One of them discreetly adjusted the flat plane of her breast.

"I'd love to score with one of them," Chaplin said, her mouth full of ice cream. She nodded in the direction of the amazons. Benja looked at her in surprise.

"Really?"

"They'd probably chew me up and spit out the bones, but at least I'd get to feel something before I died."

Benja smiled. "I wouldn't have the guts."

"Nah, you wouldn't." Chaplin laughed. "You don't even have the guts to do it with a tulip."

"That's not true." Benja jumped down and dashed after Chaplin, who ran teasingly backward, out of her reach. Chaplin was always quicker.

They dropped panting onto the grass.

"Will your mother be back soon?" Benja asked. She didn't want Chaplin to go.

"She doesn't get off work for another hour. Can you go grab us some more ice cream? I want another red one."

Benja brought back a cup for Chaplin. She didn't want any more herself. She sat in the sun, feeling the heat on her forehead. Chaplin had crawled into the shade. There were patches of sweat under her arms.

"What does your mother do, anyway?" Benja asked.

"Helps sick people get better."

"Is she a doctor?"

"No, but she's read so many books that she's just as smart as the doctors."

"Is she your birth mother?"

Chaplin nodded. "What does your mother do?"

"I never met my birth mother, but I know she travels around the world, participating in masturbatathons."

"My mama did a masturbation competition once too, but she was eliminated in the first round. Is yours good at it?"

"She makes a living off it, my mothers say."

"Are you that good at it too?"

Benja sighed. "No, I'm the second worst in my class."

"Who's the worst?"

"Also me." Benja smiled, and she couldn't help giggling, although she was a bit nervous about trying to be funny.

Chaplin laughed. Benja joined her. For a while they lay next to each other in stitches.

"Have you ever tried it?" Benja asked.

"Tried what?"

"Giving yourself an orgasm?"

Since she'd met Chaplin, the things she learned in Body class had gotten a bit more interesting.

"I'm kind of hot—I should probably get home," Chaplin said, sitting up.

"Why don't you just take something off? You've always got about a hundred layers on. We can dip our feet in the water," Benja said. "We don't have to swim," she added quickly, when Chaplin frowned.

"I have to go home."

"Oh hey, cool," Benja said, pointing at a little spot of blood between Chaplin's legs. "You're bleeding."

Chaplin hurriedly slipped a hand between her legs.

"I'm supposed to bleed later today too," Benja said. "It's because we're true soulmates."

"I've got to go," Chaplin said, brushing her other palm swiftly down Benja's arm. "See you tomorrow?"

Benja sat for a while, gazing after her. Even after she got home, she could feel exactly where Chaplin had touched her arm.

That night after she'd gone for a swim, she lay in bed and thought of Chaplin. She imagined the smell of her between her legs, the way her small breasts would settle softly against her palm, if she touched them. The thought of how they'd feel under her hand put a strange sensation in her body. For the first time in her life, Benja wanted another person to be close to her.

"Dumb piece-of-shit needle," Chaplin growled, jerking at the thread so that all the stitches she'd been trying to embroider evenly on the white handkerchief were tugged into one small clump. She dropped it into her lap, took a few deep breaths, and went on in a calmer voice. "My hands are too stupid for this. My mama gets so pissed off with me." The rat sniffed at the pocket square and bit the thread. Chaplin nudged it irritably away.

"Why does it matter if you can embroider?" Curious, Benja sat down to the left of Chaplin on the couch. It was hot. Benja would have liked to be in the water, but she preferred to be with Chaplin. So they were in the house.

"I need to improve my fine motor skills, my mama says. I'm too clumsy, I've got to learn how to control my movements. My homework is making three nicely shaped flowers by the time she gets back."

"I'm no good at embroidery either."

"She'll be really mad if I haven't done them."

"Let me try?" Benja reached out for the fabric and needle, but Chaplin snatched it back. "I *have* to be able to do this," she said vehemently, then immediately apologized. "I didn't mean to get annoyed, sorry, Benja. Did I scare you?"

"Oh yeah, absolutely." Benja laughed, swatting at her. Chaplin swatted back, and then they chased each other through the house and out into the garden, until Chaplin climbed one of the trees, out of Benja's reach. She sat astride a branch, her bare ankles suddenly visible under the two pairs of jeans. There were big red marks on the skin.

"What happened to your legs?" asked Benja, startled. "Doesn't that hurt?"

Chaplin drew her legs up at once. "It's nothing," she said, jumping down from the tree. "See ya—I've got to go home."

Her mothers noticed she was happier.

"Has something happened?" they asked, and Benja couldn't help grinning.

Wera too had observed the change in Benja.

"What's going on with you?"

"I've just been having fun with Chaplin." Benja reddened.

"The girl from the slum?" Wera looked concerned.

"She can embroider too."

"Embroider?"

"And climb and read maps."

"Why don't you bring her along to church one Sunday?"

"Maybe," Benja answered.

It was high summer. The sun beat down ferociously into the garden, which was hemmed in by so many trees that it felt like a saucepan.

"We're being boiled," Chaplin wailed, rolling up one of her sleeves. As far as Benja could see, she was only wearing one pair of jeans and a single long skirt over the top.

"We could go down to the beach?" Benja said. "There's more air, and we can lie in the shade on the rocks—no swimming."

"Let's go on an adventure instead."

"Where?"

"Isn't there anywhere you've always wanted to see?"

Benja considered this. "I'd like to see the water lilies inside the pensives' greenhouse. But that's in the city slum, we'll never find it."

"I can find it," Chaplin said smugly. "We can check the maps. Nice to finally have a reason to use them. Most of the roads are overgrown, but the big ones are usually still there. And there are university buildings, libraries, churches—lots of them are still standing, or bits of them anyway, so we can use those to get our bearings. You stay here and I'll grab the maps."

"We're not allowed into the greenhouses, they're full of pensives."

"That's what makes it fun—we're not going to go running around inside a greenhouse that's got nothing but plants in it."

* * *

Neither of them had to be home before dark. For the first hour, Benja had butterflies in her stomach. There was something dangerous about moving past bodies of water, bogs, and other things they couldn't see on the maps. Several times they stopped to discuss which way to go. Chaplin seemed confident about the direction. She had drawn a big circle around the greenhouses on the map. And Wera's church, which was close by.

"St. Mark's is there," Chaplin said. The rat poked its head cautiously out of her pocket, then crawled back to safety.

"Wera's church is called the Church of Agatha."

"Well, it definitely used to be St. Mark's, but maybe that was a man's name."

"One of my mothers is named Mark."

"Back then men had their own names, and we weren't allowed to be called them. Isn't that hilarious?"

Benja laughed. "Wow, it must have been so weird in those days."

"I bet nobody wanted to hang out in some gross man church, so they had to change the name, before women started being called Mark as well." Chaplin laughed. "Wasn't their god also originally a man or something? But they changed the stories so now it's a woman?"

Benja shrugged. Even though she didn't believe in Wera's Mother-God, she didn't like Chaplin sneering at something that was important to Wera. "They also do a lot to help other people, like in the slum and all that stuff."

"What makes them think people in the slums want help?" asked Chaplin sourly. She seemed about to say something else, but was soon engrossed once more in the map.

They'd been walking for an hour when Chaplin announced they were halfway there. "Look, there's the big library tower. And the ruins are the university. The secret passageways go underneath the road we're standing on. That's where I used to live, before. Back when I was a mole." Chaplin laughed and mimed digging, hands scrabbling in front of her face. She stopped short when two elderly ladies in black, wearing faded red caps, emerged from a hole in the road.

"Quick," said Chaplin, dragging Benja down behind a pile of broken bricks. She took the rat out of her pocket and held it close to her heart.

"It's all right, stay calm," she whispered to it. Benja stared at her in bewilderment. The ladies didn't seem dangerous, although they kept switching back and forth between loud bickering and singing arm-in-arm. Then one of them would shout something again, and the other shouted back. They were old and not walking very well. Chaplin looked horror-struck.

"We can outrun them no problem," Benja said.

"Shh!" hissed Chaplin, crouching even farther down behind the rubble as she clutched the rat. Benja, unsure if this was a game, sat down next to her. She giggled quietly, but stopped when Chaplin hushed her one more time.

Only once the women had been out of sight for several minutes did Chaplin creep furtively back out. "Come on, it's lucky we're going the opposite way."

It took them two hours to reach the Church of Agatha.

They hid behind a large oak and exchanged a grin.

"It's down there." Benja pointed at the greenhouses, which arced against the sky. White-robed pensives went in and out. Many of them held something in their hands. It was like a mound filled with white ants.

"So many misfits gathered in one place. That can't be a good idea," Chaplin said. "Why not spread them out a bit?"

"They're supposed to be learning from the plants. Wera says they have to live in the greenhouses because it's always either too hot or too cold or too humid in there. It helps them to understand that sometimes you have to adapt to life, because life doesn't always adapt to your immediate needs."

Chaplin stared at her as though it was the most idiotic thing she'd ever heard.

"And they have to live in a glass house and grub around in the dirt to understand that?"

They crept down the hill. Running from tree to tree, a mound of soil, a heap of stones that had once been a building, then behind another tree. A pensive walked past without taking any notice of them. Chaplin and Benja glanced at each other in alarm, each stifling a laugh. Benja felt like squealing with delight. Like taking Chaplin's hand, kissing it, hugging her and twirling on the grass.

"Coast's clear," Chaplin whispered, and set off full tilt toward the greenhouse. The coast wasn't remotely clear—there were pensives wandering to and fro, like they'd been doing all along. None of them looked up as the two girls went racing past. Reaching the greenhouse, they both flung themselves behind a bush.

"Do you think they saw us?" Chaplin was practically crying with laughter.

"Oh, only about fifty of them." Benja laughed.

They sat for a moment catching their breath, then crawled on all fours through the plants.

"Do you know where the water lilies are?" Chaplin asked. Benja shook her head.

"No, but if you spot any water, that's probably the right place. If you know what water looks like, I mean." Benja couldn't help laughing at her own joke, and Chaplin's expression made it even better. They reached the end of the greenhouse and brushed the dirt and tiny pebbles off their knees.

"It must be over there, on the other side," Chaplin whispered, still on her hands and knees. "Follow me, hag." She cackled so loudly there was no way the pensives didn't hear them.

"There," said Benja, pointing toward an indoor pool. Chaplin had caught sight of it too. She was elbowing her way forward between the hanging plants. Benja, who couldn't help stopping to touch the gorgeous red flowers that surrounded her, lagged slightly behind. But then she hurried after Chaplin, who was already standing at the edge, looking at the water lilies.

"They're gigantic," she said, poking one of them with her hand. It bobbed lazily on the water's surface.

"They can support the weight of a human being," Benja said, gently stroking the nearest water lily. It was soft and firm. She pushed down on the leaf; it moved, but stayed easily afloat. It was so thick that its ribs were like bulging veins running up its sides. "Do you think I could lie on it?" Benja whispered.

"They look like they could carry an elephant." Chaplin was watching her with interest.

Benja glanced to the right and left. There were no pensives in this part of the greenhouse. She lay down carefully on the water lily, making sure to distribute her weight evenly—partly to not damage the leaf, partly to keep her balance. The lily rocked beneath her, but then found equilibrium and drifted out across the pool. Benja shut her eyes; she was one with the water and the plant. Letting all the air seep out of her, she disappeared into the moment. This was what happiness felt like.

A yell from Chaplin snapped her out of the trance. Sitting up abruptly, she lost her balance and fell smack into the pool. When her head came back up, she saw Chaplin thrashing panic-stricken in the water. A water lily had ripped in two when she tried to lie on it. The leaf must have buckled under her weight. Benja could touch the bottom, so surely Chaplin could as well, but she was kicking her arms and legs, vanishing underwater and yelping in fear as her head broke the surface again. Benja swam hurriedly over, grabbed her under the arms and tried to keep her head above water. For a brief moment they were both pulled under, before Benja managed to drag Chaplin's heavy body to the edge and with a huge effort heave her out of the pool.

Chaplin was bawling uncontrollably, curled up in the fetal position.

"You're safe now," Benja reassured her, putting her arm around her.

"Don't touch me," Chaplin screamed, shoving her away with one hand while she tried to hide her wet body with the other. Her long skirt was soaked and clung to her torso. Her jeans had fallen down. Chaplin tried repeatedly to hitch them up, but the fabric was waterlogged and kept sticking to her skin. Her light-colored underwear had been pulled loosely to one side, and underneath it hung two bags of skin. Benja couldn't stop staring. Another few convulsive sobs, and Chaplin drew her legs up. More baggy skin appeared.

"I think you're hurt," Benja said, leaning forward to get a better look. "Is it painful? You've got something—" She reached out her hand, and Chaplin let out a howl like nothing Benja had ever heard before. Yanking her skirt back down, she pushed Benja away so hard that she tumbled into the water again. She was gasping for air when her head came back up, just in time to see Chaplin get to her feet, stumbling in the wet skirt so that the tattered underwear revealed not just two pouches between her legs but also a bulge. She tugged frantically at her clothes, trying to rearrange them, then raced out of the greenhouse in such blind turmoil that she barged into two basket-carrying pensives. They gazed after her in confusion, picking up the contents of their baskets from the ground.

The rat floated lifelessly past Benja. Drowned.

Suddenly the water felt cold. She got out shaking. She was hyperventilating, her heart pounding, vision going black. Had she really seen what she thought she'd seen? If it hadn't been for Chaplin panicking, she would have been willing to accept that she'd imagined it. After all, there were no males wandering loose.

She'd only ever seen them before in school textbooks, and the Jesus statue. One of her mothers had a painting in her room of a male member and the skin bags hanging underneath.

"It's just a bit of fun," she said, when the other mothers told her it was in bad taste, and that she shouldn't even think about decorating the common areas with stuff like that.

Benja had studied the painting several times. It was exactly what she'd seen between Chaplin's legs.

Not caring if anybody noticed her, she rushed out of the greenhouse. She ran so fast she felt like throwing up, but didn't stop until she was up the hill and standing outside the Church of Agatha. Tears streamed down her face as she went inside. Maybe Wera would be there. Two priests came over to her.

"What is it, little one?"

Benja collapsed in front of them, crying so hard she couldn't speak. Could barely even breathe.

"Isn't that Wera's little disciple?" one priest said to the other. "Go, get her!"

Moments later, Benja heard Wera's gentle voice above her. "Benja, what are you doing here?"

"She's a boy. Chaplin is a boy," Benja wept.

For the rest of her life, she would regret that she had said those words.

Everything that happened next was a blur. Someone came to get her and put her in bed at home. She stayed under the covers for a month. They thought she'd caught something in the pondwater, but Benja knew she was sick with shame: she had betrayed her best friend. Her only friend. Once Benja had gotten used to the thought that Chaplin was deformed, she knew she could have kept her secret, if she'd had time to get used to it. She had been frightened, that's why she'd blurted it out. Wera had said, after all, that the penis was also part of the Mother's creation.

Everybody said she'd done a good thing. A brave thing. She was right to have run straight to church and told them what she'd seen. When they thought they were out of earshot, they murmured to each other that she must have been seeing things. Only Wera believed her and recruited several people from the church to search the slums, trying to catch the male.

"I've heard about him before," she said, but as a Christian priest her word wasn't taken very seriously, and talk soon died down among the general population.

Nobody said anything about what happened to Chaplin, and Benja couldn't ask, because by the time she had recovered from her long bedrest, she'd stopped talking.

Several months went by before she dared go near the sweet clover house again. There were no signs of life at the mint house. No clothes hung out to dry, no trumpets blaring. She snuck back several times, but was greeted only by the blank gaze of the windows in return. Soon she stopped visiting the area at all.

She dreamed every night about her friend. The dreams were less frequent over the years, of course, but never a week went by that Chaplin didn't appear in her subconscious. Dancing with her in her dreams, laughing with her. They kissed. Made love in the sweet clover. She was usually a girl between her legs, but sometimes a boy. The more time passed, the less it mattered.

Benja didn't go back to school after that summer. Never passed her exams. She grew feral, roaming around the slums, to the water and the woods. Her mothers, driven frantic, tried their best. She refused to go anywhere near Wera anymore, although the priest tried doggedly to stay friends. If Wera hadn't told, Chaplin would have been there still, Benja was convinced.

As the years went by, her mothers simply let her take the paths she chose. They stopped asking where she'd been, or why her clothes were torn. She never answered anyway. They gave her new clothes to wear, put out food for her, then went on with the lives they needed to live. But it was clear from the way they looked at her and then at each other how concerned they were.

Benja didn't actually know how she felt. She just was. She cried every day with her head underwater, allowing herself to drift off like a plant, hoping to float so far from shore that she wouldn't be able to swim back in. But she always could.

After ten years, aged twenty-five, she boarded the train and didn't get off until she was in Zealand. All she brought were the shears and the desire to vanish. For a brief moment she felt wistful at the thought of leaving her childhood sea and the neighborhood she knew so well, but she took comfort in the fact that there were plants too that had no need of roots.

She found her way to the old patriarchal district. The slums were the only place she had ever thrived. There she lived off the small animals she caught in makeshift traps, and insects she wasn't sure were really edible.

When the winter came, she crawled into the shell of a house on the outskirts of Vesterbro and gathered enough things to consider it a home. A hole-riddled mattress in the corner, a wonky cup, and a board to eat off. In an abandoned house, she found a knife. She made it through the winter by the skin of her teeth and hoped for better times in spring. When summer came, she was still there. A little to her own surprise. Plants had blossomed around her shack, and there were moments when she almost felt alive. The nights she spent drifting on her back in the old lakes, among tangled plants, seaweed, and flotsam. It was only then and there she could stand to be human.

The few other locals ignored her. Nobody lived in the slum to make friends; they were there to be left alone. She was bothered only by a flock of crows that kept pecking at the seeds she tried to dry in the sunlight. They enraged her. They were small flying hyenas, stealing from a person who already had nothing.

"Shoo," she hissed, and scared herself. What if someone heard her?

The best day was the day she managed to catch one of the crows. She killed it with the shears, plucked its black feathers, gutted it as best she could, and roasted it over a fire. It didn't taste very good. Still, she was pleased, and felt invincible. The next day she caught another. And another. But soon came fall, and before long it was winter again.

She wasn't sure exactly when it dawned on her, but one day she knew she was waiting to die. That this was why she'd left the place of her childhood. So that at least she could spare her mothers the anguish of finding her dead.

From that moment on, she stopped looking for plants to love, or plants from which she could take seeds. She stopped going down to the water. Stopped trying to catch more crows.

Before long she was so thin that even her mothers wouldn't have recognized her. She only had energy enough to sleep. Soon she was letting the crows take what they wanted.

It was in this state that Eldest found her.

If Eldest hadn't found her in the Vesterbro slum, she would be dead by now, she was sure of that. But Eldest had persuaded the other sisters at the convent to let Silence move in.

"She can look after the plants—she's got a wonderful knack with everything that grows, you should see the way the plants sprouted among the rocks where she was trying to live," she said, putting an arm around Silence. "Isn't that right?"

Silence, who wasn't called Silence yet, attempted to smile, but had forgotten how.

"IF ONLY THERE WERE MORE OF US, THERE SHOULD BE MORE of us," Medea wailed, throwing off her dogskin. Dragging Eldest's dead body down the stairs and into the garden was sweaty work. Eldest's foot had bumped into the shelf where Medea kept her elixirs against bad breath. Apparently she fought fire with fire, because the stench of rot had spread throughout the house, so intense that it had followed them out into the garden.

Wicca was still sound asleep on the floor as they carried Eldest past her. Whatever sedative Medea had given her, it was working.

"There should be moonlight, really, but I don't want to wait, not if somebody's coming to take us soon." Medea was still whining. She adjusted Eldest's blue skirt so that it spread out neatly. Silence slid two blue bows into her hair, the ones she had worn when it was thicker. Now the clips were barely hanging on. They placed her on the bench in the garden.

"Since there's no moon, we'll have to use what the sun sends us." Medea stretched out her arms and spread her fingers like antennae, as though to catch its rays.

They positioned themselves on either side of Eldest. Madam swooped down, alighting with a mournful gabble on Eldest's head. For the first time, Silence felt as if she heard its own voice.

"Alone I am a cell, a small part of the earth," Medea chanted. "I send you my love, and I receive yours. Together we are strong."

She rocked her body side to side, and Silence copied her. She gave Silence a knot of lit sage. The smoke was soon drawn up into the winter cold and was not enough to overpower the reek coming from the house. Medea strewed withered leaves over Eldest's body, as well as a handful of dried snakelets.

Silence had attended the burials when the other sisters died and didn't remember having seen the baby snakes before. But since Medea was the oldest now, she supposed she could add whatever elements she thought best. Silence didn't think Eldest would care much for the snakes, actually.

The cold was boring up through the thin soles of Silence's shoes. Besides, she was worried about the boy. He'd seemed stable before they went up to get Eldest, but he might be getting feverish again by now.

At long last Medea was finished with her gesturing and witch song.

They drew a heavy blanket over Eldest, covering all but her head, where Madam still sat motionless.

"Well, that's that. We'll have to bury her as soon as the frost allows," Medea said. Back inside, she came to an abrupt halt in the kitchen. Wicca wasn't where they'd left her. Silence ran into the front room. The boy was still there. Breathing a sigh of relief, she laid a hand on his brow. He was warm. Medea darted from room to room.

"She isn't here!" she panted. "We'll have to search the streets, because if she's still a bit woozy and she collapses somewhere, she'll freeze to death."

They searched for over an hour. She wasn't there.

"She must have made it out, which means it probably won't be long before she's back with reinforcements," Medea said. "We've got to hide the boy." She hurried into the living room. He woke briefly as she picked him up, but soon dozed off again. "And I need to get as much out of him as I can. Can you grab that blanket?"

They put him in the room behind the secret wall, where Eldest had been lying just hours before, switched on the radiator, and tried to help him drink some tea. He coughed weakly and slept on.

"You stay here with him, and I'll go down and prepare for the extraction," Medea said. "It's now or never." She sped as fast as she could down the stairs.

Silence looked at the boy and sighed. Soon he would be taken from her. She lay down next to him and cried without a sound.

She must have fallen asleep, waking to unfamiliar voices in the kitchen. Someone was coming up the stairs; doors were being opened. She jolted upright. The boy was still sleeping heavily. She heard approaching footsteps. Silence scurried into the corner, so that the door would hide her if it opened.

It did.

Through the gap she saw Wicca come in, accompanied by a tall woman. The woman knelt down by the boy on the couch, her back to the door and to Silence.

"He's got a fever," she said, and injected something into his arm. "But he'll pull through."

"Eva, you see that, don't you?" said Wicca. "It's Kali's child. Look at his hair! And when he wakes up you'll see he has the same eyes. Right age too. Do we really need to turn him in?"

The woman put her arm around Wicca. "I'm not sure if I'm as certain as you are, but I guess there's no harm in waiting an hour or two. Why don't we have a cup of something strong—I've brought supplies. The cold here is unbearable. Don't these witches ever heat the place?"

The woman stood up and came back toward the door. As she passed the gap, she caught sight of Silence. They locked eyes. The woman stiffened. So did Silence. Then she and Wicca swept on down the stairs. Silence was left with the shock of having seen a ghost. She had just glimpsed Chaplin.

EVA

There was a throbbing in the stitches between her legs, the way there always was when her emotions got the better of her, although it had been years, decades even, since the final operation had healed. There was nothing to be afraid of. She wasn't even bothered by the scar tissue anymore. Yet she was aware of each and every stitch.

Eva took five deep breaths. Just as her mother had trained her, as a way to make the anger, the shock, the rapid pulse or whatever she was feeling stop. She closed the door to the small convent toilet behind her and sat down on the seat. It was cracked. She only hoped it wouldn't break, because she had to sit down for a moment.

She had just seen Benja.

The walls were closing in around her. She had spent so much time locked up as a child that she felt constricted in narrow rooms. Like this toilet. But right now what was on the other side of the door was more frightening still.

"Are you okay?" Wicca knocked on the door.

"Just a minute." She had to pull herself together. But how? Benja was the only living person who knew her secret. She'd been dreading this day since she was fourteen, running full pelt out of the greenhouse.

Eva took five more breaths. Slipping her hand into her pocket, she felt the rat give her a reassuring nip. Her whole body was throbbing now. She swallowed hard. She had to throw up. She opened the lid, and the smell brought the vomit surging up. She continued until her stomach cramped, then she flushed, the way she'd seen in old films. There was no water.

"Eva?"

"Coming."

She wiped a hand across her mouth and opened the door.

"You look terrible."

"I must have eaten something that disagreed with me."

It might not even have been Benja. Eva tried to put her mind at ease. What would Benja be doing in a witches' convent in the slums of Frederiksberg?

But there she was again, standing behind Wicca, looking straight at her. Chewing on her bottom lip, just as the old Benja used to do. The Benja who knew precisely what was once between her legs. The Benja who could take from her everything she now had.

"Do you have two glasses?" Wicca asked Medea. "We'd like to have a drink while we wait for the medicine to take effect, so that he doesn't have a fever when we take him in. But we've got our own. I'm not having any more of your devil drink."

"I don't feel very well," Eva said. "Is there somewhere I can sit and rest?"

The little witch led her into the front room, where the whole ceiling had birdcages hanging down from it. Most of them were occupied by black crows, which glared sleepily at her. Another kind of bird, one with a blue bow tie, bobbed good-naturedly on its perch. "Rest," it cooed. "Rest. Rest. Rest."

"It'll quiet down soon," Medea said, throwing a blanket over the cage. The bird squawked disconsolately. "Can I have a minute with the boy alone?"

"That's fine," Eva said. It would give her time to recover.

"To say goodbye, of course," the witch added.

Her stomach was still rumbling queasily. Eva tried to focus on the fact that she was a doctor. Eva. A doctor come to fetch a rare thing: a wild boy. She had colleagues who knew her to be capable, she had friends who loved her, she lived in a beautiful round district in a well-organized room. She had carried all of that across the convent threshold. Now Benja had taken it all away. In an instant she was once more the revolting and malformed Eva. Filled with shame and lies.

"Of course you can say goodbye." Eva's voice shook. *Fuck.*

Wicca sat down next to her on the couch.

"Are you going to throw up?" Wicca took a bucket from behind the couch and passed it to Eva. There was birdseed at the bottom.

Benja stood in the doorway, looking at her. Eva's stomach clenched as she tried to retch up something that wasn't there. She closed her eyes and took a deep breath. The smell of animal shit was in her nose. It reminded her of living in the slum.

HER MOTHER HAD ALWAYS SAID THAT WHEN SHE WAS LITtle she'd loved tugging at her penis. From the first moment she was old enough to reach it. Or her *kuk*, as her mother called it, because she was Norwegian, and in Denmark they didn't use the Norwegian word. Just in case somebody happened to be eavesdropping on their conversation, despite their solitary way of life.

"You used to lie there pulling at your kuk bold as brass, it was disgusting," her mother said, and even as an adult, the thought of it made Eva ashamed to the depths of her soul. Even though she had no kuk now, and no memory of having pulled on it.

The shame of being born as she was had been the cornerstone of her childhood. She couldn't tell if it had lessened over the years, or if she'd simply gotten so used to it that it was now an integral part of her personality. At any rate, it wasn't something she thought about every day, not anymore.

But it was her first memory, the shame. That and tall dark-green spruce trees topped with snow, white hills, and the crunch of frost underfoot. She couldn't have been more than three, because by the time she turned four her mother had moved them from the woodland cabin in Norway to the woodland cabin in Denmark.

"We weren't safe there anymore," her mother said, whenever Eva asked why they'd left everything and everyone she knew in Norway. "My mothers were starting to look at you strangely. It was only a matter of time before they figured out what you were."

Eva cringed when her mother talked about her like that, so before long she stopped asking about life in Norway altogether.

Of course her mother's mothers had looked at her strangely. She was a freak.

The years in the Danish cabin, which sat on the outskirts of the Aarhus slum, ringed by trees, bushes, and other greenery—those Eva remembered clearly. Running down the overgrown paths, rolling in the grass, sneaking out to climb the trees. The climbing she only did when her mother napped at lunchtime, or had gone to get more food. Eva was forbidden from using too much of her strength.

"Your muscles are deformed. They'll grow too much if you're active, so you mustn't use them more than absolutely necessary," said her mother, who squeezed her arms at least once a week. Then she would either nod appreciatively or breathe in the angry way she had if she thought she could feel a change.

Eva remembered her mother sprawling naked in the sun, in the little patch of ground they'd cleared outside the cabin. She remembered longing to throw off her underwear, to feel the grass tickle her buttocks and the sun warm her groin, but she wasn't allowed. She had no memory of trying to take them off, but she must have tried, as a young child. Underwear had to remain on. Always. And she had to wear two pairs.

The cabin wasn't far from the water, and every morning, all year round, they went down to the shore, where her mother undressed and went into the water.

"To wash away the miseries of the night," she said. Sometimes she would take a dip and come straight back to Eva, waiting obediently by the water's edge. Other times she'd float around for hours, disappearing under the surface until Eva screamed in fear, terrified she'd never see her mother again.

"Calm down," her mother soothed her, after she resurfaced and waded ashore. "I'm rotten inside and out today. It takes a while to be cleansed."

Eva wasn't allowed in the water. It was a rule that could not be bent.

"The tape might disintegrate," was the explanation, which was plausible enough. The only tape they could ever find was old and didn't stick well. Water would make it peel off, and her kuk would become visible in her underwear. Which was the worst thing that could happen. The very worst.

"You never know when someone else might come along," her mother said. "If they spot the kuk, they'll take you. And you'll never see me again."

So water was dangerous, it was fluid lava; water meant the world as she knew it might fall apart.

All Eva's nightmares revolved around somebody discovering the kuk. It peeped out from the edge of her underpants. Or dangled suddenly from her shoulder. Once it hung out of the middle of her forehead; other times it sat on the table or adhered stubbornly to her mother's arm. No matter where it appeared in the dream, the outcome was the same. Somebody saw it, and Eva was dragged shrieking from her mother and flung into a hole where she couldn't breathe. Often, in the dream, her mother didn't even bother to fight for her. It was Eva's fault, after all, for allowing the kuk to escape. But Eva had no control over the kuk. None whatsoever in her dreams, and sometimes not even when she was awake.

It was a loathsome thing to be given.

"Why am I the only one that has one, why don't you?" Eva had cried as a child.

"You were born not quite right, baby," said her mother gently. "We'll fix it, if I can figure out how."

Those were the good days.

If her mother was in a bad mood, if Eva had washed, or if the tape gave way before she could put a new piece on, so that the kuk could be seen under the fabric, she stared at the kuk with revulsion. Sometimes her mother would jab at the bulge with her finger, twisting her bottom lip, with a face that looked as though she was about to throw up.

Eva never touched it. When she was old enough to tape it up, she always kept a rag between the kuk and her hand, so she wouldn't be soiled if she touched it. When she dabbed it after peeing, she was careful not to let her hand come in contact with it. The times it did, she washed her hands until the skin was fiery red.

The first thing she did when she woke up was sniff her hands to make sure they didn't smell of kuk. When they did, she wept with disgust.

They lived in the cabin until at last the structure was so rotted and aged that one fall a storm effortlessly peeled off one side of the roof. Eva was ten years old. With the wind squalling and the rain lashing down, her mother didn't dare stay in the house, so they spent a long, chilly night in the shelter of the trees, which groaned above them. Eva clung to her mother under blankets that weren't waterproof, terrified the rain would loosen the tape between her legs and that the rest of her life would come crashing down around her ears as well.

Meanwhile her mother sat with stoic composure, legs crossed, defiantly berating the storm.

"You're not getting me," she shouted at the gusts of wind that threatened to knock them over.

When Eva woke from a restless and shallow sleep, the storm had dropped, and her mother was rummaging through their belongings, gathering up the most important things.

"We're not safe here anymore," she said, tying a blanket full of kitchen utensils onto Eva's back. "We've got to move on."

They moved into the old subterranean passageway near the university buildings in Aarhus. Her mother had once heard a rumor about its existence, although she'd not believed it. They said rats lived there, and beasts, and people who did not wish to be seen.

The rumor was true. The old underpass and the little rooms connected to it, which centuries ago had been used for student parties, as cloakrooms, toilets, and other things, were now inhabited by small animals that darted into hiding when Eva and her mother entered, dragging their belongings. The few humans who lived there looked away. It wasn't hard to find a room where they could live alone. Few people wanted to spend a life in darkness.

The underground passageway was a stark contrast to the freedom of life in the cabin. There was no need to worry about Eva using her muscles too much, because there was nothing to use them on.

They slept on two thin mattresses left by a previous occupant. Cooked over a small fire pit in the corner, where a makeshift chimney had been dug through to the open air above. The smell of smoke lingered for days after they made food. Which they didn't, much. Usually her mother would find something for them to eat in an abandoned building, or at the places where kindly souls fed the animals in the Aarhus slum. A park surrounded the dilapidated university buildings; in days past students had lounged and read there, or kissed behind the trees. Now it was the animals' turn to enjoy the green hillsides.

Eva shifted her feet when Wicca brought in two glasses and sat down at the other end of the couch. She took the glass of aquavit handed to her, although she didn't want it. The nausea wouldn't go away. Benja had vanished, which made Eva more uneasy than when she'd stood there staring. She'd probably gone to tell everybody Eva's hideous secret. And that they could find her in the front room of the convent.

The little witch in the gold cloak was busy in the kitchen. If Benja had said something to her, presumably she would have reacted. Gotten frightened, gone to fetch someone, threatened her. The witch might be campaigning for better conditions for the men at the Center, but there was no way she'd want someone with that much testosterone roaming around at will.

Benja flitted across the doorway, glancing briefly at Eva before she was out of sight again. Were they coming to get her now? Tears stung behind her eyelids, threatening to settle in the corners of her eyes and slide down her cheeks.

"I've had a thought," Wicca said, looking expectantly at Eva.

She couldn't cry now. There was no reason for her to cry. Wicca would start asking questions.

"Hello?" Wicca batted Eva's knee. "What's up with you? It's like you're not even here."

Eva knocked back the aquavit in one gulp. It burned all the way down her gullet and into her stomach. She leaned back, shut everything out. Giving the spirits a chance to stay down.

"Why are you being so weird?"

"What thought?" Eva forced a smile.

"You know how my mother's upset that we don't have a real

male for the Easter ritual, and she's angry with you because you won't help get one from the Center?"

"It wasn't my decision that we're not talking anymore." Eva closed her eyes. The aquavit squelched uncomfortably in her stomach.

"Well, now she's angry with me too, because I had a little mishap at church, with that bewitched snake I bought from Medea. My mother said they might not let me back." Wicca wiped away a tear. "What am I going to do if I can't be a priest? I mean, I'm a Walborg!"

She poured them both another aquavit. Eva took the glass, but put it on the floor. Wicca downed hers.

"I was thinking the two of us could bring her a male. The boy, I mean. She'd have to forgive us then. Kind of perfect timing, don't you think, this little male showing up? It's the Mother's will."

Wicca got up and started pacing around the living room. One of the crows squawked testily as her head bumped into its cage.

"And it's Kali's. I know it's a son, and it's not the same as a child. I know I can never have a real relationship with him. But it's all I've got left of the woman I loved. The woman who's dead. I can't just give it up again."

Eva cleared her throat. It had been a relief, not having Wicca's mother breathing down her neck for the last couple of years. She had always felt as though she owed her something, and the church. She probably did.

"I promise I'll look after him," Wicca continued. "He can live with the extra snake. The verger and I can take turns keeping watch. Even if I have to sit by his pen every night for the rest of my life!"

"You can't have a boy in church, Wicca." Eva stretched her legs wearily. "It's too dangerous."

"My mother's right—we'd be the most visited church in the whole country if we had a male at the Easter ritual."

"He might look sweet right now, but before you know it he'll be stronger than you, and unpredictable. Men are slaves to their hormones. They do whatever their testosterone demands of them. You can't raise them like girls, make them understand what's best for the community. Their gender trumps all rational thought."

"We can medicate him. You can teach me everything you know about keeping them calm, like you do with the young males at the Center."

"Males are only allowed in captivity. You're not going to get permission from the Center or anyone else to keep a man just because of a religious event."

"But nobody knows he exists. If we don't ask anybody, we're not breaking any rules."

"What will you do to make sure nobody finds out about him?" Eva asked tiredly.

"I can dress him as a girl," Wicca said, smiling, "and teach him to speak in a higher voice. It's not that hard to fool people."

Eva looked down. Wicca kept going. "You can get the medication from the Center—nobody's going to notice. Anyway, they love you so much you wouldn't get in trouble even if they did."

"They don't all love me. My new manager doesn't, for one."

"I thought you and Nanna were best friends—practically joined at the hip? Or did that change after she got promoted to manager?"

Wicca picked up Eva's glass and downed it. "I'll go and see if the boy's any better," she said, heading toward the door. "Think it over. You'll see this is a unique opportunity—it's as if it's been sent straight from the Mother."

Eva put her feet on the floor. She tried to stand up, but had to lean back again instead. She wanted to get away from here. From the truth, from Benja, the convent, the boy, and Wicca's absurd suggestion.

When she got up that morning, she'd thought her only problem was the one she had with Nanna at the juvenile unit. If Benja shared her secret, if it got back to Nanna, Eva's life was over. She'd lose everything she'd built. The mere rumor would be enough to jeopardize her career. Nanna would love to see her slip up—would love to have an excuse to fire her.

It hadn't been like that at first.

Nanna was a doctor too. Like Eva, she specialized in the juvenile males. She was a few years older and had worked at various Centers across the country, as well as in Norway, where she'd studied their experimental approach.

"In Norway they provide their males with more space to move around, and they're kept active for several hours a day, both physically and mentally. They're given a say in the groups they mix with too. Not all of the males are interested in that, but among the ones who are, a small but significant increase in the number of non-medication-induced erections was observed," Nanna told them at the job interview. Eva, as the longest-serving doctor on the unit, had been on the hiring committee. She had advocated strongly for Nanna's appointment, given her experience with this experimental approach. The fact that Nanna had shiny hair, smelled of lemon balm, and allowed her gaze to rest a fraction longer on Eva than on anybody else at the meeting—that might also have had something to do with it. But mostly it came down to professional interests.

On Nanna's first day, Eva had butterflies in her stomach. She put on the sweater with the embroidered trim, which she knew accented her breasts nicely, and painted her lips with the rose-colored lipstick Wicca always said made her eyes sparkle.

Nanna had lit up the moment she saw her. "I'm really looking forward to working with you," she said, putting a hand on

Eva's arm. She could feel its warmth through the fabric. "You're very good at your job, they tell me. Perhaps you can teach me a few tricks." Nanna ran her fingers over the embroidery on the sweater. "This is lovely—did you do it yourself?"

Eva nodded ruefully. "I guess I might as well admit that my hobby is embroidery. I've yet to meet anyone who doesn't roll her eyes the minute I start talking about it."

"I'd love to hear more about how you make such tiny, delicate stitches." Nanna smiled. "And why."

That was the first time they ate lunch together. It lasted ages, because they were laughing so much. Before returning to the juveniles, they agreed to have lunch again the next day. Soon it was a habit. One Eva lived for. Not since Benja had she been so at ease in the company of another human being.

Nanna's way of working with the males was inspiring. She played with them, teased them affectionately, and whenever she walked into the common area the juveniles would flock to her with devoted faces. She was never afraid of them, like many of the other staff, who wanted the males pre-medicated and guards standing by before they'd go anywhere near the herd.

"Why would they try to hurt me?" Nanna said when she was questioned. Most people thought she was overconfident. Naive.

"I bet the first women didn't think the males of their own species would attack and subdue them for centuries either," their colleagues said. "Just you wait, one day it'll go horribly wrong. It always does, with human males. At some point their emotions overwhelm them." Others agreed, sharing their knowledge of soccer matches in the olden days. "Have you ever seen footage of sports events? Men used to gather by the hundreds. Their hormones can't cope with emotions like defeat, so if their team lost they used to lash out at the opposing fans. If one of the males starts to feel a sense of ownership over you, they'll be at each other's throats."

Eva knew that several of the guards and carers smirked about Nanna behind her back. But Eva thought she was wonderful with the males and was always singing her praises to the management.

"You've got an unusually good rapport with them too," Nanna said to Eva, during the long shifts they shared. "It's as though you expect them to answer when you ask them something."

The days at the Center felt like a game, all flirtation and talking shop. Under their care the juveniles thrived; even the management noticed that the unit was functioning better than it had ever done before, and workplace gossip was that either Eva or Nanna would be the obvious choice the next time there was a rotation among the senior staff.

Long days in the underpass made ten-year-old Eva fractious. No sun could get in, so she had to make do with the pale shine of whatever light sources her mother could find, most of which had been discarded by someone else, and so glowed only faintly, or not for very long. That year she discovered for the first time what it meant to be lonely. The feeling clung to her until the summer she met Benja, but that was still several years in the future.

Eva spent her time underground taming one of the many rats that had been set loose to clear the area. While her mother was out looking for food, Eva taught the rat to nudge a ball, to balance on a string, and give kisses on command. At night it slept by her side, in a miniature hammock she had made for it out of a pair of underpants she had outgrown.

Her mother hated the rat.

"I saw a male rat the other day eating the face of a female one. We'd better get you fixed, or I might wake up one morning to find you've chewed my face off." She laughed hard.

Eva did not. She tucked the rat into the pocket of her outermost jacket.

Her mother went out every day to scavenge for food, light, and also tape. Their supplies were low and of even poorer quality than they were used to.

"You just sit still," she admonished. "If anybody comes, don't move—and keep the blanket over your legs."

By the time her mother came back, boredom had made Eva angry. "There's nothing to do," she snapped. "Why can't I go outside?"

"You know why. Stop whining."

"I'm not whining," Eva shouted, and she slammed her fist into the wall behind her. "I can't take it just sitting here anymore." Anger roared through her, fizzing into the far tips of her fingers. Her mother observed her thoughtfully, then squatted down in front of the mattress she was lying on.

"I've been dreading this day since the moment I decided to keep you."

Eva looked at her through narrowed eyes.

"Next month you'll turn eleven, so this is probably the testosterone inside you starting to wake up," her mother said. "Take a deep breath in and out. Don't let it get the better of you."

It frightened Eva to see her mother so grave.

"What's testosterone?" she asked, as tears welled up. It was bad enough she had the kuk—now she contained other dangerous things as well.

"Testosterone is what makes you a male. I think we've got our work cut out for us."

Eva shook her head. "Please don't let that happen, Mama. I don't want to have the kuk *and* be a male." She was crying uncontrollably.

Her mother put a reassuring arm around her. "I've got a plan, I'm just not ready yet. While we wait, it's important to be careful no one finds out, and to never speak to anybody."

"I only talk to the rat."

"And you've got to practice reacting to the testosterone. If you feel yourself getting worked up, you've got to push it back down, never give it any room." Suddenly her mother thumped her, hard, on the thigh.

"Ow!" Eva gasped.

"Does that make you angry?"

Eva shook her head.

"Good," said her mother, satisfied. "From now on, we'll have to train. And stop those tears, someone might come in. Everybody knows males are more sensitive and react more strongly when they're upset. You don't want to get people thinking."

She had begun to hit Eva without any warning. On the arm or leg, at first, before waiting to see her reaction. Once Eva had learned to control that feeling, she began to slap her when she least expected it. Sometimes even at night. Other times her mother stabbed her with a needle, and when she got older, she burned her ankles.

"Are you angry now?" she always asked, watching attentively. The first times, many times, Eva roared in shock and pain and also rage, of course. But she learned to control everything she felt, and in time she could take punches, kicks, needles, and coals with no response but a friendly smile. Her mother was proud.

"Soon there'll be nothing left to do but take care of *that.*" Her mother cuffed her, hard, in the groin. She struck the parts that were most tender, which would normally have brought tears to Eva's eyes. Now she nodded and smiled.

"Yes, Mama," she said. "Now how about I make us some tea?"

Her mother got the job she'd been hoping to get, in order to carry out the plan. She was assisting at the hospital. Probably cleaning, Eva thought as an adult, but her mother made it sound as though she were saving human lives.

"It won't be long before I know so much about surgery that I can remove the kuk and make you normal."

Eva had flung her arms around her mother's neck the day she came home and said those words.

"Oh, soon, Mama."

"I just have to read up a little more," her mother said, and she dragged home stacks of old books from the hospital's musty library.

"Are you allowed to take those?" Eva asked.

Her mother yawned. "Nobody's going to find out. I've never actually seen anybody in that part of the library. The dust is so thick it's not easy to tell what anything is. The books are old knowledge about men. Nobody's interested."

Eva flipped through one of the books. "Be careful, that's hundreds of years old," her mother said. But she let her daughter read them, and over the next three years, Eva learned as much as her mother had about how to surgically remove kuks, as well as other things you didn't want to be there.

"Why on earth would anybody want to remove their breasts and become a male?" Eva asked in bewilderment one day, when she came to a chapter about a woman who desperately wished to be a man. It made so little sense that she couldn't help laughing. And her mother laughed too.

She brought home other books for Eva. Mathematics, and languages with strange words that she tried to sound out in the long hours when her mother was at the hospital.

Once a month she was allowed outdoors. Especially in winter, when her layers of clothing attracted less attention. Eva lived for the hours when she saw the sky and felt the air swirl around her cheeks; when the sun dazzled her eyes and she watched beautiful people go by without knowing what she was. She was rapturous at the world's existence.

"Stop that," hissed her mother. "Do you want everyone to know?"

Eva hardened herself and took her mother's hand. Together they strolled down the old tracks where the area called Trøjborg had just been combed, after the last pieces of the past had vanished into the ground. More beautiful roundhouses with egg-shaped roofs had shot up like toadstools every time Eva went outside.

"Do you think we'll be able to live here one day too?" she asked hopefully.

"Maybe once we've fixed you."

It was always with a heavy heart that she let herself be guided back down into the tunnel.

"We could always move to Norway, Mama," she said, the day after she'd been allowed aboveground for an hour. It was years since they'd talked about her mother's homeland.

"Norway?" Her mother snorted, and Eva was immediately cowed. She hadn't noticed it was one of her mother's bad days. "What do you want to go there for?"

"It's colder in Norway," Eva tried, although she knew the conversation would go nowhere. "I could be outside more, because I'd have to put more clothes on anyway."

"Norway's no better than here. Yes, they're a bit more liberal when it comes to rearing males, but they'd never accept one free-range."

"We could try. Maybe your mothers would like me?"

"They'd tie a stone around your kuk and throw you into the fjord."

A tear was threatening to run down Eva's cheek, and instantly her mother slapped her. She stood straighter.

"You're right, Mama, we'll stay here." She put her hand into her pocket, where the rat nibbled at her finger.

All those hours alone took a toll on Eva. She couldn't be bothered to get up when her mother left. Couldn't be bothered to get up when she came home. She lost interest in the books. She'd flick through them sporadically, but couldn't muster the energy to flick the rat away when it started gnawing at the pages, even though she knew it would infuriate her mother. Probably it would mean another slap, or a kick to the shin, but she'd almost rather that—at least that was a real thing, happening. In any case, she no longer felt physical pain.

Two elderly women in black had moved into the room next door. They both wore red caps. Eva had only seen them from the back. When she heard them coming, she hid under the blanket, although she'd never caught them peering in. They didn't seem dangerous, but you never knew. They bickered all day long. Except when they were laughing. Or singing loudly about Jesus and the Mother.

At times when Eva was most bored, she would repeat the words they said. They spoke Danish, not Norwegian, as she and her mother did. But if she was ever going to fit in in one of the round districts, she'd have to know the language. She tried to make it sound the way it did when they talked. Their words were soft, the Aarhus rhythms heavy and fun to mimic.

"Oy, was it you who took my shorts?" one of the ladies shouted.

"Oiwassi choo took my shors?" Eva whispered, taking pains to pronounce the words exactly as the woman had.

"Don't you fucking call me a hag," the other one replied.

"Donchoo fuckin callmeeya hag," repeated Eva.

"I didn't call you a hag, you hag."

Then they laughed hoarsely at each other, while Eva was annoyed she didn't understand what *fucking* meant and wished she could ask them to repeat it.

It was never long before they were engaged in a new quarrel for Eva to practice. She'd pretend to be having the arguments with the rat, and after a while she wasn't whispering the words. She said them out loud.

"Who are you talking to?" asked her mother, who had just returned from her job at the hospital.

"Just the rat," Eva said, sliding one of the pages it had gnawed to bits underneath the flimsy mattress.

Her mother set down a new stack of books with a groan. "I found them at the very back of the library. They've got drawings and pictures that show precisely how to remove a kuk." She turned to one of the pages and pointed at an image. Eva gazed at it curiously.

"Do you think you can figure it out?" she asked.

"It might kill you. But at least I'll have given it my best shot." Her mother laughed.

Eva took a deep breath, to stop the anxiety spreading in her belly.

"Removing the little doodah is one thing, but if I'm also going to turn the skin back and make an opening, then pad it so it looks like real genitalia, then I'm going to have to do a lot more reading."

She sighed resignedly. "Well, let's just hope for the best. And now I need a nap. It's been a long day."

Eva nestled up to her mother's back, letting the rat crawl up and down her arm. The two cap-wearing ladies were walking down the corridor, toward the outdoors. Eva watched them go by through the gap in the door, which was so wide her mother didn't even have to open it. She could sidle in and out. During the first year underground, they had been careful to make sure no one saw them. They'd draped a blanket across the gap, but after three years they'd started to ease up on security.

"Hag," the ladies screeched at each other. Irately, at first. But then they laughed throatily, their voices fading up the steps and out of the hole. There had once been a staircase and a door, but now it consisted of a piece of metal that you dragged aside when you wanted to go in or out.

Eva felt a stab of longing—she wished she had someone she could call a hag, someone who would laugh about it. Who might swat at her because it was fun to swat, and not just because she wasn't allowed to feel it.

Her mother slept all evening and all night, and by the time Eva woke up she'd gone to work. There was bread on the table, which her mother had brought home from the hospital along with the stack of books. One whole side was covered in mold. Eva picked off the green bits and put them in front of the rat, then began to nibble on the part that was still light-colored. She found some lard in the cupboard, which she smeared on and ate without caring that it tasted rancid. The ladies next door were already squabbling.

"Fuckin killoo in yoor sleep, I will," Eva repeated to the rat. The rat didn't take the threat seriously, still munching away at page seventy-three of an ancient mathematics textbook that evidently tasted better than the bread. Eva couldn't blame it. As she sat down on the bed, she felt the tape come loose and the kuk fall out. She shuddered. Eva hated it when it moved. Rummaging around in the corner for another roll of tape, she discovered they only had one left. There was hardly anything on it, and it was the worst kind. Her mother had said several times she'd take some from the hospital, but she hadn't done it yet.

"You'll just have to stay under the blanket," she said, not understanding that Eva mostly taped it back for her own sake.

She sat down on one of the two chairs that had been there when they moved in. Tore a strip of tape off the roll and stuck it to the end of the kuk without touching it. She pulled back in a practiced motion, positioning it and the two limp balls between her cheeks. But the stupid tape slipped, and the kuk slapped lazily onto the chair.

"Ugh," hissed Eva, and at the same moment she glimpsed the back of the two hags passing the gap in the door.

Had they seen the kuk? They were quiet, for once. Then they began to sing one of their songs. Terror spread through Eva. She rushed over to the bed, crawled underneath the blanket, and tried to breathe slowly so she wouldn't react. It didn't help. She was shaking with fear; she didn't even notice the rat chewing on her hair. She had to get out of there before they came back with reinforcements. They would toss her into the hole, and not even her mother would help her out of it.

Quickly she packed up the bread and rat. Put on underwear that was technically too small for her now, but which was as constricting as possible. Without the tape the kuk was visible, but two pairs of underwear and the woolen skirt covered all the bulges. Minutes later she was hurrying down the walkway in the opposite direction from the ladies.

SHE FOUND A WINDOW AJAR IN THE OLD LIBRARY TOWER ON the other side of the road and managed to squeeze herself through. For reasons that were perhaps mostly nostalgic, the tower had been renovated whenever cracks appeared in the wall or the roof lost a tile. Nowadays it was a museum devoted to patriarchal-era research and other superstitions, but from what Eva had seen, there was never a line to get in. In fact, she'd never noticed anybody going in or out through the door. Her mother had told her an elderly woman came and opened up every day, sat there for a few hours, then went home before dark.

Eva closed the window soundlessly, sat on the floor, and let the rat out to look around. Her heart was thudding so hard she was afraid the lady upstairs would hear it.

The room was square, ten or so feet along each wall. One was covered by a bookcase full of cardboard tubes, boxes, and some books. In the opposite corner was an old sink with a rusty basin. Otherwise, it was empty.

The rat darted away, but kept coming back to make sure she was still there. From time to time she peered furtively out of the basement window, which had a view of the hole leading down to the university underpass.

It was still several hours until the time her mother usually returned. *How quickly would the cap-wearing ladies sound the alarm?* she wondered. If she was lucky, they hadn't seen anything, and she could sneak back home later. Preferably before her mother discovered she'd been gone, so she wouldn't have to explain the accident with the kuk.

As darkness fell she heard movement upstairs, a click as the door was locked, and footsteps receding from the library tower. The museum lady hadn't noticed her. She stared appraisingly out of the window. All was silent. The cap-wearing ladies had probably come home without her realizing and were already bickering away in the room next door. She'd been scared for no reason. Eva couldn't help laughing at herself.

Just as she hoisted herself up to climb out of the window, she heard a vehicle. It was an unusual sound, especially in the slum. The roads were bad, where there were any roads at all. It wasn't easy getting past the rubble and other debris scattered around the buildings. Private modes of transport weren't used much outside the slums either—if you were going somewhere too far to walk, you took the train.

Startled, Eva dropped back onto the basement floor. The engine cut out by the underground passage. Cautiously, she looked outside. Three people got out. Two of them were the ladies with the caps. The third was dark-skinned, with a high ponytail in long, snakelike coils down her back. She wore a green cloth over her shoulders with a yellow *W* on either side. Eva's heart was pounding. Her mother would be getting back from work soon. She knew she shouldn't cry, but she couldn't help it. How could she have been so reckless with the kuk? If they couldn't find Eva, they'd probably take her mother. They might throw her in a hole, even though she didn't have a kuk, just because her daughter did. For a moment she considered running out there, revealing herself to save her mother. But she was too much of a coward. She cried about that too. The rat fidgeted in her hair. She kissed its head, wiped her nose on her sleeve, and looked out of the window.

Her mother had arrived. She was standing beside the dark woman with the ponytail. The hags were nowhere to be seen. Her mother gave a strident laugh. After a little while the ponytail got into the vehicle and drove off the same way she had come.

As soon as she was out of sight, her mother rushed down into the hole. Eva sat down on the cold basement floor. She had absolutely no idea what to do next.

She woke up as the sun was rising. The rat was scattering shreds of paper. Eva took out the bread and ate the last of it.

It wasn't yet fully light. Her mother only set off for work once she could see where she was going, as she always said. Eva looked out of the window. The cover over the hole shifted, and her mother appeared. At the same time, Eva heard steps on the floorboards above. The museum lady had arrived.

Her mother dragged the cover back across, straightened up, and began to slowly tramp down the path that would lead her past the library tower. Eva held her breath. When she was close enough to hear Eva calling, she knocked cautiously on the pane. Her mother looked around, until at last her gaze fell on Eva. For a moment her eyes widened, then she nodded briefly and kept walking. Eva felt like shouting, like chasing after her, but stayed where she was. Perhaps this was the nightmares coming true. Her mother had no intention of helping her, not after she'd let the kuk fall out.

She wept noiselessly on the floor until it got dark again. Not even the rat could make her stop. She felt neither hunger nor the cold, only that she was lost.

After it had been dark for a couple of hours and the lady upstairs had gone home, her mother crawled puffing and wheezing through the window.

"Good hiding place," she said, tossing Eva some bread and a blanket.

"Mama," she whispered, throwing herself into her arms.

Her mother pushed her away. "What were you thinking? Those old crones are convinced they saw a male. They were absolutely beside themselves, crying and screaming. It's a good thing they're nuts. Wasn't difficult to persuade the priest you didn't exist. That you were just a figment of two crackpot old ladies' sick imagination."

Eva couldn't hold back the tears; they trickled down her cheeks until her mother struck her hard across the temple.

"This is a great spot you've found here. I'd better head back to the underpass, or they might get suspicious. Tomorrow I'll put some food outside the window, but otherwise you won't see me until I've found a safe place for us."

She disappeared into the hole across the street.

And then time stopped.

When Eva thought back to the period she spent in the library tower, she could have sworn she was there for months. But her mother said it was only four weeks. Maybe five.

Every day on her way home from work, her mother put a bag of food and a source of light outside the window. Usually the light was only enough for a minute or so, but it was nice to have, for those brief moments when it was so dark she thought she was dead.

Every morning her mother would collect the same bag, now containing Eva's feces. She peed in the rusty sink. She didn't know where the urine went, but she hoped it wasn't somewhere that would give her away.

She cried the most in those early days. Quietly, in the hours that were light. Louder, when she was alone in the building. The rat sat on her shoulder, nuzzling her ear, and if it hadn't been for that, she would have gone insane. She carried books from the bookcase into a corner and used them as insulation on the floor, covering herself with the blanket her mother had brought.

After the first week passed, she ran dry of tears. It wasn't due to any bright spark of life; more that she was gripped by an inner defiance. She was dirty, her skin itched, and her hair fell in matted clumps around her face, getting in her way as she fell greedily on the food in the bags. To hell with everything. Maybe she would die alone in this hole, but at least she'd find something to do until it was all over.

On one of the shelves she found an old rubber band, which she used to tie back her hair. It was a relief not to have it in her eyes—for about half a day, until the rat gnawed the band in two and her hair fell once again over her face. She tried to cut it on the edge of one of the shelves, but it didn't work. Frustrated, she began to search through the various items lying around. The books were moldering at the edges, chewed by animals and dissolved by time. The pages crumbled when she tried to turn them. In the dark hours she would drag some of the metal boxes over to the corner where she slept, ready for when the light came and she'd have to keep still again.

Boredom had won out over loneliness. She eked every last bit out of the boxes, only allowing herself to open one every other day. She wanted to suck all the entertainment she could out of their contents. Unfortunately, most of it was illegible, ground away by time, and what she could read was too dull to hold her attention. Instead she counted words and letters, read it backward, slantwise, and upside down.

The third week she took off all her clothes. The tape had long since given up, so she peeled the sad remnants off and put them in one of the food bags with her excrement. The kuk flopped around in her underwear when she moved. She released it. Let it hang between her legs, disgusting and skinny. She was glad it was too dark to see it and was careful not to touch it. It smelled worse than the rest of her. She tried to walk with her legs spread so the kuk wouldn't slop against her thighs, but it still did. After moving gingerly for a while, she gave up. Nobody could see her in the dark, and she'd probably die down there anyway. She swung her hips. The kuk swung with them. She couldn't help but laugh—it felt so silly. And forbidden. Before long she was strolling openly around the room, letting the kuk flop left and right and into whatever it pleased. In the dim morning light she could make out the contours of the rat, sitting on the table, nibbling on the remains of the rubber band.

"Kuk right, kuk left, kuk up, and kuk down. Welcome to the world's first and only kuk show," Eva sang.

The rat ran up onto the shelf and tugged a few pages out of a book, then set about gnawing. The rubber band had grown too bitter.

Eva paced back and forth across the room, but she got so cold she put her clothes back on. As she dropped down into the corner, she wished she was able to cry. Instead she unwrapped the last hunk of bread from the evening meal. Tossed a piece to the rat.

As light filled the basement room and footsteps sounded overhead, Eva opened another of the boxes from the shelf. Its contents were different from what she'd found in the rest. Inside the box was a stack of folded paper sheets, which she lifted out gingerly. The pages were decorated with crisscrossing lines. Each one had a name. *Åboulevarden, Skt. Clemens Torv, Fiskergyde.* It was an old map of the slum. Crowded with roads that had since been swallowed up by nature. They edged around and among each other, some long and broad, others short and narrow. For hours she turned one of the maps over and over, comparing it with other maps, and soon understood that she was on Victor Albecks Vej. And that she had formerly lived under Vestre Ringgade.

"Ha!" she exclaimed loudly, then immediately put her hand over her mouth.

When she heard no commotion or running overhead, she looked back down at the map. She traced the old roads around the city with her finger, stopping where something sounded interesting. *Cathedral, ARoS museum, the Old Town, Botanical Garden, Greenhouses.* Also in the box were old brochures and magazines, disintegrating from dust and moths and the ruthlessness of time. But much of it was clear enough that Eva could go sightseeing with her forefinger.

She pretended she was bumping into people, stopping a minute to chat.

"Lovely weather today," she said in a bright, quiet voice, making an effort to sound Danish.

"Gorgeous," she answered before quickly correcting herself. "Gooorjus."

The next few days were spent studying the maps, imagining the life that had been lived on those streets under the tyranny of men.

When the lock clicked and the lady disappeared into the slum, Eva packed away the maps, shook off the cold and the silent hours. She played with the rat and went for walks around the room, until at last it all began to feel so small that she scraped a hole in one of the burns on her ankle out of sheer boredom.

The next day, without knowing it, she turned thirteen. Her mother didn't remember either, putting the usual food bag outside the window on her way home from work. Eva spent the day trying to call back the rat. It had scuttled through a crack between the door and the jamb. Kneeling, she tried to peer through. No light came in; it was impossible to see what was on the other side.

When the rat still hadn't come back after dark, she broke the door open and used some of her mother's meager light to reveal a room identical to the one in which she stood, except that the bookshelves were stacked with large tubes and dusty magazines. The rat was sitting at the very top of one of the shelves, with another rat, darker in color. They were eating a piece of cardboard. The strange rat made off as Eva approached.

"There you are," she said affectionately to her rat, which allowed itself to be lifted down. It clung to Eva's hair as she opened one of the cardboard tubes, curious, and drew out a poster of a man with a cane, black hat, and moustache. He surveyed her with mingled earnestness and humor.

All the pictures she had seen of men were either from medical texts or the aggressive images in the schoolbooks her mother had sometimes procured for her.

"Charlie Chaplin," she read at the bottom of the poster. "Do you think that's his name?" she asked the rat. "I like it."

The rat squeaked and darted up the shelf. "You can be Charlie, I'll be Chaplin," she told it. "Are you going to see that other rat again? You're not allowed to like it more than you like me!"

She took the poster into the corner, unrolled it, and put a box on either side to hold it flat. She grabbed a couple of the magazines as well. It was too dark to read the words, but in the few seconds of light she had left, she made out something in the pictures she hadn't seen before. Darkness engulfed the pages before she could really understand what was happening in them, but she felt a peculiar tug in the kuk. Instantly she felt such a surge of disgust with herself and with the pictures that she threw the magazine aside. She lay down on the bed and called over the rat, which thankfully came to her and nestled in her palm.

She woke early the next morning. The rat wasn't there. She called for it softly. It fussed near the gap, and soon it was in her hair. Content, she slept a few more hours, not waking until the lady opened the museum upstairs.

Eva turned onto her side with a yawn and looked at the poster of Charlie Chaplin. She lay on her back and sighed deeply. The hours until darkness fell and she could move around again felt endless. With another sigh she reached for the magazine she'd tossed aside. Men with big kuks were penetrating, erect, between women's legs. Shocked, Eva turned the pages, finding one horrible scene after another, until at first it made the kuk twitch and then made her hands touch it. Afterward, when abruptly it stopped feeling nice, she was struck by a loathing for the kuk that was ten times worse than it had ever been before. In tears, she hurled the magazine as far away as she could, crawled under the blanket, and hugged her knees.

As soon as it got dark, she stood up and put the magazines back on the shelf in the other room. There were piles of them. The ones at the top were dusty and fragmented by time, so it was impossible to see what was happening in the pictures, but a few layers down, all the foulness came out. Some were less violent: they were black and white, and mostly of people—of women—standing there naked. Whereas the ones in color showed men tormenting women. She didn't understand why it made the kuk feel good, but she did understand that she shouldn't tell her mother. And that she must never look at the magazines again, and certainly not touch the kuk while she was doing it.

The next morning she touched it again. She wasn't even looking at the pictures.

"I'm disgusting," she cried to the rat, which had eaten one of Charlie Chaplin's legs while Eva was under the blanket, too ashamed to show her head.

The rat didn't care. It pattered up her neck and settled down to sleep in the hollow between her chin and the bulge on her throat that had slowly begun to grow.

That night there was a tap at the window. Eva woke with a start. She crawled, terrified, to the other end of the room, certain she had been discovered and was about to be taken to the hole. It was probably what she deserved, anyway, after having her fun with the kuk. The rat followed. She hid her face in her hands and tried to breathe without making a sound.

Another tap.

"Eva," her mother whispered. "Are you there?"

Eva lifted her head in surprise.

"We're leaving."

It took Eva a moment to understand what her mother was saying in the dark. She hurried to snatch up the maps she had looked at the most.

"Coming," she whispered toward the window. A minute later she climbed out, with the rat in her hair and the maps clutched to her chest.

"Oh, for—you've still got that thing, have you?" her mother said, pointing at the rat. "And you'll have to carry all that crap yourself, if you absolutely have to bring it with you. I've got a bag hidden in the bushes behind the corridors, you'll have to carry that too."

Concealed by the dark, they walked down what Eva now knew had once been called Ringgaden. When the sea blocked their path, they turned left.

"I found a house for us in the Risskov slum," her mother said, scowling with disapproval at the rat perched on Eva's head. It was looking out across the water, which glimmered in the moonlight.

It was their first morning in the Risskov slum. There were only two houses in the neighborhood still standing amid the mounds of stone, old gardens grown wild, and abandoned vehicles, now upended and staring vacantly out of the earth. The house her mother had chosen for them had once been two stories, but the second had collapsed onto the first, which was evidently supported by strong foundations and determined pillars, since it hadn't given way under the weight.

They had slept on the floor under the same blanket. Her mother wouldn't let the rat anywhere near, so Eva kept it secretly under her top, waking every hour to make sure it was still there.

"We had it good in that underpass. It was warm, out of the way of prying eyes. Nobody asking questions, and no roof threatening to bury us alive. It was stupid of you and your kuk to ruin it."

Eva cleared her throat. Then she cleared it again. It had been a while since she'd spoken to another human.

"It didn't do much for your conversational skills, did it, sitting in that basement?" Her mother gave her a cup of tea.

"Jesus, you stink." Her mother wrinkled her nose. "As soon as I can find some more water, we're going to scrub you till your skin bleeds."

They sat down on two chairs, which creaked beneath them. Eva put the hot tea on the table between them. It was more stable than the chairs.

She wanted to share all the thoughts and experiences she'd had in the basement, but she'd lost the habit of talking to someone who could answer, and the idea made her nervous. Besides, she didn't even want to think about what would happen if she mentioned touching the kuk. Her mother might throw her into the hole single-handed.

"Are you going to say anything, or what?"

"I . . ." Eva began.

Her mother looked at her expectantly. "Yes?"

"I think . . ."

Her mother poured herself more tea impatiently. "What do you think?"

"I think we should hurry up and get rid of the kuk. Then we can go and live in that new round district at Trøjborg."

Every hour she wasn't working or sleeping, her mother sat on the small raised platform outside their house and read the medical books. Once it must have been a porch, although most of it had sunk into the ground. Previous residents had laid new slabs, so there were still parts of it you could walk out onto from the kitchen door.

Underneath the house was a basement. You could go in, but it wasn't possible to stand upright.

"If you go down there, it's at your own peril," said her mother. "Whole place could come down around your ears at any moment. Still. Then at least I wouldn't have to keep reading about men's revolting anatomy."

Eva couldn't stay away from the basement. It was filled with things she'd never seen before, although some of them she'd read about, like the trumpet. While her mother studied, Eva tried to get a sound out of it. She blew and blew, but the air simply passed with a sigh through the brass.

She sat down with it in her lap beside her mother, who turned a page and squinted, examining a picture that could be unfolded out to double size. It was a drawing of an enormous kuk, with arrows pointing to the places it was supposed to be detached from the body. In this picture, the two bags had already been removed.

"This won't be easy," her mother said, stretching. "The worst part is that I only get one shot. And it says you're supposed to have injections of estrogen before the operation. Maybe I can get something at the hospital." She yawned. "I need a nap—grab me that blanket, will you?"

She had washed Eva and all their things in the stream, and they had both carried water home in whatever they could find that was watertight.

Eva went and got a blanket, which luckily was dry by now. She placed it over her mother, who was already snoring, then dozed off herself against the doorframe. She was soon in the middle of one of the dreams she'd started having a lot of since the basement. The kind where the kuk moved without assistance, and tried to get out of the tape, out of her underwear, and into the open. Demanding that she touch it.

"Disgusting!" her mother screamed. She had woken up while Eva was dreaming. The slap hit her ear, and for once it made Eva flinch.

"And you're actually outside, where people can see it," her mother shrieked. "That kuk's coming off even if it kills you!"

The next day, Eva managed to get a sound out of the trumpet.

The slum was pitch-black when the sun went down. The only light they'd seen was in the house opposite—the other one still standing. A small, pale light that was gone the next time Eva looked. It was only in the beginning. Then it stayed dark.

When her mother was at work, and she was supposed to stay indoors, she crept up the path to the house. She knew she shouldn't, but curiosity drove her to be disobedient. Besides, she'd lived successfully in hiding for so long in the basement, undiscovered by the footsteps upstairs, that she didn't see why she shouldn't be able to sneak up and spy on whoever had lit that light.

The woman was lying in a funny position on the couch. Her eyes stared vacantly into space, and a dark fluid oozed out between her legs and onto the upholstery.

Eva went back and kept on practicing making sounds with the trumpet.

A few weeks later, the dead lady was carried out by a group of women all wearing snake-green stoles around their necks. They were yammering the same songs as the crazy ladies with the caps used to sing. That night, the rat had nine babies in Eva's bed.

At first she tried to hide it from her mother, but they squeaked too loudly for that to work.

"Should we kill the males?" Eva asked. There were five of them. "The females haven't done anything."

"Hmm." Her mother hesitated, looking with displeasure at the nest of rats. "Maybe I can practice on their kuks?"

Eva had her first estrogen injection one day when the sun was shining. Everything was going to be fine, she knew it. The injection was the start of a new life, a life in which she and her mother would be normal. She sat for a long time in the sunlight behind the house, trying to discern whether there was a *before the injection* and an *after the injection*. Was she like everybody else now? She examined her skin, hair, arms, legs, and feet. She avoided the area around the kuk.

The first thing she noticed, a few weeks after the first dose, was that she had acquired two small lumps on her chest, underneath the nipples. They were sore.

"I've got breasts!" she cried euphorically, rushing over to her mother, who pressed down hard on them both. Eva winced, but didn't pull away.

The next thing she observed was her skin becoming softer. Her sweat began to smell different, sweeter. So did her urine. Her jaw, which had been strong before, was rounder now. The same thing happened to her hips.

"We left it right down to the wire with those injections," her mother said. "Your voice was about to break, and after that we'd never have been able to change you. If we're lucky, you'll also stop growing as quickly as you have been lately."

It was as though the kuk knew its days were numbered, because over the next few months it stopped moving on its own. The few times when it did at night, and white liquid came out with no help from Eva's hand, it felt different. The explosions were not as intense, although they lasted longer and throbbed all throughout her body.

"I think they've gotten smaller," Eva said to her mother as they were eating breakfast together, the third month after she'd started taking estrogen. "The bags under the kuk have shrunk. Maybe it'll go away on its own, and you won't have to cut me?"

"I don't think we'll be that lucky," said her mother, munching on a piece of stale bread. "Small balls still make enough testosterone that the kuk will make you a male."

Eva shuddered. "When are you going to take it off?"

"Soon I'll try to cut one of the male rats. It'll be interesting to see if it survives."

It did not.

"It squirmed, so I accidentally cut its stomach instead," her mother said, as she went out into the garden and threw the little body into the bushes. Eva nervously stroked the rat in her pocket. Now that its young had grown bigger, it was back at her side. The females had vanished into the slum. The five males were in a cage, yelping with hunger.

"I found another book on penile amputation. I'll page through it before I experiment on number two," said her mother, drinking her tea without blowing on it first.

An hour after her mother had removed the rat's genitals, it was still breathing. She smiled in satisfaction and examined the tiny stitches she had made. "Not bad, not bad," she sang. "Go out for a walk, I'd like to enjoy this moment by myself."

Eva sauntered whistling down the path. At last life was beginning.

It was in that mood she met Benja.

That was where she died was the first thing she said to her. Benja had her nose in the stain on the couch, just where the lady had been lying in her own stool.

Then Eva pretended her name was Chaplin.

When she got home that day, the male rat had bled to death, and her mother was in a foul mood. "Didn't I tell you not to wander off?"

When the third rat died too, her mother got so frustrated she gave Eva a double dose of estrogen. "Maybe you're right. Maybe it will shrink the kuk."

They weren't that lucky.

Eva had hot flashes instead, headaches and nausea. Her tender breasts ached even worse, and her ankles swelled. She cried now because Chaplin seemed sad on his poster, which she'd taken from the basement under the library tower. She hadn't noticed it before. She was annoyed with the rat when it ate a corner of the paper, making Chaplin's other foot disappear. The week before she hadn't minded when it ate his entire hat.

At first, Benja was mostly a nice distraction while Eva waited for her mother to finish practicing, so that real life could begin. But as the days and weeks passed, she started to seek Benja out, and not just as a way to kill time. She dreamed of her at night, and sometimes the kuk dreamed too, but she preferred not to think about that when she woke up in the morning. The relief of knowing she would soon be rid of the deformity made her treat the kuk more gently. She didn't hate it as intensely as before, and every now and then she let herself enjoy the moments when it pulsed.

The fourth rat bled out on the day Eva successfully embroidered a red flower that satisfied both her and her mother. When the rat expired, its hindquarters soaked in its own blood, her mother had just been praising her, telling her the estrogen was clearly helping with her fine motor skills, which meant that at least they knew the monster inside was on the retreat.

"Shit," her mother said. "But I've just been reading about another technique I think might work. Why don't you let me try it on you? Just for fun."

"Maybe we should put it off for a bit?" Eva chewed her bottom lip anxiously, poking at the male rat. It toppled lifelessly onto its back.

"The bigger you get, the greater the risk that somebody finds out about you. Take off your jeans."

Eva always did as her mother said, but when she stuck the knife through the skin of her groin, she gave a loud scream and hid behind one of the chairs.

"Good, I'll try it on the last rat first. But you've got to stay inside from now on. No more running around putting up those silly signs or wandering through the slum. Remember what happened with the ladies in the university underpass."

Eva nodded and promised to stay indoors. But the next day she went out anyway, to eat ice cream with Benja in the square after her mother had gone to work. If she wore the jeans plus the skirt, she'd be safe, she thought. Even when the wound opened and she bled through two layers of clothing, she acted like it was no big deal so that Benja didn't suspect a thing.

Maybe if she hadn't gotten cocky everything would have been fine. Or if the estrogen hadn't made her sweat. It was a hot summer, and she felt as though she might literally die unless she got some air on her legs. She had ditched the jeans and put on a loose-fitting skirt instead. She had left the house, even though she'd promised not to. She had walked all the way through the city to the greenhouses, purely to impress Benja with how well she could navigate in the old parts of town. When they reached the university, disaster had almost struck when they ran into the two old ladies. Eva had flung herself behind a pile of broken bricks and dragged down Benja too, her heart thudding so hard she was scared it would burst out of her chest. She should have taken it as a bad omen, but as soon as the hags were out of sight, she shook it off.

"Come on, let's keep going," she said boldly, and they went on toward the greenhouses. They'd been in a giggly mood, crawling through the jungle of plants, past staid-faced pensives. They were still giddy when they reached the pond and found the leaves could carry them. Carry Benja, anyway.

Eva had never been swimming before, in a pond or in the sea. The shock as the water engulfed her made her panic. Up became down, and down became up. She screamed for her life, swallowing a lot of water. By the time Benja finally got her out, she was sobbing with fear, humiliation, and gratitude. She was so agitated that she didn't realize the tape had come off and the kuk had writhed free, until it was too late. When she looked into Benja's eyes, she could tell she'd seen it. She knew the secret nobody could be allowed to know. In desperation, Eva ran. She ran as fast as she could, bowling over a pensive as she went, racing on out of the greenhouse, up the hill, past the university passageways. She cried the whole way. She knew she shouldn't show so much emotion, that it only betrayed the testosterone in her, but she was so terrified she couldn't help it. Besides, things couldn't get any worse than they already were.

Her mother was beaming, walking toward her as Eva came

scrambling through the ruins. Why was she there? She was meant to be at work. Instead of scolding Eva for not being home when she was supposed to, her mother took her hands.

"I've got it. It suddenly hit me at work what I had to do, and I rushed straight home. It worked on the last rat. It's alive. It's woken up and is moving normally. It isn't bleeding. We're ready. We can get that thing off you. Right now!"

"She knows," Eva stammered, out of breath. "She saw it. Benja saw the kuk. Very clearly."

The joy faded from her mother's eyes, giving way to fear and then to anger. "Maybe it's no more than you deserve," she hissed. "And after everything I've done for you."

She threw the books and anything else that might give them away into the lake behind the house. They took only the most important things with them. No more than they could carry. The rat didn't come when Eva called, and after floods of tears she had to leave Risskov without it in her pocket.

By the time the Christians burst into the house, crosses held aloft, Eva and her mother were already making for Zealand as fast as they could. For a while there was a rumor going around that a Christian girl had seen a boy. But it was quickly dismissed as yet another foolish vision dreamed up by religious cranks.

THE MYNA BIRD WAS PERCHED ON THE BACK OF THE COUCH, nipping at Eva's forehead.

"Ow," she gasped, pushing it away, but that only made it fly up and land on the other side of her, where it started pecking at her ear.

Eva felt like smacking the thing but thought better of it. She closed her eyes and didn't react, even as it flapped around her head.

Benja aimed a cuff at the bird, which screeched and flew into the kitchen. She had come into the living room without Eva hearing.

"What's wrong with that bird? It's terrifying." Eva tried to keep her voice calm. She could hear it shaking. Benja's presence made her nervous.

Benja looked at her seriously.

"What kind of bird is it?" Eva tried. It was always possible Benja hadn't recognized her. "I heard it talking before—did you teach it that?"

Benja sat down mutely beside her on the couch. She cleared her throat. Coughed. She seemed about to speak, but closed her mouth instead, staring desperately at Eva.

"Have you lived here long?"

Benja put a hand to her throat.

"I live with Wicca, who's friends with Medea, but maybe you already know that?"

Benja tried to say something, but all that came out was a rasp.

They looked into each other's eyes. In an instant all the years that had gone by vanished. They were Chaplin and Benja, swinging their legs and cracking up over the littlest things. Best friends who lay in separate beds in separate houses, waiting for morning so they could see each other again and come up with more fun ways to pass the time. Both smiled, and Eva held out her hand to take Benja's, then changed her mind and drew it back. The moment passed, and once again she was the person Eva feared most in the world.

Wicca poked her head into the room. "Eva, you coming?"

"I'll be there in a minute, I just have to . . ." Eva dug her nails into her forearm. Right now it was more important than ever to keep her cool and not reveal how flustered she was. Not like at the edge of the pond in the greenhouse, when she had panicked and ruined everything.

Eva left Benja on the couch, went past Wicca, past the dogs, past the little witch, who had set out a long row of test tubes on the kitchen table, each labeled with a red or yellow dot.

She opened the front door and went outside. Let the winter cold creep into her body. The door opened behind her. Benja's footsteps were quiet.

"Why are you following me?" said Eva wearily. "Do you just want to destroy me?"

Benja shook her head.

"What do you want from me? Anything."

"So . . . rry," Benja stammered out in a croaky voice. "I didn't mean . . ." She cleared her throat and continued hoarsely: "Didn't mean to tell anybody."

They stood in silence for a minute.

"Do the others in there know?"

Benja shook her head. "It was . . ."—she broke into a lengthy coughing fit—". . . a shock, I only told . . ." She held up one finger. "But it was enough." She looked down at the ground. "I'm sorry," she repeated.

"You're the only one who knows. My mother did too, of course, but she's dead now."

"I won't tell . . . ever."

"Thank you." Eva felt the tears well up, and straightened her back. There was no reason to make things worse. "I have to see to the boy," she said, and went back into the convent.

When Eva and her mother got to Zealand, they settled in the Brønshøj slum. It was almost entirely subsumed, but there were still a few stubborn houses clinging on, and her mother hid Eva in a ruin on the outskirts while she found a place sheltered enough to survive. After it got dark, the kind of dark it only got in the slums, she led Eva to the ramshackle house she'd found empty. It was a risk, because around that time there'd been another brief wave of nightwalkers in the most neglected areas.

They made it without anybody showing them much interest. Eva lay down in the corner, and her mother made a semicircle out of pebbles around her bed.

"If you step across that line, I swear I'll throw you in the marsh myself, with a stone around your neck."

Eva had no reason to doubt she meant it. Besides, she had no desire to go anywhere until she was normal. Maybe not even then.

"Please cut it off, Mama," she whimpered. "I don't care if I die."

"There's nothing I'd rather do, but I didn't bring the sharpest of my knives. And I don't want to risk getting a new job, because they might have heard about us."

Talk of a Christian girl who'd seen a boy in an Aarhus greenhouse had even reached her mother while she was out searching for food. But people in this part of the country also found it hard to take the Christians and their notions seriously. Surely it was no more than an adolescent girl's overheated imagination. After all, who hadn't fantasized about bumping into a male in the wild, about abandoning herself to the danger of it all?

* * *

They ran out of estrogen before her mother found a new solution. Bristling hairs began to peep out from Eva's chest and legs.

"Mama," Eva said desperately. "Am I turning into a male?"

Her mother examined the hairs closely. Sniffed her armpits and sighed. "We'll have to make do with the tools I have. Luckily, I managed to trade for some anesthetic, but I don't know what we'll do about the estrogen. If we can get those skin bags off, we won't need so much of it anymore, thank goodness. They're pumping you full of testosterone day after day, and it's tough stuff—it never gives up. If we don't take those balls off, who knows what you might do?"

The next day when Eva woke up, her mother wasn't there. Hungry, she looked around for something to eat. There was nothing inside the pebble circle. On the table a few feet away was bread and lard. But she didn't dare go over and take it, although her mother had denied her food yesterday as well, and her belly was rumbling. Maybe it was a test, putting the food out like that; maybe taking it would be the thing that finally made her mother wash her hands of her.

She used the wait to tame a new rat. It was a fast learner. By the time her mother came home a few hours later, it was sitting in her hand. Her mother cast a swift glance at the bread and nodded approvingly.

"We'll do it today. It's good you haven't eaten anything. Your stomach has to be empty, otherwise you'd choke on your own vomit while I'm fiddling with the kuk. There's already plenty of other reasons you might die. We don't need to add to them."

Her mother had brought bandages, needles, and everything else they needed.

"Where did you get that?" asked Eva, impressed. "Did you find a new job?"

"I set up my own clinic, and I've already got some generous clients. Go and wash so we can get started."

"I won't feel anything at all?"

"The male rat stayed still, so if the anesthetic works as well on you, then you won't."

"What about when it's healed?" Try as she might to stop, during all those hours alone in the pebble circle she'd not been able to help touching the kuk.

Her mother shrugged. "The kuk is just an overgrown clitoris. What I don't know is whether you'll be able to feel anything in it afterward. I'm planning to move the top of it. See if I can sew it on, try and give you a clitoris. Life's pretty boring without one. But first and foremost, of course, you need to have a life to enjoy."

I'm going to die was the last thing Eva thought before the anesthesia blotted out her senses. The idea neither scared nor saddened her. Mostly she felt relieved. Best-case scenario, she would wake up and be like everybody else. Worst, it would all be over. But it wasn't really that bad, because there'd be no more fear, no more feeling like she was wrong.

While she was under anesthesia, her mother scraped both the overgrown clitoris and the pouches empty of their filling, throwing the contents to the newly tamed rat, which ate most of it. Then she used the skin to create an internal sheath, shaped a pair of labia and moved the urethra so that it sat approximately where it should. She had to check her own body a couple of times, because the whole area between Eva's legs suddenly confused her.

Eva didn't bleed out or lose the ability to urinate. But her mother had to give up on shaping a clitoris.

"You'll have to find other ways to get some peace of mind," she said, as she was explaining how the operation had gone. "Best to lie still now and not move for a couple of days. I've put a rod up there to stop the whole thing from collapsing. You'll need to keep it in for at least a week."

"So I don't have a kuk anymore?" Eva whispered. She tried to feel for it, but the whole area was wrapped in bandages. Everything hurt, from her belly to the middle of her thighs. "Am I going to be normal now?"

"Assuming you don't bleed to death like the first rats, there's a good chance you will be. By the way, someone's coming over before it gets dark, someone I've got to fix something for. I'll put a blanket over you and hide you behind a screen. Nobody needs to know you exist."

Through a gap in the sheets of cardboard her mother had placed in front of Eva's bed, she saw somebody enter the decaying living room and greet her mother. The person's hair was clipped short and close, the shoulders broad, the arms muscular.

"Let me take a look at it," her mother said, and the person muttered something Eva couldn't hear.

"Yes, it's split. The skin wasn't able to tolerate it. If you're lucky, it'll stretch a little more, but only time will tell. I'll get you sewn up so it'll last at least a month, and then you'll have to come back. Did you bring the estrogen? And the other thing we talked about trading?"

The next day Eva was covered up again, and they had more visitors. Her mother bustled around, and the visitor cried. When there was silence, her mother removed the cardboard and gave Eva a slice of freshly baked bread with the most delicious toppings she had ever tasted.

"I think we hit the jackpot. There's a whole street full of them, and they had no one to do a proper job sewing on their silicone dicks. Well, now they've got me. And they have plenty to trade. Absolutely anything—I only have to name it, and they'll get hold of it. I got something for your pain, the estrogen, and a bag of food. It's too bad I couldn't milk you for testosterone, because I could have sold them that for sure. Anyway, let me see how you're getting on between your legs."

One week later, Eva was on her feet for the first time. It hurt, but the joy of being alive and kuk-less eclipsed everything else. Her mother had removed the bandage and the rod.

"Look, Mama," she said happily, taking a step. "There's nothing dangling."

Her mother smiled vaguely and sat down, tired.

After a month, Eva could walk around the house. Except when there were clients at her mother's sewing business—then she hid behind the cardboard.

They had never eaten so well. Eva only had to say what she wanted, and the next time a manlady came knocking with a problem, it would be brought to her. Only, she had a hard time imagining what she might like. Other than moving to a round district and starting their new life. But her mother put her off whenever she mentioned it.

"The kuk is gone, why don't we move?"

"I can't deal with any of that right now, Eva," said her mother. "Leave me alone."

Soon her mother couldn't even bring herself to get out of bed when the manladies arrived, asking for help with their silicone penises.

"Eva," she called. "Can't you do it? I'm too tired."

Eva peeped cautiously out from behind the cardboard. The manlady, whose name was Lars, gazed at her in astonishment. He had enormous breasts, which lolled half out of his neckline.

"That's my daughter," said her mother, eyes still closed. "She's better at this sort of thing than me."

Eva's hand shook as she went to pierce the needle into Lars's skin.

"Have you never seen a penis before?" he asked.

Eva shook her head.

"Scary sons of bitches, I'll give you that, but this one always does what I tell it, don't you worry."

Eva smiled at him gratefully, took a deep breath, and sewed up the skin that was threatening to tear.

"That's perfect. You've just landed yourself a regular customer," Lars said, giving her a bag of food, estrogen, and the various remedies her mother had ordered to help the manladies with the problems that arose between their legs.

Her mother never used any of them. From that day on, it was Eva who served the manladies. Although she'd never visited the Street, she got to know them all. They weren't the kind of friends she'd imagined she would have when she became like everybody else, but it still felt nice having someone to talk to. Her mother didn't say much now. She slept for a few hours at a time, then lay staring at the wall.

Lars was Eva's favorite customer. He always had time for a chat. Apart from Benja, he was the only person who had ever shown an interest in how she was doing.

He often brought a nursing baby with him.

"Could you hold her a minute?" he said one day when the little girl was crying, and the skin over his penis was hurting too much to rock her back and forth.

Eva was worried that her mother, who had lately become more aggressive about noise, would wake up and complain about the crying. Hurriedly she took the child out of the stroller and held her close. As though by a miracle she stopped crying, reached a hand up to Eva's face, and let it rest there while a smile widened across her little face.

"You're good with kids," Lars said.

"I've never held one before," said Eva, looking in bewilderment at Lars and then at the child, which babbled for a few minutes before drifting off in her arms.

"Little ones can tell what's in your heart," said Lars. "And you must be an angel."

"I don't know about that . . ." said Eva awkwardly, thinking of what she'd been born with.

"My penis thinks so too," Lars grinned. "It's never hung so well before."

Eva placed the little girl into the stroller and sat down between Lars's legs. "It definitely looks better than when I first saw you, but there's something about the angle of it when you're standing with your legs spread." She poked critically at the fake, and Lars grunted. "Maybe it's because you don't have the pouches behind it, they'd give it the right support. Looks a bit lonely, hanging like that . . ."

"Yeah," Lars said, "I know men have testicles, but women aren't interested in those. So I'd rather not go through a painful operation just to put in two useless whatsits."

"I can understand that," Eva said, turning away. She was uncomfortable having her face this close to a penis, even when it wasn't real.

Lars got to his feet and gingerly did up his pants over the fresh stitches. "For someone who'd never seen a penis until recently, you know a surprising amount about them."

"My mother taught me," Eva said quickly. "Everything I know, I learned from her."

"Of course," said Lars. He drew a blanket over the baby and moved toward the door. "See you the next time things go wrong down there."

ONE YEAR LATER, THE WOUNDS WHERE THE KUK HAD BEEN amputated had healed, and it was impossible to tell there had ever been a deformity there. Unless you got too close. She just had to keep people at a distance for the rest of her life.

"Aren't you getting up, Mama? We've got some yummy vegetable pâté in the basket from Lars," Eva tried. But she knew she'd end up eating it by herself.

Her mother didn't respond. Eva snuggled up close, daydreaming about how before long they'd be living in a beautiful oval house. Just as soon as her mother felt better. Neither of them had been out of the house much since they moved into the Brønshøj slum. All her mother wanted was to lie in bed.

"I'm tired," she said, whenever Eva suggested they eat together, or go for a walk, or clean up the hovel they were living in. Eva herself took only short walks around the neighborhood. She preferred not to leave her mother for more than fifteen minutes at a stretch. When she got bored, she played with the rat. Taught it the same balancing tricks as the old one. And she enjoyed entertaining Lars with it when he came to have his penis repaired.

"Animals and kids and people with fake dicks, we know who to stick with." Lars laughed and gave her a long hug before he left. "How are you holding up?" He shot a concerned glance at her mother, who hadn't moved during the hour he'd been there.

"I've got the rat, and I can look forward to your next visit," Eva replied.

"You know where we are," Lars said. "I always have a little one you can look after if you get lonely."

* * *

One day Eva woke to find her mother getting out of bed.

"Why don't I make us some food, Mama?" Eva said hopefully, standing up. Immediately she started rummaging through one of the bags Lars had brought the day before.

"I need to go out."

"Out?"

"They say fresh air does wonders," her mother slurred, pulling a blanket around her shoulders.

"I'll have something ready for when you get home."

Her mother didn't look back as she left. Eva watched her through the dull windowpane, most of which was covered with blankets, cardboard, and other insulating materials. She saw her mother pick her way among the ruins. Tripping over a hunk of masonry, she got clumsily to her feet and disappeared behind some trees covered in greenery.

Eva sat waiting for hours, with two slices of bread and fresh water in the jug. She had combed her long hair and spent the time plaiting her six braids into a single one down her back. When it grew dark, and her mother still hadn't come back, she began to worry. She'd occasionally spent a night away before—but not since the fatigue, when she only lay in bed. For two days, Eva went from window to window, trying to see if she could spot her mother.

The third day she went out. Not very far at first. Then a little farther. The next day she searched the whole of the Brønshøj slum.

Somebody had found her in the marshes, face down. Eva, standing in the background, listened to them discuss who the woman might be. Eva said nothing. She felt her legs quiver beneath her and stumbled away. On her way back to the slum she passed out right in front of the Christian church, which stood large and grandiose on cleared ground. Everything around it had been swallowed up long before anything else in the slum, making room for both a roundchurch and a tower. People laughed at that. The Christians spoke of the miracles of the Mother Goddess. Everybody else remarked on how the rat population had swelled noticeably during the years when they most wanted to build a church, and how, funnily enough, the Japanese bamboo had decided there was particularly good growing soil in the precise circle the Christians had earmarked for their orchard.

Eva woke up on a church pew beneath the largest apple tree. There was a thick blanket over her, and above her sat a heavily pregnant woman, watching. The first thing Eva did was put a hand between her legs to check that she was wearing jeans, and if the sutures had burst. They pinched a little, but they were intact.

"There, you're awake," the woman said. "We found you outside the church. Did you suddenly feel ill? Are you from the slum? Are you hungry? Oh, my name's Waleria, by the way." She pointed at her belly. "And the little one in there, her name will be Wicca."

WALERIA WAS TWENTY-FIVE AT THE TIME, AND WICCA was the first and only child she would have.

"So I hope she'll be like you," she said, lying next to Eva on the big round couch. Eva was, as usual, studying. She had begun at one end of the W clan's large family library, which included books both new and old.

"Where did you get all these?" asked Eva.

"You'd be surprised what the people we help in the slums have lying around. We find some absolute gems in the old basements. Most of it's too damaged for us to want it in the library, but anything that's unspoiled we take with us. We've been collecting since the Evolution."

"It's hard to imagine you've been living in the same place for all these hundreds of years."

"Where does that accent come from?"

"I've moved a lot, so I don't really know," Eva said, trying to sound as Danish as possible.

"Aarhus?"

"Yeah, I've lived in Aarhus."

She had said as little as possible about why she had no mothers to help her. They'd gotten sick. They'd walked out. She had set off for adventures on her own.

Waleria had brought her back to the W clan's shared home, and since she had nowhere else to live, they let her move in.

"I could tell right away you were something special," Waleria always said, when she was explaining to other people how they'd met.

"I was a wild animal," said Eva, shaking her head.

"Exactly."

"Suffer the little beasts to come unto me, as Jesus says."

They both laughed.

Eva had learned about the Bible after she moved in. Her mother had never told her about it, and only now did she understand who the two ladies in the underpass had been singing about. It was hard to believe the Bible was a true story, she thought, but it was pleasant reading, and to show her gratitude she often went along to events at Waleria's church.

Every Tuesday she spent a few hours in the Brønshøj slum, where she had appointments with the manladies.

"Couldn't you settle for a smaller insert than the one you have now? Then it wouldn't constantly be splitting the skin," she asked Lars several times.

"And undermine my whole livelihood?" he answered with a smile. "I have always been and will always be the one with the biggest penis on the Street. They don't pay me for my happy-go-lucky disposition, you know. Nobody embroiders it as delicately as you do. One of these days you're going to cover it with little flowers, like the ones you sew on those handkerchiefs. Anyway, if it wasn't constantly splitting, I wouldn't have an excuse to hang out with the best penis seamstress in the country, would I now?"

Waleria made sure Eva went to school.

"You've got to use those brains for something. Anything else would be a waste for humankind," she said. "Where did you go to school in Aarhus?"

"A few places," Eva said. "My mothers taught me most of what I know."

"Impressive," Waleria said. "You know a remarkable amount about the body and how it works. Maybe you'd like to be a doctor?"

* * *

Wicca started school the same day Eva finished her training and got a job at the Center in Lolland. She had specialized in male anatomy.

Every Tuesday she left early to work for a few hours at the slum house in Brønshøj, which on the outside still looked like a tumbledown shack but inside was gradually resembling a small clinic.

"Alas, I'm losing my favorite nanny," Waleria said in her speech at the banquet in the church celebrating Eva's new job, attended by the priests and congregation. "And when you get tired of doctoring men, I'm certain you'll go far. Some people think you've gone the easy route by studying male anatomy, which doesn't have all the same complexities. But I know your knowledge of the body far exceeds the ordinary. In the long term, you won't want to waste it on a herd of males at Lolland."

Eva thrived at work. The only part she didn't like was examining penises up close. She tried to avoid it, and when that wasn't possible she always wore gloves, but even then she couldn't help but feel disgusted when she touched them. Unfortunately, that proved necessary more often than she liked, because at the time the Lolland Center was carrying out a research project on why males couldn't become erect unassisted. They knew it hadn't been a problem for the first generation of Center males hundreds of years earlier, but the situation had gradually deteriorated, and nowadays males never became erect without being medicated first.

Eva still woke up erect in the morning. She clutched the space between her legs, terrified, and was always relieved to find it had only been a nightmare. Still, the erection was there. Since there was nothing to tug, it passed quickly. Another problem was the itching. It was worst under the balls—which weren't there either, of course. She found both hydrocortisone and natural remedies in the cabinet at the Center, but they weren't much help. In any case, it was hard to figure out where to apply the cream when the part that was itching didn't exist.

Living in the church's roundhouse with Waleria, Wicca, and the other Christians was, in many ways, all Eva had ever wanted. The only thing that bothered her was that her mother had also been part of that dream. At first, she missed her every day, struggling with the guilt of knowing she was living a comfortable life while her mother had wasted away in miserable hovels in the slums, all because she'd given birth to a deformed daughter.

No one at the Christian roundhouse eyed her mistrustfully, or interrogated her about whether she was normal. Yet the fear of discovery never went away. When she had to pee, she always waited until the last moment before pulling her pants down or dress up. If anybody came in midstream, she stayed seated and acted as though she wasn't done. The others teased her, joking that she didn't get up until she'd air-dried. She was mindful always to take menstrual containers for a few days every month and dip them in the blood samples she took from herself. She had considered stealing discarded blood from the males' samples at the Center, but if she was caught taking testosterone-rich blood out of the building, she'd be fired. It would be seen as an unacceptable perversion.

Eva had examined herself long enough in the mirror to know there was no immediately apparent difference between her parts and everybody else's. But she also knew that inviting anyone to get too close was not an option. She still never went swimming.

"I don't like water," she said, if the others tried to coax her into joining them at the beach on hot summer days. They accepted it, like so many of her other little quirks. Like her obsession with embroidering the little scraps of fabric she called handkerchiefs. She taught the children from the congregation to sew neat crosses and Agatha's severed breasts in fleshy tones.

"Why don't we find you a girlfriend?" asked Waleria and the other Ws. They were always suggesting someone in the congregation they thought would be perfect for her to do a little round dance with, as they called it.

"I'm busy with school," she said, putting them off. "With work." Or "I promised to be with Wicca."

Over time they got used to her being uninterested in a relationship, either short term or long. Some people were just like that.

As far as Eva was concerned, life was easier now they weren't pestering her about girlfriends; except that a girlfriend was the one thing she most wanted. Someone to be close to. Someone to share her secret. Which was probably why she let her guard down with the new doctor, Nanna, albeit only for a moment.

Every time Nanna told Eva she had an unusually good rapport with the juveniles, she lapped up the compliment. Because it came from Nanna, and because Eva knew she cared as much about her job as Eva did.

Normally she didn't like people making that sort of comment. She was good at her job because she devoted herself to it and had studied as hard as she could. But in moments of weakness she couldn't rule out the possibility that the reason she understood them so well was because she had originally been born with a kuk. What if the day came when somebody made that connection? As a result, she often pretended to be slightly worse with the males than she really was, if other people were around. Except for Nanna, whom she wanted to impress.

After a few months, she invited Nanna for dinner at the roundhouse one night. Wicca was gushing.

"This is the first time Eva has ever brought someone around—you must be something special. Nobody is ever good enough."

Nanna had smiled at Eva, making the kuk that wasn't there twitch and her heartbeat quicken.

The fantasies came, of course. Muted in the evenings and in full bloom while she slept. There was nothing she could do about it. And contrary to what Wicca believed, it was far from the first time Eva had fallen in love.

The first time was with Benja, when in hazy infatuation she'd thought she might share in the life that others lived and meet someone who'd like her just the way she was. The next person she fell in love with was Lars, but only from afar, thankfully; he never knew. After that came a few sweet-scented women at medical school. Nanna wasn't even the first of the doctors, nurses, and other Center employees to turn Eva's head. To figure in her dreams and be conquered in her mind. She imagined telling them all the things that no one was allowed to know, stroking them lovingly from neck to back to cheeks and in between their legs, asking them to turn around and doing the same along the front. The one thing they all had in common, except for Benja, was that she'd never let them get too close. Physically or emotionally. She had kept her feelings to herself, had never touched them inappropriately, and if you asked them they would have known nothing of the tempestuous love that roiled in Eva whenever she went near them.

So, when she was attracted to Nanna, she didn't consider it a problem. She just wanted to enjoy it while it lasted, to feel the love that thudded in her chest and kuk, which stiffened in her mind. She knew from experience that after a few weeks—or maybe months, if she was lucky—her imagination would be exhausted, worn down to nothing but indifference, or at most a trace of melancholy, if she happened to bump into the chosen one.

The trouble with Nanna was that she was equally in love with Eva. She made no attempt to hide it. Every chance she got, she stood as close as possible to Eva. Took every opportunity to touch her. Knocked on her office door at least once a day, where she sat seductively on the couch with her legs spread and mouth painted crimson. Eva had to dig her nails into her skin to stop herself from running over there and kissing her, holding her tightly. Stroking her hair. Putting herself between those legs and making love to her with everything she didn't have. It was torture. Eva knew there was only one thing to be done.

"Walk you home?" asked Nanna, with one of those smiles that shattered Eva's heart.

"Sorry, I'm receiving two newborn males this evening," she answered offhandedly.

"I can stay, it'll speed up the categorization process."

"No thanks. I'd rather do it by myself."

"Do you want to go to dinner tomorrow?"

"I'm already meeting someone."

Eva behaved as haughtily as she could, but inside she was sobbing, wracked with desire and loneliness, locked away with her secret, hopeless of ever sharing it with anyone.

One morning she found it necessary to be so blunt that Nanna ran out of her office in tears. The next day she came to work with red eyes and a tormented look, and after that she stopped addressing Eva directly.

Eva had to call in sick for a week. She didn't have the strength to lift a cup, couldn't bring herself to eat, and only the fear that the angles would start to show on her hips again made her decide to get up and put food into her mouth. To put on her yellow work clothes and continue her wretched journey through life.

Lately the atmosphere between her and Nanna had grown so tense that it was agonizing for Eva to be around her. The situation was not helped by the fact that Nanna was the one who'd been promoted, and it was now up to her to decide whether Eva kept her job.

Moreover, Nanna had stopped merely ignoring her and started getting snide. It felt as though she was perpetually trying to catch Eva in a mistake.

"You haven't given that male enough vitamin D, you can see from the color of his skin."

"Were you the last person in the lab yesterday? You didn't clean up."

"The way you handle the males starts them off on the wrong foot here."

It was a long list, the things that Nanna picked on. Sometimes she was right, sometimes she wasn't. Worst of all, it seemed as though the tactic was starting to work on some of her colleagues, and Eva sensed them looking askance at her and whispering about whether she was doing her job properly.

She often left work early, making some excuse about it being that time of the month. She went home with a churning fear in the pit of her stomach, running over in her mind all the things she had to do better with the males. She had to avoid making a serious mistake at all costs.

She had considered, of course, switching to a different Center. But she was well-liked by the senior management, and they had no reason to investigate her background more closely or wonder whether she might be different from anyone else. She didn't know what she might encounter somewhere new, especially if Nanna managed to spread disconcerting rumors about her. So she stayed where she was and tried to make herself as invisible as she could.

THE BOY HAD WOKEN UP AND WAS EATING A GREEN LEAF Medea had given him. On the table stood a box filled with test tubes. Some of them contained blood; others hair, nails, saliva, and something Eva couldn't identify. The boy had small Band-Aids where the witch had pricked him.

"What are you going to do with that?" asked Eva.

"Use it as medicine for my snakes."

Eva hid her smile. "What can you cure with hair and teeth and boy's blood?"

"We'll have to see," Medea said, looking tired. She poked another leaf at the boy, who eagerly opened his mouth and ate it.

"And what's that you're giving him?" Eva couldn't help her curiosity.

"They're ash leaves dipped in honey. To build up his immune system."

"Of course," Eva said, with an indulgent smile.

The boy opened his mouth for another leaf.

"He's feeling better." Medea stroked his crooked-shorn hair.

"Is my Eldest coming back soon?" the boy asked. "I want to sing with her."

"He speaks in sentences?" said Wicca, taken aback. "I've never heard a male do that before. At the Center they only use primitive constructions."

Medea gave him a glass of water, which he downed in a few seconds. He swung his legs over the edge of the couch and hopped down. His eyes were clear and his movements free. There was no sign of fever.

"Where is she?" he asked again.

"Your injection must have worked," Wicca said to Eva. "Look, he's fine."

"I think it was my herbs and drops that did it, actually," Medea said. Like the others, she was watching every step the boy took. He put on his raspberry bag, stood in the middle of the room, and launched into one of the songs he used to sing with Eldest.

"He sings with words?" Wicca gazed at him in astonishment. The males at the Center hummed sometimes, but there were never any words in their songs. "Eva, please let me have him, he'd be a smash hit at the Easter ritual."

Eva shook her head. So did Medea.

"Maybe he's the new Jesus. The Mother must have led me to him." Wicca knelt before the boy, who sang at an ever-increasing volume in the spotlight of their attention, and began to dance. Slowly, at first, then faster, then at full speed. Past the table, up over the armchair, three chassés to the right, then to the left. The bag hung at his hips, and every once in a while he gave it a prod with his rear so that it flew around him in an arc. He laughed delightedly. As though risen from the dead, fizzing over with joy.

"Imagine what my mother would say if I gave her a Jesus for the Easter ritual. She'd forgive all the fuss I caused with the devil snake. You owe me that, Medea!"

"I've seen what you do to your Jesuses. I don't want that for him," Medea said.

"He's Kali's son, so he belongs to me more than he does to you." Wicca leaned forward to touch his fair hair, but he was too spry and darted away from her. He threw off the tunic he'd been wearing while he was sick and leapt around naked in front of them. His appendage thrashed merrily back and forth with the raspberry bag.

"Males are unhealthily preoccupied with their genitals. They can't get any distance from them," Eva said, looking away. "You think he's sweet now, but when he grows up he's going to rape you, beat you, manipulate you. At worst, he'll kill you. Testosterone is not to be played with. That's why we keep males medicated and separated from the rest of us."

Benja gave Eva a long look.

"I heard this rumor," Wicca said. "It's been going around among Christians for decades. People say there's a boy living somewhere in Jutland, a hidden boy. It's been years since he was first sighted, but several people have seen him. He must be an adult by now, and nobody knows where he is. If he can live in hiding without endlessly going on rampages, then this boy can live in the church!"

"That's just a myth," Eva said quickly. "It's impossible."

The boy danced past them, tugging at his penis, twirling and laughing so loudly he could barely stand. Eva felt sick.

Medea threw him the tunic.

"Put that on," she said. He ignored it. Thrilled to have all eyes on him, he swung the bag onto his belly, and with a magician's sense of the dramatic, he whisked the pruning shears out of the bag.

Benja let out a gasp of surprise. The rat fussed in Eva's pocket. It had slept throughout her visit to the convent, but now all of a sudden it was jittery.

Benja tried to catch him and grab them back, but he was too quick.

"I don't think Jesus would do *that*. He doesn't steal." Wicca sat down on the edge of the couch, disappointed.

The boy gave a scream. The rat snake had come slithering in, like the twilight outside. It glided along the wall, approaching the couch and the boy. He pounced on it with a yell, and in one violent movement he stabbed it with the shears. The snake writhed, trying to bite him, and he pulled out the shears to impale it one more time. Medea shouted and ran over, but too late. The snake was lifeless at their feet. The boy leaned into Medea's arms, crying.

"Why did you do that?" she shouted.

"It's dangerous," the boy sobbed.

"You killed it," Medea said. "You murdered my last rat snake!"

"Now she can come back and sing with me," he wept.

"What did I say," whispered Eva, thin-lipped. "Testosterone is dangerous."

THEY WRAPPED THE BOY UP WELL AND WALKED IN A GROUP toward the train. Benja accompanied them for a few streets, then turned right toward the lakes without saying goodbye.

Wicca got off the train at the Brønshøj slum.

"I'd better talk to my mother," she said. "She's got to get the church to show me mercy."

"I'll be seeing you," Medea tried.

"No, you won't," Wicca snapped, before the doors slid shut and she stomped off down the path toward the church.

Medea, Eva, and the boy rolled on toward Lolland in silence. The boy, who was wearing a sister's robe and had a hat covering his chopped hair, stared in puzzlement at Medea. She'd been unable to look at him since he killed the rat snake. He squeezed her hand and peeped cautiously out at the staggering world that rushed past the window.

"Do you think they'll make us pensives?" Medea asked.

"I'll say I found him on a back street in the slum," Eva said, thinking of Benja, who might talk if she mentioned the convent.

The sun shone so intensely that the yellow gates of the Center stung their eyes. The boy hid behind Medea.

"I'm not going through that gate with you," she said.

"No, of course not," Eva said.

"Here," Medea said to the boy, giving him the snake-skull amulet she wore. "Can you make sure he always keeps it on?"

"Of course," Eva lied, knowing the first thing that would happen was that all his clothes—and thus the amulet as well—would be burned, to minimize the risk of infection. Even the newborn males were disinfected upon delivery to the Center.

"Do you think they'll let me visit him one day?" Medea asked, blowing her nose.

Eva shook her head. "You can't choose a specific male when you visit the Center. All I can do is make sure you're not matched with him if you choose the type he's categorized as. Anyway, you'd need to have passed the right exams—have you?"

Medea shook her head. "But I just want to talk to him, maybe tap him a bit."

"I'm sorry." Eva almost felt bad for the little witch.

Medea sniffed. "I know it's silly, it's only a male. But I get sad when one of the male dogs dies too." She stroked the boy's hair. "At least I can keep Pythia healthy for a while now, I think . . ." Then she turned and walked back toward the train.

The boy cried and tried to follow, but Eva held on to him tightly.

"It's not dangerous, I promise you, and there are lots of others like you, boys you can play with. There are no snakes. You don't have to be scared."

The boy was twisting desperately to free himself.

Eva looked at him. She wasn't used to the young males having such strong wills. Doubt crept in. She knew, of course, that a boy couldn't live out in the open, but could she allow him to become a Center male? He spoke, he sang, he thought. Just like her, when she was deformed. He was different from other males his age. The mere fact that he was toilet-trained was curious. Most males only learned that once they reached sexual maturity.

There was also a good chance the other juveniles would tear him to shreds at playtime. It didn't happen often, but then again it wasn't unknown, if the boy was too different. It was hard sometimes to find the right doses of tranquilizer to keep their aggression in check, because they grew at such different rates. The boy had given up trying to squirm out of Eva's grip. He looked at her with wet eyes.

She could kill him. Free him from the suffering incurred by being born the way he was.

Eva looked around. She could put a hand over his mouth behind the bushes. Suffocate him slowly. Say she'd found him in the slum and wanted to bring him to the Center, but that he must have eaten something poisonous, that he was already unconscious when she found him. There'd be a huge fuss about a boy being found outside the gates, but nobody would care that he was dead.

She took a step back from the path, glancing around to make sure she hadn't been seen, and jumped when she caught sight of Nanna in the doorway, scowling interrogatively at Eva and the boy. She hurried back onto the path. Took five deep breaths, the way her mother had trained her not to feel. Then she held the boy by the hand and walked firmly toward the entrance.

MEDEA

Come here, Medea communicated telepathically to the male dog. It eyed her skeptically.

"Come on," she said out loud, holding out a piece of lovecake. The male swallowed the dry crust without tasting it. Soon it was nuzzling up to her devotedly, with all its weight. She had to reach out and grab the wall so she wouldn't be knocked off her feet.

A rat scuttled past. Grabbing—with only minor difficulty—one of the stones she'd put out, she closed one eye and took aim. The male nudged her arm as she threw, and the stone hit the doorframe just as the rat bolted under the door and was away.

"Oh well," she said resignedly, putting all her weight into shoving the male dog. Just enough to get her hand into her pocket and take out the syringe. She stuck the needle into its thigh. Blood ran red into the vial. She put the syringe back into her pocket and glanced down between its legs.

For several months, she'd been treating Pythia with what she'd tapped from the boy. It had worked better than she'd dared to hope. The drops of his blood made Pythia lustrous, and it didn't take more than a couple of weeks on the blood cure until she was moving once again at her youthful speed.

The problem was that the supply of fluids was diminishing far too rapidly, and before long she would run out. So she was now trying different options from the male dog.

The dog's blood didn't have the same effect as the boy's, so maybe something else was required. There was no telling how many lovecakes she'd have to feed it before she could get something to experiment with from between its legs.

* * *

Madam flew over both of them, landing on the male dog's head. It opened its beak and barked loudly. The male thrashed, trying to make the bird let go—but gave up. Since Eldest's death, the myna had focused all its affection on the male dog. It liked to sleep between its front paws and barked and growled too to get its attention.

There were no crows left in the cages. They might have all flown off, of course, but Medea quietly suspected Silence of having eaten them.

The first time Medea had caught Silence plucking the feathers from a dead crow, she'd scolded her. Silence had ignored her and hacked off the bird's feet.

Medea was too busy with Pythia to worry about Silence, or the birds, for that matter, so she contented herself with a sigh whenever she saw her sink her teeth into yet another roast bird, in a kitchen overflowing with black feathers.

She hadn't seen much of Silence in the past few months. She'd changed. She didn't smell of rotten lake water anymore, and once or twice she'd even smiled at Medea; and then on top of that she'd heard her humming to her plants.

"Will you cut my hair?" Silence asked one day. It was still strange to hear her voice.

"Have you got scalp fungus again?"

"No, I just want you to take it off."

"Bald?"

"Do you think it would suit me?"

Medea had never known Silence to take an interest in her appearance before.

"I'm meeting someone," she said, smiling happily.

"Who?" Medea began to cut her hair.

"Chaplin. I mean, Eva—the woman who was here. We know each other from before."

"You're going to Himlingeøje?" Medea asked, surprised.

"Here, you can use the shears to get the little hairs at the back of my neck."

"Say hi to Wicca for me," Medea called as Silence went out, but she wasn't sure she'd heard.

Medea missed Wicca and her body. What they'd done together, and the way Wicca had looked at her when she wanted sex. She hadn't heard from her since that day on the train, when she said she never wanted to see Medea again. There were times when it got her down, not having a human body to rest against anymore, because Wicca had given her something the snakes never could. Still, the joy it brought her to see Pythia back to her old self eclipsed everything else.

It was more than a week before Silence returned to the convent. After a while Medea had thought they must have made her pensive, and that it was only a matter of time before they came and took her too. But then Silence turned up after all, clean-scrubbed, happy, and with a loaf of bread she'd gotten from Eva.

"Where have you been?"

"With Chaplin."

"This whole time?"

"Yes, why not?"

"Isn't it getting time for your monthly bleed?"

Silence left just half a cup outside her door, then she was gone again. This time for three weeks.

"Does Wicca ever talk about me?" Medea asked, when Silence was abruptly standing in the kitchen.

"I don't talk to her," said Silence, petting the little female, which was yowling with delight that she was home.

"Do you think she'd see me?"

"Chaplin says Wicca's only allowed to be a priest at the church if she never goes anywhere near you or your snakes again."

Medea took her mattress down to Pythia and began to sleep

there regularly. She decided she wouldn't think about Wicca anymore.

Lars was back on his terrace outside the old supermarket. Fall was on its way, and already he was lighting the lanterns at five in the afternoon. His breasts were packed away under a woolen shirt.

"They stopped producing milk while I was pensive. It's not easy to crank it back up again, so I'm considering dropping that service," he told Medea, sighing, when she and the male dog dropped by on their way to gather roots. The little female had trotted after Silence the last time she left; she'd probably taken it to Himlingeøje. Either way, Medea hadn't seen it since.

"They also forced me to remove my penis, but I've made an appointment to have it sewn back on. Do you still make those lovecakes?"

"Do you really want to risk it, after last time?"

"Could you maybe make it as a drink instead?"

"If you can get hold of some more menstrual blood for me."

He could.

And it wasn't long before Medea was delivering little bottles of lovecocoa. Best served warm.

"There's only one thing I want in exchange," she said, after he'd finished lauding its effect on his clients. "Are you able to get me the blood of a male?" she whispered. "A real male, I mean."

Lars shrank back. "Look, I know we like to live pretty near the edge on the Street, but whatever you've got in mind, I want no part in it. You'll have to make do with menstrual blood from the working males around here."

He glanced down the Street. "There they are, the scum," he said, walking up to the railing. A herd of ratgirls was coming toward them, baskets empty. They'd been working extra hard lately, filling the area with waves of rats that gnawed everything to ribbons. They looked exhausted. Medea sometimes thought it was only a matter of months before the convent came apart around her ears. She tried to brace the walls with things she found in the nearby ruins but was always finding new holes. Without the rat snakes, it was a losing battle.

"You look tired, and cold," Lars called out to the ratgirls. "I've just come to the end of quite a long term as a pensive, where I learned how nice it feels to do good things for other people. May I offer you a mug of hot cocoa?"

The ratgirls exchanged uncertain glances, but when the one in charge accepted, drawn in by the aroma, the others followed suit.

Within a few weeks the rat population had nosedived, and the ratgirls only visited the area to see Lars. By the time the winter came, the rats were gone.

It was a relief for Medea, but she found it difficult to be happy. Pythia was ill again, getting sicker with every day that passed. She'd fed her all the other snakes, in the hopes that they contained something that might substitute for the testosterone-rich blood. Nothing helped. The vivariums were empty. Only one snake was left now: the white male cobra. That would give Pythia one good week. But it would be her last. And then it would be over.

When Silence came home in early January with the little female at her side, she found Medea crying on the kitchen floor. In the old days she would have stepped over her and gone up to her room. But now she crouched down a few feet away and looked at her with concern.

"What's wrong?"

"I don't have any of the boy's blood left, and Pythia's sick again. I've tried using the dog's blood, and its semen, but it doesn't work. Soon I'll have to feed her the last cobra, and then she'll die. And I can't get hold of blood with testosterone in it, because they won't let me anywhere near the boy." Medea flung herself over the male dog and sobbed so loudly that it got to be too much for Silence. She stood up and went to her old room, where she picked up the last few things she wanted before moving in with Eva.

"The female's staying with me," she said, and left. Medea lay on the floor for more than an hour, her face buried in the dog's fur. Then she went downstairs and fed Pythia the male cobra, her last meal. First, however, she removed the cobra's tongue, which she made into a new amulet that she hung around her neck. As Pythia swallowed the white snake, Medea raised her arms to the skies, praying to her gods, the universe, and all the energies of the souls that Pythia might be saved. When night came, they huddled in the corner of the basement.

When Pythia died, Medea would die too.

She was woozy from a lack of food and water, and from lying in the dark. She didn't hear the person and the little dog moving around in the kitchen upstairs. Or the male mounting the female, or the footsteps coming down the staircase and past the empty vivariums, or the door opening to Pythia's room.

"Here." Silence placed a syringe in front of her. "It's the blood of a human male. The testosterone might not be as pure as you'd like, because there's estrogen mixed in. But it's from an adult, so it should be at least as strong as the stuff you got from the boy."

Medea picked up the syringe, confused, and stared questioningly at Silence.

"If you never ask me where it comes from, I can come and bring you a syringe once a week."

Silence was already on her way out of the room. In the doorway, she stopped and turned. "The male dog just mated with the female. If she has pups, I'll have to move back into the convent with her. Eva also says she misses the slums sometimes."

Then she was gone.

Medea opened Pythia's mouth and let a few drops of blood fall onto her tongue. Pythia hissed softly and opened her eyes. Life came slowly back into her drowsy gaze.

ABOUT THE AUTHOR

Simon Klein-Knudsen

Maren Uthaug is an award-winning author of four novels and has a daily cartoon strip in Denmark's largest newspaper. Her critically acclaimed second novel, *Where There Are Birds*, was awarded the Danish Broadcasting Corporation's Novel of the Year Award in 2018, and her third novel, *A Happy Ending*, received the Readers' Choice Award. Born in the town of Uthaug, Norway, she lives in Copenhagen.